Ebook ISBN 978-1-80048-773-4

Kindle ISBN 978-1-80048-772-7

Audio CD ISBN 978-1-80048-765-9

MP3 CD ISBN 978-1-80048-766-6

Digital audio download ISBN 978-1-80048-768-0

Boldwood Books Ltd
23 Bowerdean Street
London SW6 3TN
www.boldwoodbooks.com

For Joe, Joey and James – thanks for everything

1

The first rule of Wife Club is that you talk about Wife Club *all the time*.

Today is my friend Rachael's wedding – the last person in our friendship group to get married – and it's an interesting one.

There are four of us. Me, Rachael, Lindsey and Sally, and we've all been friends for a long time, and I mean a long time. Pudley village is only a small place, so the four of us being the same age landed us in the same nursery group and we stayed friends all the way through school, into adulthood. We're all thirty now, and while I may not feel like we're as close as we used to be, I think it's impressive that we're all still friends.

The reason we're drifting apart is the aforementioned Wife Club, and some of us perhaps not being quite as into it as others.

It's funny that Rachael is the last one in our group to tie the knot because she's always been the most enthusiastic about doing so. So much so that we had a bit of upset last year when Sally got married.

Well, Rachael was a bridesmaid for me, and then for Lindsey, so when Sally wound up getting married next and asked us all to be bridesmaids, Rachael had a total meltdown because, you know what they say, three times a bridesmaid, never a bride. I mean, they say that, but it's not true, is it? It's clearly not true because Rachael was eventually persuaded to be a bridesmaid for the third time, and her wedding ceremony just finished, so it's obviously bullshit.

We're currently in that weird stage between the ceremony and the wedding breakfast, right after the photos are taken, when everyone sort of mills around for a bit before taking their seats. I could do with a drink, but after having our bridal party photos taken, we're still standing in the semi-circle we stood for our last photo, just chatting by a large hotel staircase that provided the backdrop, making the most of our time with Rachael before she's back to being a busy bride. I remember exactly what it's like at your own wedding, no one really lets you have a minute, you're just constantly talking to people, thanking them for coming, smiling, working your way through the formalities.

'I can't thank you all enough for being my bridesmaids,' Rachael gushes. She's got big bride energy right now – you know, that super smug level of extreme happiness where you know the world has no choice but to revolve around you? I don't mean to sound so cynical – or maybe I do – but this wedding was planned down to the tiniest detail (excluding the groom, of course) long before Rachael even met Kevin. That's Rachael, though. She's always been the sensible one, always worrying about anything and everything to cover all bases. Don't get me wrong, it's been useful over the years, especially when we've all tried to coordinate trips or plan parties, but she does drive us all a little mad sometimes. I know no feeling like the heavy weight on my chest when Rachael hands us one of her itineraries – a more recent addition to her organisational tactics, thankfully – knowing full well we'll all have to stick to it or she'll have one of her meltdowns.

'I just hope that, by the end of the day, my wedding lives up to all of yours,' Rachael replies. She has a look on her face that somehow shows that she *knows* her wedding is so far so superior. That's what she believes, anyway. I'm not sure I agree.

'No one was ever going to be able to compete with our street food fair,' Sally half-jokes.

No one was ever going to be able to compete with Sally's wedding full stop. Her husband's dad invented something completely boring but worth an absolute fortune – I think it's a type of adhesive, because the whole family make 'sticky' jokes constantly – so there was no expense spared for her majorly tacky big day (Christ, even I'm doing it now).

She's still getting her money's worth from the wedding, though. She almost always finds a way to mention it. Today it's going to be too easy. Back in February, at Lindsey's dad's wake, she was seriously reaching, but she got there in the end. Some tenuous link between the Tunnock's teacakes they had out and her two-thousand-pound wedding cake – she had the same baker as Meghan and Harry, don't you know.

Crass as it is, you've got to hand it to her, it's impressive how she always finds a way to bring it up. That's Sally, though, she's always had the vibe of a snooty rich person, even before she was actually rich.

Lindsey is probably the one who has changed the least, she's still a big hug of a friend, always smiling, always preferring baking to bitching. There's nothing that girl doesn't think she can fix with scones. But she, like the other two, has grown increasingly sensible over the years, in a way that just doesn't seem to be happening for me.

'Thankfully, I didn't let Kevin make any decisions or the colour scheme would be Man City and we'd all be doing karaoke after the wedding breakfast,' Rachael says with a snort.

Sally shoots her a not-so-subtle look. Rachael quickly turns to me.

'Not that there's anything wrong with karaoke at a wedding, Poppy,' she reassures me, visibly cringing.

'Sorry, I shouldn't have mentioned your wedding at all, should I?'

'It's fine,' I insist.

It isn't awkward when people mention my wedding. It's awkward when they mention it and then cringe themselves inside out, before trying to make me feel better with pitying looks and soppy words – which ironically only ever makes me feel worse. I've never really viewed my life choices in a negative light. It's only when I see them reflected back at me in the eyes of others, all contorted like I'm looking at them in a funhouse mirror, that I start to wonder if maybe I have made a mess of things.

'I'm excited for the food,' Sally says, changing the subject. 'I had to taste test so much food – for our street food fair – that I was worried I wouldn't fit into my Vera Wang dress.'

We all look at her.

'I did, though,' she reassures us, as if we didn't know. 'I've always been a size 8.'

It turns out it is in fact possible to roll your eyes without moving them because I just did it. Well, I think I did. It's also possible I just rolled them properly and no one noticed because no one's eyes are on my size 12 body today. I say size 12. I'm a 10 if I'm feeling optimistic. A 14 if I've eaten too much. A 16 for my top half in certain high-street retailers. My point being, claiming to be a certain size 'always' (come on, she wasn't born a size 8, was she? *Was she*?!) means nothing. Not only because sizing isn't universal but because it doesn't define any of us. It's all about perspective. My feet are a size 8 but, when I tell people that, they usually just give me pitying looks for that too. It must have been a nightmare for this lot, watching me dance in open-toed shoes at my karaoke wedding.

'As long as you're not cooking,' Lindsey teases Sally.

'Well, that's why I thought that a couples' cooking class might be fun, the first one is in a couple of days, so we can go to a few before we jet off on our honeymoon to Hawaii...'

Rachael says this like we don't all already know where she's going, and it's worth pointing out that she isn't even off on her honeymoon until February.

'...so we can all learn to cook and er...'

Well, that's the first I'm hearing about this cooking class, which obviously means I'm not invited. Rachael can't hide that she knows she's put her foot in it.

'I actually think... er...' Rachael peers into the reception room next to us, her eyes darting back and forth. 'Yes, I think it's time to take our seats. We have little seating maps, dotted around, with QR codes on them, so you can scan them to find where you're sitting.'

This room is *not* that big.

'Bridesmaids and groomsmen are over there,' Lindsey says, pointing in the direction of the top table.

It's family only at the actual top table, Rachael told us. There's a not-quite top table for close friends. Trust me, I've heard her talk about this wedding so much, for so long, I know it all. Nothing could surprise me.

I'm about to follow the other girls when Rachael places her arm on mine, holding me back. She waits a second or two until it's just us.

'Poppy, I actually thought it might be cool for you to sit somewhere else,' she eventually says with a smile.

'What do you mean?' I ask. Perhaps I can be surprised. I'm also pretty sure I know what she means already but I want to hear her say it.

'Well, you know, I thought you'd like to sit at a table where you can meet some new people,' she explains. 'And, to be honest, with the tables only seating six, with the other girls and their husbands...'

That's four.

'...and then two other people, that's six, and with you just being on your own...'

I bite my tongue. It's her wedding day.

'So, which table am I at?' I ask coolly.

'Table twelve,' she replies.

'Twelve?' I squeak back at her. 'How many tables are there?'

'Oh, only twelve,' she replies, confirming that I am on the last table. 'It's over there.'

Table twelve couldn't be further from the top table without being out in the car park.

'Honestly, you'll be much happier there, people to meet, lots of singles, and other divorced people too!' she says, like that's going to be the answer to my prayers. 'Enjoy the food, hun.'

She dashes off before I can say anything. I don't

know what I'd say to her if she hadn't. Not on her wedding day, anyway.

Table twelve. I can't believe it. The sad singles table. Has it really come to this?

Perhaps it has, given that I'm the only one in our group who is single. Not only was I the first person in our group to get married, I was the first to get divorced, too. And boy, they don't ever let me forget it.

2

In some ways, Rachael's wedding is like every wedding I've ever been to. The bride wore white, her dad gave her away, and all the guests are taking their seats in the function room, which is laid out beautifully with large round tables covered in pristine white cloths, topped with big bunches of flowers that match the bride's winter bouquet. The thing that makes this wedding different from all the others – and it does really feel different – is the fact that it's New Year's Eve. Never mind the fact that I'm pretty sure every wedding I've ever been to has taken place in the summer, meaning I always associate the events with long, warm sunny days instead of cold, dark dreary ones like today, but I've never actually been to a wedding that overlapped another occasion, like a birthday or a national holiday.

For me, this wedding sort of covers both. Obviously New Year's Eve is New Year's Eve, which is the case for everyone here, but the clock striking midnight doesn't just kick off all the phoney new beginnings and short-lived healthy eating bullshit we all flirt with each year, it also marks the start of my birthday, pretty much to the minute.

The night I was born was kind of a funny story – not that I remember anything about it, obviously, but it's a story my parents enjoyed telling year after year. My mum was always a bit of a wild card. Despite having a super serious job in the legal profession, you wouldn't recognise her outside the office. She was fun and reckless and said whatever she wanted, did whatever popped into her head without giving it too much thought, and rarely worried about consequences. That's why at pushing nine months pregnant with me she didn't think twice about going to a fancy-dress New Year's Eve party with my dad and their friends. No prizes for guessing that my mum went into labour before the clock struck midnight, and I was born shortly after, making me the first baby born in Lancashire in 1991. What makes the story funnier is that my dad, assuming my mum had gone home early with my auntie, didn't even realise my mum had gone into labour, so he stayed out partying all night – something out of character for him, as he's always been the straitlaced, sensible one. This was before everyone had a mobile phone (wow, saying that makes me sound so old) so he didn't even know I was born until he was walking home the next morning, still dressed as John McClane from *Die Hard*, when he noticed the local newspaper and there I was, their first baby of the year, in the arms of my mum who – hilariously – was still half wearing her Madonna cone bra. Needless to say, after spotting that, my dad got himself to the hospital faster than you could say yippie-ki-yay, and he somehow became even more sensible after that.

I like to think it was my chaotic entry into this world that paved the way for my yo-yo life. It's always nice to blame it on something, isn't it? Well, when you get married *and* divorced by the time you're twenty-five, it feels a little bit better being able to put it down to something other than who you are as a person. My mum, when she was still with us, always used to say I took after her, albeit reluctantly. She never tried to talk me out of getting married, she was all for it. She also helped me pick up the pieces when I got divorced.

I always think of my mum more at this time of year, with Christmas and my birthday soon after. I wonder what she would think of me, if she could see me now, slinking sheepishly up to table twelve, the loser table.

I say loser table – I don't think we're losers just for being single. I just know that will be the way Rachael sees us. She'll think she's doing some kind of public service, putting us all together like this. Isn't it annoying, when people find love, and it makes them aggressively want to find it for you too? If her heart was in the right place, sure, why not? But I'm really starting to feel like my single status is – hmm, how would Sally describe it? – throwing off the aesthetic of the group. I'm already being left off the guest list for activities they're planning – not that I'm all that gutted to be missing out on a couples' cooking class that sounds like a nightmare, but it would be nice to have been invited.

I'm the fourth person to arrive at table twelve. With three men already in their places, anxiously awaiting their fellow table mates, clearly already wise to the concept of the singles table, I feel a little bit like I'm on Blind Date – or almost-Blind Date, anyway. Blind in the sense that I didn't know I was going to be served up to the eligible bachelors at the wedding.

Oh, the relief on their faces when an actual girl sits down at the table.

'Hello,' I say with a brightness that does not at all genuinely reflect how I'm feeling on the inside.

'Hi,' the man directly in front of me says.

'Hello,' the man to his left says.

The man to the right just gives me a slight wave.

Good God, it's going to be a long day, and I mean that in both respects. It's going to feel like a long day, if this is the level of chat the men at this table have to offer, but it's genuinely going to be an actual long day, given that this wedding is doubling up as a New Year's Eve party.

'And you are?' the man in the middle asks, rather formally.

He's probably in his late thirties. His dark hair is

starting to go grey at the sides, which wouldn't be a problem, except the product he's used to slick it back hasn't worked, causing the sides to stick out wildly, making him look a bit like a rockhopper penguin.

'I'm Poppy,' I tell him. 'You?'

'Simon Alistair Ainsworth,' he says, extending a hand for me to shake. 'Car insurance salesman.'

I shake his hand only to come away with one of his business cards.

'Oh, right,' I say, a little bemused by, well, basically everything. 'I can't drive, so...'

I hand him his card back and he takes it with such a look of disdain.

'What, like you're on a ban?' he asks. His tone quickly shifts to something rather light-hearted, for something so serious. 'Big fan of the old Venetian water?'

That's not something people call Prosecco, is it? I glance down at my glass, which I have just drained in the last few seconds, but how could I not at a time like this?

'Not banned,' I confirm. 'Never learned. Didn't fancy it.'

'Ignore him,' the man to his left says. 'I'm Pete.

And, if we're dropping our jobs when we introduce ourselves, I work in pharmaceuticals.'

'You work *in* a pharmacy,' Simon corrects him.

'I *own* a pharmacy,' Pete replies, irritated.

'You *own* the building,' Simon continues. 'On a *mortgage*.'

'I take it you two know each other already,' I say, trying to ease the tension.

'We're brothers,' Pete says.

'Twin brothers,' Simon corrects him.

I glance back and forth between them. Pete looks about ten years younger than Simon, in fact, the two of them don't look related at all. Simon reads my mind.

'Non-identical,' he says with a sigh.

'Simon's the serious one,' Pete informs me. 'I'm the fun one.'

I nod. I don't really know what to say to that.

'What's your name?' I ask the third fella.

'Craig,' he tells me simply. He doesn't smile, he doesn't blink – he doesn't look at me for more than a second or two before he looks back down at his drink.

I wait for him to say more than that, but he

doesn't. He's either not remotely interested in me, or absolutely terrified of talking to me, and I can't quite put my finger on which one it is.

'So, what do you do?' Simon asks me.

'I manage a framing company,' I reply.

As is always the case, my table mates come down with a bad case of second-hand boredom.

'Like, picture frames and that?' Pete asks in disbelief.

'Yes,' I reply. I don't get chance to elaborate.

'Well, that doesn't sound very exciting,' Simon replies with a snort.

It is actually cooler than it sounds. For one, it's the family business. My parents may have met while they were studying for the Bar, but my dad hated being a solicitor almost right away, so he quit to start his small framing business. It's a much bigger business now, which I like to think I helped with. We're not just a little shop any more. We specialise in all sorts of custom frames, made from cool and unusual materials from all over the globe. Everything from fancy resin frames to eco-friendly ones made entirely from waste materials. We have these fun, colourful plastic framed mirrors that sell like crazy on Etsy because they're made from plastic that has been cleaned out of the sea. I know, it might still sound boring, but I do find managing a business fun, especially for someone as easy-going as my dad.

'It sounds like you're a bit of a square,' Pete jokes.

'We actually like to think we're pretty edgy,' I reply.

Oh, God, there it is. My first time making the joke my dad always makes about how cool the company is. Maybe I am boring. No one even laughs.

'That's a nice dress,' Simon eventually says. 'I love all things blue.'

'He really does,' Pete quips with a wiggle of his eyebrows. Simon doesn't get it.

'You were one of the bridesmaids, weren't you?' Simon continues.

'I was,' I reply.

'So, why are you sitting here?' Pete asks.

'Probably because she's a single loser like the rest of us,' a female voice chimes in.

I glance next to me as a woman takes a seat alongside me. At first, it worries me that I'm going to have some competition at the singles table, and from a woman who is my exact opposite. I'm on the taller side for a woman, with long, straight blonde hair (although it's pulled into an uninspired up-do today, just like the other bridesmaids). My rival is short, with big, bouncing brown curls, the type that can only be natural. She has occasional purple highlights throughout her 'do, which match her form-fitting dress. Of course, I'm not remotely interested in any of these men, so she's not really a rival.

There is one seat left at the table, though, on my left. Surely whoever sits here is going to be the most eligible bachelor by default. Well, Simon, Pete and Craig aren't exactly my type. I'm not even sure what my type is, but it isn't these guys. Oh, imagine if my dream man comes and takes a seat next to me. So long as he prefers blondes, and doesn't ask too many questions, I might stand a chance with him.

'You seem like a handful,' Pete tells her.

'You don't,' she claps back. 'The name's Kat.'

Pete looks a little embarrassed, but not beaten.

'I'm Pete,' he says. 'This is my brother, Simon.'

They seem to pitch themselves as though they come as a team, or perhaps they do this to offer themselves up as multiple choice. Which brother do you want, A or B? Either way, it must get awkward. I also get the impression that they seem to think they couldn't be less alike but, despite their obvious differences, the more I hear from them, the more alike they seem. There are some definite prominent family traits – one of which is audacity.

'What do you do?' Simon asks her.

'What do I do about what?' she replies.

I'm sure she knows what they mean.

'*For work*,' Simon clarifies.

'Oh, I'm sort of between gigs at the moment,' she says casually.

'Like *unemployed*?' Simon replies.

The words taste bad in his mouth.

'No, not *like* unemployed,' she replies. 'Just unemployed.'

He seems to have more of a problem with it than she does.

'And I thought your box reply was boring,' he tells me.

'Frames,' I remind him.

'Well, that's even worse,' he snorts.

We're clearly not the calibre of women these men are looking for. It's fine because, like I said, they're not exactly my type either, but it's a sad state of affairs when everyone at the singles table seems to repel everyone else. I'm sure it's not true, that this is just a terrible way to try to get people together, but it does make you start to wonder exactly why everyone is single. Craig doesn't talk, so that one is easy, and Simon and Pete aren't exactly charming the pants off us. I wonder what's wrong with me and Kat? Kat is clearly gorgeous – surely a little thing like her being between jobs wouldn't put a man off? Then again, I'm not even sure if they are put off, it just seems like they're being mean, high school style.

'This is Craig,' I tell her, changing the subject.

Craig nods in acknowledgement.

'Does this one not talk?' Kat says with a laugh.

He seems really uncomfortable, so I chime in.

'And I'm Poppy,' I tell her. 'Nice to meet you.'

'You too,' she replies. 'I was going to ask: bride or groom? But you were clearly a bridesmaid, and I know my cousin Kevin doesn't have any female friends.'

'We were friends with Kevin growing up,' Pete says. 'So we can confirm that.'

'Not just because he's kind of a loser,' Kat continues. 'But that Rachael. Jesus Christ. She keeps him on a tight leash, doesn't she? I'm pretty sure she once warned me off him and I'm his fucking cousin.'

'Well, if you're his *fucking* cousin,' Pete jokes.

Oh, boy.

'Erm, I'm fairly certain Poppy is quite good friends with the bride,' Simon points out, assuming Kat hasn't realised she's slagging off my friend.

'Oh, yeah, right, so you'll know what I mean,' Kat continues. She wiggles a single finger next to her temple. 'Psychoooo.'

I mean, is she wrong? As an adult, Rachael has always been really highly strung and seriously emotional. She worries about everything. She lets people get away with nothing. When Sally asked her to be a bridesmaid, she wanted us all to stop talking to her and boycott her wedding, for God's sake. Still, she's my friend, so I'd never say anything.

'Looks like this is my seat,' I hear a voice say behind me.

Is this him? The man of my dreams?

I turn around to see Rachael's little brother Liam standing there. So much for the man of my dreams. Liam is ten years younger than me. It's so strange that, at twenty-one, he doesn't look much older than he did when he was still in his teens. He still looks like a kid, although an older kid than the one Rachael and I used to babysit when we were teenagers, but, still, not by much. I'd guess he's styling himself on Harry Styles, with his long-ish messy brown hair, and his green patterned shirt is a little more out there than anyone else is wearing. It definitely suits him though.

'Hi, Liam,' I say, just about masking the disappointment in my voice. It's not his fault he's a kid instead of a single Chris Hemsworth with low standards.

'Hi, Poppy,' he says brightly. 'It's been forever, how are you?'

Liam leans forward to give me a kiss on each cheek. I hadn't expected him to be so mature. Then again, the last time I spent more than a few minutes with him, he used to eat grass.

'Great, thanks,' I reply. 'How are you?'

'Can't complain,' he says with a smile.

'What are you doing sitting here?' I ask him. 'Shouldn't you be at the family table?'

'I think Rach wanted to stick all the singles together out of the way,' he replies. He doesn't look offended, he looks amused. 'This will be the most fun table, anyway.'

'I'll drink to that,' Kat says. 'But I need another drink first. Poppy, let's go.'

She gestures towards the bar with her head.

'Okay, sure,' I reply.

Kat hooks her arm with mine and leans in to talk to me as she leads me towards the bar.

'Right, do you fancy any of that lot?' she asks, cutting to the chase.

'No,' I reply plainly.

'Neither do I,' she replies. 'But you know what men are like. If we're their only two options, we'll be looking like Cara Delevingne and Kendall Jenner to them.'

I don't know which one I am. I'd assume the blonde one but, y'know, obviously I'm a million miles from being close to either.

'We need to stick together,' she insists. 'Have each other's back. Make sure neither of us gets so drunk on all things wedding that we think maybe, just maybe, we should lower our standards, just this once, just in case it's love. Because chances are, it isn't, and we'll only regret it tomorrow when we have to change our phone number or name, or entire identity. Sound good?'

I laugh.

'Sounds great,' I reply.

'Okay, let's get a bunch of drinks, because the bar is only free for so long, and we're going to need to be hammered to put up with those three.'

Well, of all the people at the sad singles table, I have to admit, the last person I was expecting to hit it off with was the only other single woman.

3

Simon and Pete – or the Brothers Dim, as Kat calls them – are doing just as she expected. Grafting into overtime to try to win us over. I don't get the impression that either one of them especially fancies either one of us. I think they're just at a wedding and they fancy a woman, any woman. And while I'm sure that the six of us at this table are not the only singletons in the room, we're the only ones Rachael has put together with her sort-of blessing.

I've tried talking to Craig a few times while we were eating, but he's not really interested in conversation. I even asked him how he knew the bride and groom and from the few words he uttered in reply,

I'm genuinely none the wiser. I'm not taking it personally because he has no interest in talking to Kat either.

'You two could be sisters, you know,' Pete tells us.

'Oh, could we now?' Kat replies.

You can tell she isn't remotely interested in any of the men at the table but she seems like she's always down for a bit of a flirt and a good time. I used to be a bit more like that. I definitely used to be way more fun. I think it's a by-product of my friendship group maturing and leaving me behind. We don't go on wild nights out or for boozy brunches any more. None of them want to do anything without their counterparts, and I'm being left out of more and more, just because I don't have a significant other. Emphasis on the word significant, because I'm seeming insignificant without one.

'Oh, yeah,' Pete replies. 'It's every man's fantasy: two sisters.'

'*Is it*?' I can't help but blurt.

'Oh, yeah,' he says again. 'But because you're not actually sisters, it's a more agreeable fantasy.'

Seriously, is this guy for real? Is this all that's out

there for me as a single girl? The last of the men and their weird fantasies?

Kat nods as cheeky smirks spread across the boys' faces.

'So, if I said I wanted you and your brother, right now, what would you say?' she asks.

Craig just stands up and walks off. Thankfully, Liam is already off somewhere. Can you imagine if he reported this back to Rachael?

'What?' Simon asks, a look of genuine disgust cemented on his face.

'Well, no, that's sick, isn't it?' Pete replies.

'That's sick?' Kat confirms. 'But two sisters isn't?'

'It's different with girls,' Pete protests.

'It really isn't,' I insist.

'We're just going to have to agree to disagree,' Pete says. 'Anyway, you're not actually sisters.'

'And we're not actually interested,' Kat claps back.

Simon huffs.

'Come on, bro, let's go get some drinks,' he says.

'Right behind you,' Pete replies, his fragile masculinity causing him to cringe at his choice of words.

'Bloody hell, Rachael must hate you as much as

she hates me,' Kat says, taking down the last of her Pimm's cocktail. 'Ugh, that's good. I'm getting another. You want one?'

'I don't think I've had a Pimm's in years,' I tell her. 'One summer it was pretty much all I drank. Wimbledon was on, and they had this pop-up Pimm's bar in Manchester that served nothing but Pimm's cocktails and strawberries with cream. My ex and I somehow made this pop-up bar our local. You got the strawberries for free when you bought a pitcher of Pimm's and we thought we were getting so much for free – until we realised we'd spent about £100 on Pimm's in two weeks.'

'Well, the bar is still free, and you won't just be getting a drink, you'll be getting a walk down memory lane too – what do you say?'

Kat waggles her eyebrows at me encouragingly.

'Go on, then,' I reply.

'Amazing,' she says. 'Back in a sec.'

I don't think I've ever had Pimm's on New Year's Eve – or outside Wimbledon season – and I've certainly not had any since my ex and I sickened ourselves on it. I mentally shake myself. I shouldn't be thinking about Zac today, although I always inevitably do end up thinking about him at weddings, for obvious reasons. These days more than ever because, even though we were the first ones to get married, we never turned into whatever my friends are now. We were fun. We had wild nights out and even wilder nights in. Then again, we were only twenty-four when we got married. If it was anything that broke us, it was having to grow up too much too quickly. We were divorced before I turned twenty-six.

'Hi, Poppy,' Liam says as he sits back down next to me. 'It's good to finally get you on your own for a chat.'

Liam has so much confidence. The way he carries himself, the way he talks. It's a kind of self-assurance that I'll bet means he knows exactly how to walk back to the seats after he's taken his turn bowling, which has to be one of the ultimate tests of self-confidence. I didn't have that much confidence at twenty-one – I don't have that much confidence now.

We chatted plenty while we were eating. In fact, if I wasn't chatting with Kat, or spectating her weird interactions with Simon and Pete, I've been chatting with Liam, catching up, hearing all about the estate agency he works for and his plans for climbing the career ladder.

I smile. It's nice to see him grow up so happy in his skin and so full of ambition. And eating food, instead of grass, obviously.

'You know, I always had a bit of a crush on you,' he tells me.

'Really?' I squeak.

'Yeah, I don't know when it started, probably when I was about twelve or thirteen,' he replies. Beyond the grass-eating years when I used to babysit him, then. 'To be honest, I still do.'

'What?'

I'm getting the wrong end of the stick.

'I still fancy you,' he says. 'I still really fancy you and, look at us now, both here at the singles table, next to each other, getting on like a house on fire.'

Okay, so I don't have the wrong end of the stick. I have the right end of the stick – a stick I don't want anything to do with.

He isn't drunk so he must be joking, so I laugh. He doesn't laugh though.

'I'm so much older than you,' I remind him, cutting to the chase.

'Only ten years,' he points out.

Only ten years?! Ten years is a big gap when it's between twenty-one and thirty-one.

'Haven't you heard of the French rule?' I joke, referencing the supposed guideline that you should never date anyone who is younger than half your age plus seven.

'No, but I've heard of the French kiss,' he replies, taking my hand in his, stroking it.

The room is alive with people all busying themselves with celebrating, drinking, dancing, chatting. No one is looking at us, but I feel my cheeks flush at the thought of someone just happening to glance over right now and seeing me – seeing this, whatever this is.

'What are you doing?' Kat asks him. 'Helping her to the bathroom? She's not that old.'

The sight of Kat with two massive glasses of Pimm's couldn't be more welcome.

'We'll continue this later,' Liam tells me, eventually letting go of my hand.

'Was that kid cracking on to you?' Kat asks me when we're finally alone.

'I think he was,' I reply.

I'm amused but only the tiniest amount. Mostly I'm just mortified.

'You didn't seem like you were interested, hope I didn't overstep the mark,' she replies, nudging my glass towards me.

'You saved me,' I tell her as I gratefully accept my drink.

One sip and I'm right back to that summer with Zac. I need to push him out of my mind. It's like Kat said earlier, about getting drunk on all things wedding, being surrounded by so much love and talk of happy ever afters really makes you look long and hard at your own situation. The more romantic gestures you witness, paired with the more you drink, and then single men surrounding you start to seem a lot more attractive. Well, still only the ones you didn't used to serve spaghetti hoops to while he watched *The Simpsons*, but you take my point.

'I've been to three weddings this year and this is my third time at the singles table,' she tells me, widening her eyes for effect. 'I'm basically – and tragically – an expert at how to survive these things.'

'Are you an expert on how to handle all your

friends being married and leaving you out?' I ask, only semi-seriously.

'Oh, my friends gave up on me a long time ago,' she replies. 'We don't hang out like we used to.'

'Same,' I say, almost excitedly. 'They're all doing this stupid couples' cooking class in a couple of days, and they haven't invited me, just because I'm single. How out of order is that?'

'Honestly, stuff like that boils my blood,' Kat replies. I can tell she means it. 'Was it *Rachael* who organised it?'

You can tell exactly how Kat feels about Rachael by the mocking way she says her name. I can't say I'm her biggest fan at the moment, either.

'It was our other friend, Sally, who booked it all, I think,' I reply. 'But they're all going.'

Kat cocks her head and smiles.

'Can I borrow your phone?' she asks.

'Erm, yes,' I reply. 'Sure.'

I unlock my phone and hand it to her. A little trusting, considering we've just met, I suppose.

I watch as Kat taps the screen. Her smile just keeps on widening and there's a mischievous look in her eyes. Eventually she hands me my phone back.

'I've told them you'd love to go to couples' cooking with them, now you've got a date,' she informs me.

'Erm...' For a moment I just laugh awkwardly. '*I* have a date?'

I notice Simon and Pete standing a few metres away from us, at the side of the room, nursing beers as they so clearly ogle female wedding guests.

'At least let me pick which one,' I say with a sigh. No idea which one I'd choose.

'Not them,' Kat says with a snort. 'Me.'

I give her a look.

'Not like that, you silly cow,' she replies.

'Oh, no, I didn't mean... I didn't think... I just meant... you'd go to a crappy couples' cooking class with me, just to prove a point?'

'You'll be amazed what I'd do to prove a point,' she says with a smile. 'Especially this point. Just because we're single, doesn't mean we don't exist.'

I smile. I completely agree.

'Poppy,' I hear Sally call out from behind me. That's the problem when you're at the side of the table with a view of nothing but the person on the other side and the wall behind them. You don't hear anyone coming.

'Oh, hi,' I say as normally as I can, but even I think I sound like I've just been caught out doing something I shouldn't.

She looks at Kat and then back at me.

'Can I borrow you, babes?' she asks. 'Over here.'

'Yeah, sure,' I reply. I turn to Kat. 'Back in a minute.'

'Bring a couple more of these back with you,' she says, holding up her almost empty glass.

Sally frowns at her. Like Kat isn't her sort of person.

'What's up?' I ask Sally, as I realise she's leading me over to the others.

'You said you've got a date for couples' cooking?' Sally prompts excitedly once we're with Rachael and Lindsey.

'Erm, yes, I do,' I say kind of awkwardly.

'Who?' Rachael asks almost suspiciously.

'Well,' I laugh. It's a weird sort of laugh – certainly not my laugh. 'You're the one who sat me at the singles table. So, thank you for that.'

'Oh, my goodness!' Rachael claps her hands and

dances on the spot. 'I just knew you'd hit it off with one of them. Who is it? Is it Craig?'

Craig is the last one it would be because he will not talk to me. Perhaps that makes him my best bet.

'You'll just have to wait and see,' I reply. This is a problem for future Poppy, not for now.

'That's amazing! So pleased you can hang out with us again. *So* exciting,' Rachael replies. 'But not as exciting as my first dance. Which is happening pretty much now. Ladies, go get your men.'

I feel a little pang of anger deep in my stomach, at confirmation of the fact that my friends haven't been including me. And don't you just love how quickly the conversation went back to her?

'Let's hope we remember all our training from Marcus,' Sally says as she leaves.

Marcus was – I think – a professional dancer on *Strictly Come Dancing* or similar. He gave Sally and Seth dance lessons for their first dance. I am not being bitchy when I say this, honest, but you couldn't tell. Some people just aren't natural dancers. I'd know, I'm one of them.

'Poppy, wait,' Rachael says. 'I need a favour.'

Oh God, what could she possibly need from me?

She's asked basically nothing of me in preparation for the wedding, instead asking Lindsey and Sally because, y'know, their weddings were successful in that they produced marriages that are still going strong. I swear, it's like she thinks I'm cursed.

'Oh?'

Strong response, Poppy.

'Liam was pestering me to let him sit at the singles table,' she says with a roll of her eyes. 'I knew it would only be you and Kevin's oddball cousin, Kat, but he was insistent.'

'Okay...' I say, kind of awkwardly, given what I've learned from Liam today.

'Kat seems like a bit of a goer,' she continues. I'm not exactly sure what she means by that. 'I don't want her getting her claws into my baby brother.'

'I don't think he's her type,' I reply.

'Everything is her type,' Rachael insists. 'Anyway, it's time for the first dance, and, well, I don't want him with no one to dance with, and I don't want him dancing with *her*. So, I told him you'd dance with him.'

'Me?' I squeak.

'Yeah, so, if you can just do that for me, please,'

she says as I watch her attention on me slowly draining. She's looking around the room, probably trying to get eyes on Kevin, or see if the floor has cleared for her first dance.

'Do I have to?' I ask quietly.

'Liam,' she calls out. 'Liam, here. Poppy wants to dance with you.'

She dashes off.

'Oh, does she now?' Liam says once we're alone, through a huge grin that makes me feel beyond uncomfortable. 'I knew you'd come around.'

'Rachael asked me if I'd dance with you,' I point out.

'Maybe she can see what a good couple we make,' he suggests.

'I really don't think that's it,' I reply. 'This is it, okay? Just one dance, because Rachael asked me to, and in return I won't tell her about anything you've said today. Deal?'

Liam just smiles. I think he's picking his battles.

'Just one dance,' he says unconvincingly. 'That might be all it takes...'

The music starts and Rachael and Kevin take to the dancefloor. They're dancing to a cover of 'God

Only Knows' by John Legend. It really is beautiful in here, with the twinkling lights above us, the smooth music – there's such a sweet smell in the air, which you could be mistaken in thinking was coming from the giant wedding cake, but I (and only a couple of others) know that it's not real, it's a cardboard construction covered in something that looks like icing. The cake we're all going to be served later is some cheap and cheerful thing hiding in a back room.

'Ladies and gentlemen, if you'd like to join the bride and groom on the dancefloor,' the DJ announces.

'May I have this dance?' Liam asks, extending his hand.

I sigh.

'I'm doing this for your sister,' I remind him.

Liam wraps his arms around my waist and holds me close. I quickly put a bit of distance between our bodies. This is weird. So, so weird.

'I wish you wouldn't look at me like that,' he says with a heavy sigh.

'Like what?' I reply. 'Like you're my friend's little brother?'

'Well, yeah,' he says. He sounds almost annoyed. 'I'm a man now.'

'Look, there's nothing to be offended about, I'm not saying you're not an adult, I'm just a much older adult,' I point out.

'Oh my God, it's just ten years,' he replies. 'You need to chill out.'

'Right, okay,' I say with a roll of my eyes.

We just dance for a few seconds before he starts again.

'Do you think maybe this is why you're single?' he asks with a genuine curiosity.

Now *I'm* offended. I open my mouth to speak but he continues.

'Like, y'know, if you were less choosy and that,' he continues.

Wow, has it really come to this? A thirty-year-old divorcee getting advice from a twenty-one-year-old boy, and the general gist of that advice seems to be: just accept the first person who gives you the time of day. Forgive me for setting my sights a little higher than that.

Liam, Liam, Liam. He has such potential to be a good guy, the kind women (more his age, who didn't babysit him) would go crazy for. I feel like he's squandering it, with all this bravado, this brand of self-confidence that seems to exist exclusively in men. I'd say he needs me to knock him back, to show him that not every woman he wants is just going to fall at his feet, but it will be like water off a duck's back, I'm sure. If I'm getting any kind of impression from Liam right now, it's that if he ever did meet a woman who didn't fall at his feet, he'd just put something in their way for them to trip over. Example: telling them they're single because they're being too choosy.

'Cheers, Liam,' I say. 'You've given me a lot to think about.'

'Sure,' he replies with a sympathetic nod and a slight smile. The nod suggests he hasn't detected my sarcasm. The grin implies he thinks this is working.

'Mind if I cut in?' a voice from behind us says.

'Sorry, you're not really my type, and we're kind of having a conversation here,' Liam replies, rather rudely. I'm telling you – male confidence.

'I was talking to the lady.'

Liam narrows his eyes angrily then looks at me.

Once again, it isn't Chris Hemsworth coming to save the day. It is Kat, though – my actual superhero.

'I would love to dance with you,' I tell her. 'You don't mind, do you Liam?'

'I don't,' he says through a tight jaw.

He definitely does.

Kat steps in to replace Liam and I instantly relax.

'That boy is really starting to get on my nerves,' I tell her once we're alone. 'Bloody Rachael basically told me I *had* to dance with him.'

'She's off the goop, that one,' she replies. 'Imagine the look on her face if you banged her brother.'

I shudder at the thought.

'Are you not tempted to do it, just to wind her up?'

I laugh but Kat isn't kidding. This only makes me laugh harder.

'Probably not worth it in the long run,' I say.

'Fair enough,' she replies. 'Well, don't worry about it, I'm working on a plan to bust us out of here.'

'Bust us out of what, the wedding?' I ask.

'Yep,' she replies. 'I have a plan. There's no way

I'm spending New Year's Eve in here with this bunch of saddos.'

I have no idea what Kat could possibly be planning. We're at a country hotel in the middle of nowhere, and it's New Year's Eve. Even if she did 'bust us out', where the hell is she going to bust us to? I feel awful for saying this, given the fact I'm at the wedding of one of my oldest friends (even if she has kind of abandoned me for having the audacity to be single in my thirties), but the idea of going somewhere else to see the New Year in sounds wonderful. I doubt Rachael would be mad, if she even noticed, because other than forcing me to dance with her infant brother, she's not exactly making me feel like a priority guest, sticking me on the singles table, away from the other bridesmaids. If anything is going to annoy her about this situation, it's probably going to be the fact that the only two people to hit it off at the singles table are me and Kat. If a platonic relationship is the best she can do, when she's oh-so concerned about her poor, sad, single friends, well, that won't do, will it? Especially now she's basically confirmed that they've been doing things without me.

I can't wait to see their faces when I turn up to

couples' cooking with Kat. Well, what are they going to do? Stop inviting me places? They've clearly already done that. I may not be able to get a partner but at least I've got a partner in crime. Although I don't imagine my friends will be happy for me about that.

4

My single status, generally and at this wedding, has been a big talking point amongst my friends for months now. They've been really helpful – too helpful – so helpful they've been driving me crazy with it, and up until now I've been quite polite about it. I mean, I haven't torn anyone's hair out for repeatedly mentioning the fact that I'm single, again and again and again, which I think shows real strength.

Similarly, with all their super helpful suggestions of what I could do about this 'massive problem', I've been reasonably chill too. I didn't throw my phone out of the window when it was lovingly suggested I should download a few dating apps to try to find someone, nor did I flip out when Sally casually mentioned the agency she'd heard of where they will find you a plus one for special events (I was never quite sure whether they were intensive matchmakers or if you were essentially hiring a date, but wasn't massively fond of either option). Even today, being shoved on the singles table, with no prior warning – I took it like a champ. But this, here, right now... this is too much.

In a move that is both ridiculous and offensive, Rachael has decided that the best thing she can do for me is – I cannot believe I am saying this – rig the bouquet toss. Yes, that's right, she genuinely believes that it will help my sad, single status if I am the one who catches her flowers. I know whichever lucky lady catches the bouquet is supposed to be the one who gets married next, I'm just not sure that's how it works. As though catching them is going to make a man suddenly appear out of nowhere, and he's not only going to be interested in me, but we're going to get married, too. I know her flowers were expensive (because she told me a million times) but I doubt they can guarantee romantic results like that.

'Just stand in the front, at the middle, and I'll

make sure it goes to you, okay?' Rachael whispers to me. 'The DJ is going to announce the toss any minute. Just be front and centre.'

'Rach, you really don't have to do this,' I insist, still polite as ever. 'Honestly, I don't even really believe in this tradition. I didn't do it at my wedding.'

'You never know, maybe that's why it didn't work out?' she says.

She utters these words so casually I want to kill her. Rachael knows exactly why my marriage didn't work out and it certainly wasn't because I never threw my fucking flowers at her.

My shoulders fall.

'Fine, whatever,' I reply.

Well, as much as I want to flip out and throw the flowers right back at her, what's the point? Making a scene at Rachael's wedding is the sort of psychotic single girl behaviour she probably fears I'll soon succumb to. I don't want to give her the satisfaction.

'Okay, single ladies, if you want to make your way to the dancefloor, the bride is finally ready to part with her bouquet,' the DJ jokes.

To be fair, it is after 11 p.m. I know this is a wedding-meets-New Year's Eve party, but even so.

Rachael has really got the bang for her buck out of these bad boys, clinging on to her wedding bouquet for most of the day.

As instructed, I make my way to the dancefloor, which is slowly clearing so that Rachael can do her bit for the single ladies. Except, after standing here for a few seconds, it becomes embarrassingly apparent that I am in fact the only person here. I'm not the only single woman at this wedding, surely, but I'm the only one standing here, 'hoping' to catch the bouquet.

Rachael assumes the position, so I shuffle over to her.

'Do you want to just hand me them?' I whisper.

'Don't be silly,' Rachael insists. 'That's not how it works.'

I glance around the room. All eyes are on me and I don't think I've ever felt such crushing embarrassment. No one is even laughing at me – or the absurdity of the situation – instead they're all wincing, cringing, offering me pitying looks and sympathetic smiles. I'm tragic – properly tragic, the kind that is so sad it's not even funny. Now, finally, here in this moment I can safely say that I have hit rock bottom.

This is it. The lowest of the low. And the fact that Rachael is making me go through with it really feels like we're turning a corner with our friendship too. Why is it so important to her, that she would make me look like such a tit in front of everyone?

'Well, er, okay,' the DJ says, in that DJ voice they all use. Even he's embarrassed, and he just badly sang 'Agadoo' from start to finish because someone requested it and he realised he only had the instrumental version. 'Okay... erm... go... I guess.'

The DJ's uncertainty is balanced by the inevitability of me catching this bouquet. And to think, Rachael actually thought she needed to rig the bouquet toss. Somehow this is so much sadder.

'Here we go,' Rachael announces excitedly, as she turns around. Credit where it's due, she's giving it her all, as though she had twenty excitable singles behind her, ready to go. 'One... two... three!'

I half-heartedly hold my hands out in front of me, half-tempted to let the flowers hit the floor instead of catching them, but I'm worried this won't come across as the protest I would intend it to be, instead making it look like even when I'm the only single girl on the floor, I still can't catch the bouquet.

The last thing I want to do is make myself look even more single, as though that were a thing.

I sigh, emptying my lungs, holding out my hands, just wanting this to be over with. What happens next takes me by surprise. I can see the blue and purple bouquet heading straight for my hands but then this blur of red obscures it. It only takes me a second to realise it's Kat's bright red dress – and Kat, obviously, who intercepts the flowers. She cheers wildly as she catches it, then almost violently throws it down on the floor in that way you often see American footballers do so. Well, you do in the movies, at least. I can't say I've ever actually watched it. Sports, of any description, have never been my strong suit. I mean, clearly, right? I just lost out on a rigged bouquet toss.

'Woo!' Kat screams. 'I did it.'

The audience, who were already spectating a bit of a freak show, don't quite know how to react to this, so they don't. It's that good old polite English mentality of just ignoring things and having no visible reaction. I guess it's better that way.

Kat turns to me and grabs my hands. As the DJ awkwardly but quickly hits play on a song – any song – Kat makes me dance by moving my arms.

I glance over her shoulder at Rachael, who has a face like thunder. She turns her head sharply before marching off. I notice Sally and Lindsey scrambling from where they are to chase after her.

'Oh my God,' I say under my breath. I can't help but smile from ear to ear.

'I don't really know if I made that better or worse, to be honest,' Kat wonders out loud. 'But at least you weren't on your own with it.'

'I'm not sure either,' I laugh. 'But it certainly made me smile.'

'You think that's good,' she says, leaning closer, lowering her voice. 'I've found us another party to go to.'

'What? Now?' I blurt. 'Isn't it nearly midnight?'

'We'd better get a move on then, hadn't we?' she replies with a wink.

You know what, I've had enough of today, of this wedding, of having my single status shoved in my face. Wherever Kat wants me to go, I'm going.

'Okay, let's do it,' I reply.

Kat looks both ways before dragging me off. It's to make sure we're on no one's radar I suppose, but it gives me the impression that Kat often does things she isn't supposed to, and is always on the lookout for witnesses.

'Can I nip up to my room and get my coat?' I ask her.

'You're not going to need it,' she replies.

'Are you sure?' I ask. 'When I popped out for some air earlier it was freezing.'

'I'm sure,' she replies.

Kat leads me out of the function room, down a short hallway and then straight into the room next door. It's another function room, with another party in it. This one is clearly just a New Year's Eve party, with enormous gold, sparkling 2022 banners hanging everywhere, along with what must be hundreds of helium-filled balloons in a similar style. It's almost as though someone is as pleased to see the back of 2021 as I am. Don't get me wrong, when I was younger and optimistic, I looked forward to New Year's Eve, not just for the party, but for the idea of the new beginning. Who wouldn't be into the idea of reinventing themselves? Especially after a particularly bad year, or if life just didn't feel quite right. Now that I'm older, jaded and disillusioned after doing this dance a few too many times, I don't look at

New Year's Eve as a new beginning, I look at it as the end of another year where I still didn't get it right – whatever 'it' is.

I don't know how many people are in this room, but it's certainly more than were at the wedding. It's a much younger crowd too, so hopefully I can check the shame of being single at the door – the door where, thankfully, no one is actually checking anything, otherwise we wouldn't be just wandering in like this.

'So, I've scoped the place out, it's a work party, but it's a huge company, so who is gonna know?' Kat says casually, but loudly enough to be heard over the music, as she escorts me through the crowded room.

The room is glitzy and glamorous but, if you look closely, you can see the mess. Mess that comes from hours of partying. Discarded jackets and heels, prematurely popped party poppers, empty glasses, remnants of festive wrapping paper – probably from gift exchanges between those who haven't seen each other over the holidays. The people are messy too. Smudged make-up, frizzy hair, sweaty shirts on men who smell like they've had a few. Yep, this work party is in full swing. Hopefully we'll blend right in. It is exciting, being here when we're not supposed to be. It's been a long time since I had any real fun.

'And look at this,' Kat says excitedly, giving me an overly enthusiastic nudge towards the dessert table, almost causing me to faceplant into the brownies. 'You did say, when they served up the shitty wedding cake, that you'd kill for a brownie. I've saved you the hassle.'

I scrunch up my nose as I remember the traditional fruitcake wrapped in that sickly sweet white chewy icing that was served for dessert. Even Rachael herself said she wasn't a big fan, but that it was traditional. I hate fruitcake at weddings. It has no redeeming features. You can't even pick out the gross bits and eat the good parts because there are no good parts.

'Is this... ethical?' I ask Kat, kind of bizarrely, but I have had a fair bit of Prosecco and a few Pimm's cocktails, and I don't really know how else to ask what I mean.

'It's a company party,' Kat reminds me. 'And look, this is basically leftovers, everyone else has gone at it. They're all grinding on each other on the dancefloor now. Probably not their significant others –

probably just to feel alive. When I was in here before, scoping things out, a guy offered me a line. Trust me, no one is going to miss a couple of brownies.'

'What about six?' I joke. 'How many can I fit in my clutch?'

'You need to let your hair down,' Kat insists with a smile.

She's right. I grab a brownie, not wasting any time taking a plate or a napkin. It's not going to be in my hand for long.

'You're right,' I say through a mouthful.

'That's not what I mean,' Kat says. 'Well, yeah, you do need to let your hair down, but you need to literally let your hair down. That up-do sucks – I imagine the bride forced it on you?'

'A moody stylist,' I reply. 'Instructed by the bride. Believe me, I'd love to, but there's about eight thousand bobby pins in there.'

'Come here, I'll have it down before you've finished your brownie,' she says. 'I used to be a hairdresser. Well, sort of. Never quite finished the training. I was working somewhere and let's just say there was an overlap between me dating the boss and him being married. I cut his ponytail off – it felt like a fitting last job.'

Kat tells this tale so casually as she messes with my hair. I feel as though, with a story like that, surely that's the wildest thing to ever happen to a person in their life? She's telling the tale like she's talking about a boring Tuesday.

'Not that you need to be qualified to take pins out,' she reassures me. 'Or put them in, by the looks of it. She's done a terrible job. Oh, there we go.'

Kat untwists my hair, letting it hang loose. It's been up for so long that it's left me with big curls, which Kat rakes out with her hands a little.

There is a mirrored wall behind the dessert table. I can't help but admire my hair –well, anything looks better than a Nurse Ratched up-do.

'You're a regular fairy godmother,' I say. 'Can you do anything about my dress?'

'It's one of those multi-way bad boys, right?' she replies as she pulls at the slack around my shoulders.

'Oh yeah,' I reply. 'It wouldn't be half as ugly if Rachael had let me wear it the way I wanted to. You could do this twisted halter neck sort of style that I really liked, but she insisted on these "modest" short sleeves that create a sort of T-shape that isn't flattering at all if you're big up top. I feel like Johnny Bravo.'

'Come here,' Kat insists.

I should've guessed, when I offered my shoulders to her, that she was going to just undo my dress, right here next to the dessert table. I thought maybe she was getting a closer look, to see how easy it could be changed, before we maybe went to the toilets or something, but no. At least the dress is designed to be worn multiple ways, so it takes little more than me cupping my own boobs through the dress to keep it in place while Kat messes with the loose bits. It doesn't take long before we attract a couple of spectators. Two attractive men in their thirties.

'You could take a picture,' Kat suggests with a straight face. I'm sure she's kidding.

'I prefer the live show,' the shorter man with the blonde hair and the bright blue eyes says. 'You work with us?'

So much for us blending in.

'I'm Roy's ex-wife,' Kat replies, with so much confidence even I consider whether it could be true.

'His *ex*-wife?' the man replies.

'Yeah, he honoured my invitation,' she says. 'You know Roy.'

'Actually, I don't,' he says.

'Well, why don't we go find him?' Kat suggests, her tone almost flirtatious. 'And your friend can stay here with Molly, the new HR girl.'

It takes me about two seconds to realise *I* am Molly, the new HR girl.

I give her a subtle – but probably not that subtle – look.

'Have fun you two,' she sings as she wanders off with her new friend, leaving me with his old one.

'Erm, hi,' I say awkwardly.

'Hi,' he replies through an amused chuckle.

His eyes light up. The rest of his face soon follows.

'Molly, is it?' he says.

'Apparently so,' I reply.

'You don't really work in HR, do you?'

Obviously, he's on to me.

'Nope,' I give in. 'How did you guess?'

'I run the agency,' he replies with a laugh, but it's a warm friendly one – and a gorgeous one at that.

'And we definitely don't have a Roy working for us. I'm Fred, by the way.'

Fred offers me his hand to shake. He's tall – really tall in fact – he must be at least 6'5". He has dark brown hair and a thick, neat beard to match. I don't know if it's the light-hearted way he's taking us crashing his work party or his gorgeous Irish accent, but he's unbelievably charming.

'I'm actually Poppy,' I confess. 'From the wedding next door.'

Fred is still smiling, as opposed to having me removed from the party, which is unexpected. I feel like he wants to talk to me. I want to talk to him too.

'Does your friend always lead you astray like this?' he asks curiously.

'Erm...' I laugh awkwardly as I search for the words. 'We only met today. I *never* do anything like this.'

'That's what they all say,' he teases.

I laugh but it's true. I used to be a lot more fun (admittedly not Kat levels of fun) but these days not so much. Back when I was with Zac, we were always having fun, always out, living in a whirlwind. You won't believe it now, but Rachael, Sally and Lindsey were all the same. The five of us used to party until the sun came up in our twenties. I suppose we've all grown up. Well, some of us more than others, but you take my point.

'Well, don't worry, you're both welcome to stay,' Fred reassures me.

'Don't tell Kat that,' I reply. 'It'll take the shine off us being here and she'll want to leave.'

'Fair enough,' he says with a laugh. 'So, what do you really do? You know, when you're not working for me...'

'I manage the family framing company,' I say. Christ, it really does sound boring.

'It's not easy running a company,' Fred reasons, although I suspect he's only saying that because what else can he say? 'Well, it's nearly midnight...'

Worried I'm losing my audience – and in the spirit of doing things I don't usually do – my lips start moving before my brain can stop them.

'Do you want to dance?' I blurt. I did intend to sound natural and casual, honestly, but I really, *really* don't ever do things like this.

'I'd love to,' Fred says with a smile. 'Fancy a shot of something first? See the New Year in with a bang?'

Admittedly, I'd rather have a brownie (and I'd bet if Kat were here, she'd say she would rather have the bang) but I nod enthusiastically.

'Follow me,' he says with a twinkle in his eye.

Kat and her new friend are at the bar. They're not doing shots though. They're doing each other, if anything.

'Two Jägerbombs please, mate,' Fred asks the barman before turning to me. 'It's been a long time since I let my hair down.'

'It's been a long time since I had a Jägerbomb,' I reply. Ugh, even when I was fun, I never did like these things.

Fred notices Kat and his colleague kissing.

'Gosh, what would Roy say?' he jokes as he hands me my drink. 'Cheers.'

'Cheers,' I reply through a giggle.

I knock back my shot and feel my face practically scrunch closed – that's what it feels like, at least. As the burning feeling subsides, my muscles relax and I open my eyes.

Fred is laughing at me. God, he's handsome when he laughs.

'Right, let's have this dance,' he says. 'I'm expecting big things.'

'Erm, well, I love to dance,' I tell him. 'But I don't think I'm that good at it.'

'Well, that makes two of us,' he says, taking me by the hand, leading me into the heart of the dancefloor.

Being led onto the dancefloor by Fred feels amazing. Obviously, he's gorgeous, really charming, and seems like a such a nice man, but that isn't why. It's the feeling of being wanted by someone, of having no idea what's going to happen, of wishing something would. It's exciting, confidence boosting and – most importantly of all – a lot more fun than being at a wedding where I was constantly made to feel like a loser.

It's a reasonably fast song but Fred still holds me close as we move to the music. I can't help but laugh to myself – it's clearly a pop song, but I have no idea who it's by, which is a sign I'm getting old, surely?

It feels so good being in Fred's arms. I've been single for pushing a year, and my last relationship wasn't exactly serious, so it's fair to say I'm pretty jazzed to be touching a man right now. Maybe this is down to how much I've had to drink, but I almost feel as though I'm watching myself from above, up on the ceiling with all the rogue helium balloons. In fact, I actually forget it's New Year's Eve, until the DJ starts announcing the countdown.

'Ten... nine... eight... seven...'

Our bodies part and we look at each other as we continue the countdown.

'Three... two... one...' Everyone joins in, cheering excitedly, before... 'Happy New Year!'

Auld Lang Syne plays, because doesn't it always?

'Happy New Year,' I shout to Fred over the music.

He opens his mouth to reply – well, that's what I thought he was doing – but his lips only part slightly as they move towards mine. We kiss for a few seconds. It's a slow, smooth kiss. Gentle, but with the lightest flick of Fred's tongue, just enough to show me there's intention behind it. We can't be kissing for more than a few seconds – the bloody song is still playing – but it takes my breath away.

'Another drink?' Fred says casually. 'How about we make a night of it?'

'I'd really like that,' I reply.

I really would. I may not ever do anything like this any more but perhaps it's time I started.

5

What on earth is that banging sound?

I reach out and grab my phone from the bedside table. It's 8.45 a.m. – definitely not the time for banging.

My phone screen is so bright in my dark hotel room that I quickly lock it again and place it down. Around the time I realise my poor, hungover eyes can't stand the light, I discover that the banging noise is actually just the sound of my heartbeat in my ears. It's been a long time since I had a hangover like this – I don't think I've ever had a hangover like this. Wow, what a way to kick off my birthday. If this is thirty-one, I want no part of it.

I roll over, seeking the cooler part of the pillow, and a more comfortable position for my neck to see if it helps my headache. It's dark in here, which I appreciate, but as I plant my head back down on the pillow, I realise something: I'm in bed with a man. Oh my God, I'm in bed with a man. I know I was giving it the old 'I never do anything like this' last night but, believe me, I certainly *never* do anything like this. What happened last night? I remember kissing Fred, having more drinks, meeting back up with Kat and all of us having *even more* drinks. I kind of remember being back at the wedding.

Wow, I'm almost impressed with myself. I didn't realise I had it in me. Perhaps thirty-one isn't going to be so bad after all, if I'm a new and improved Poppy. Maybe the old 'new year, new me' bullshit isn't total crap? Or maybe it's just coincidence that last night was the night I decided to reinvent myself but, either way, I'm here for it.

The nerves of the old me slowly creep back. It was Fred who made the first move last night, locking lips with me. He wouldn't have done that if he didn't fancy me, would he? I need to look at last night as me getting a foot in the door. This morning, I need to follow it up with some action. Action that shows Fred I'm not only interested but worth it too.

I can just about make out his silhouette in this dark room, so I reach out slowly, placing my hand on his chest.

'Good morning,' I say quietly as I lightly brush my fingers against his pecs.

'Morning, sexy,' he replies.

I quickly take my hand back. That is not Fred. I know this because not only does it not sound like him, but I know who it does sound like.

'Oh my God, Liam?' I reply.

'You know it,' he says.

I quickly sit up, grabbing at the duvet, wrapping it around my body to protect my modesty. Oh my God. I know I was drunk last night, but I wasn't sleep-with-my-best-friend's-little-brother drunk, was I? I don't think I've ever been that drunk. I didn't think that drunk even existed. Fucking Jägerbombs!

I reach out for a light switch that I vaguely recall being above the bedside table. I only have to feel around for a moment before my fingers find it.

The sudden brightness is so harsh on my tired eyes that it makes them go funny for a second.

Flashes of lights, colours – I feel like I'm seeing into another universe. Then my eyes adjust and I see Liam lying in bed next to me, with what little I've left him of the duvet up to his waist, but he doesn't look like he's wearing anything so maybe I am in a parallel universe. I'd surely have to be to do... to do...

'Erg, it's too early for that,' I hear Kat say. That's when I realise she's lying across the bottom of the bed, fully clothed, like a weird take on a family dog.

'Kat?' I blurt.

I watch as she rolls over and rubs her eyes to try to get a better look at me.

'Jesus, what's wrong with you?' she asks.

It's only now that I look down and realise that I'm still wearing my bridesmaid dress. Oh.

'Nothing,' I insist quickly. 'Just hungover. And not expecting anyone in my bed.'

'You're both technically in my bed,' Kat points out. She yawns theatrically.

'Yep, me and Liam,' I say, kind of freaked out. 'Naked Liam.'

'I've got my boxers on,' he says, whipping back the covers to show me. God, even that disturbs me.

'Got it,' I say quickly, averting my eyes.

'Did you think you and him had... y'know?' Kat wiggles her eyebrows.

'No,' I insist. 'No, no, no.'

'You did, didn't you?' she says with a laugh. 'Don't you remember? We dared Liam to jump in the pool. He lost the key card for his room so I said he could stay here. His wet clothes are... somewhere.'

Now that she mentions it, it all starts coming back to me. God, things did get messy last night. Wonderfully, hilariously, invigoratingly messy. I feel alive – which is ironic, because I also feel like I'm dying. As horrible as this hangover feels, I'm enduring it like a badge of honour. I feel oddly proud of myself. I actually had fun for once, in forever. The only downside (now that I know I didn't sleep with Rachael's little brother) is the fact that I cannot remember what happened with Fred. I remember drinking with him, dancing with him, kissing him – and varying combinations of all three throughout the night – but I don't remember saying goodbye.

'We've got two choices,' Kat starts. She's lying on her back with her eyes closed, but she talks as though she's wide awake. 'We can either go back to sleep for a bit or we can go get some breakfast. What do you reckon?'

'Breakfast,' I say quickly. As much as I would love to sleep, there is no way I'll be able to, now that I know where I am, and who I'm with. This scenario is just beyond weird.

'Yeah, I could go for that,' Liam says. 'Unless someone wants to tempt me with something sweeter.'

I quickly hurry out of bed, adjusting my dress to make sure that all bases are covered.

'I admire your optimism, kid,' Kat tells him. 'But I think you're going to have to settle for pancakes.'

As I search around for my shoes, I can't help but marvel at just how identical mine and Kat's rooms are. I always find it a bit depressing, in hotels, when rooms are just carbon copies of one another. Then again, this is a big place. You would soon run out of ideas for making these rooms unique. Knowing the layout of the room, and all the storage spaces, means that I know where to look for my shoes, but I can't find them anywhere.

'Have you guys seen my shoes?' I ask. 'Dark purple heels.'

'You took them off somewhere last night,' Kat tells me as she wipes away smudges of black make-up from under her eyes in the mirror. 'You said you hated them.'

'I don't get girls,' Liam pipes up as he puts on his crinkled but hopefully dry clothes from last night. 'Why buy and wear shoes you don't like?'

'I took them off because I hated them, because they were uncomfortable, because they weren't my shoes and I was basically forced to wear them,' I reply, irked by a sweeping statement from a man about women and shoes.

'Ahhh,' he replies, like he gets it now. 'Rach made you wear them?'

'She made me borrow them from Sally, who is very precious about her shoes, and then yeah, she made me wear them. She said none of mine went with my dress,' I say.

'And now you've lost them,' Kat says through a smile. 'You're a rebel, I like you.'

'Oh, I'm not a rebel, I'm a dead woman,' I point out. 'But thanks. I like you too.'

'And I like both of you,' Liam says, a little too loudly for my hangover.

'You're still only getting pancakes, babe,' Kat points out. 'Right, let's go.'

'It's going to have to be a quickie for me,' I say, obviously referring to breakfast, but Liam's eyebrows shoot up with enthusiasm. 'I always go to my dad's for lunch on my birthday.'

Kat stops in her tracks.

'It's your birthday?' she squeaks as she makes a move to hug me. 'Champagne for breakfast. Liam can get it, to pay us back for putting him up.'

'Can we walk out slowly, so someone sees that I spent the night with you?' he asks.

Wow, you really have got to admire his optimism.

Kat narrows her eyes at him.

'Two bottles,' she says.

'Deal,' Liam replies.

'But you can't tell Rachael you slept in a bed with us,' I quickly say. 'I know it was innocent, and we were doing you a favour, but you know what she's like.'

'Oh, I know,' Liam says. He looks a jarring combination of amused and shell-shocked.

'Right, let's go,' Kat says. 'We'll see if we can find

your shoes in the dining room. Maybe we'll find your man too…'

Of all the things I could possibly want for my birthday, I think that might be top of the list.

6

Breakfast is in the hotel's main dining room. This means that it isn't just wedding guests who are present, it's everyone who is staying in the hotel – well, everyone but Fred, clearly.

To be fair, I don't know whether or not Fred was staying here last night. I assumed he was, given how late we were partying, but I suppose he could have got a taxi home if he lived close – not that I know where he lives, what his company was called, or even his last name. Yep, he's vanished, just like my shoes (well, Sally's shoes).

Still, I can't help but keep one eye out for Fred and the other for Rachael, because I really don't want her to catch me eating breakfast with her brother, lest she ask any questions.

Liam is sitting between us. He's got an air of Hugh Hefner about him. You know what I mean, Hugh's general demeanour when he was surrounded by his colony of bunnies, that contented smirk he always wore. Liam has that, despite being sandwiched between a couple of rabbits. I don't think anyone is looking at us and thinking anything untoward, but Liam is sitting between us grinning like the cat that got the cream – or the guy at the singles table who had the threesome. Bloody hell, imagine! Simon and Pete would have been less awkward.

Our server places our pancakes down in front of us. We've all gone for something a little different, though. Maple syrup for Liam, Kat opted for the fruit option, whereas I went for the extreme chocolate sauce and whipped cream bad boys – it is my birthday, after all.

'I need these, after the night we had,' Liam tells our poor server with a wink before knocking back the last mouthful of champagne from his glass.

I glance at Kat, as though to ask her: are you really letting him get away with this?

'He's paying for breakfast,' she reminds me with a smile and a shrug.

'Fair enough,' I laugh.

I dig into my pancakes and – oh my gosh, they are good. Thick fluffy pancakes with lashings of Nutella and peaks of whipped cream on top. Birthday perfection. The champagne is good too, but I don't want to have too much. It is still morning and I am having lunch with my dad later. I flag down our waiter.

'Can I get a latte, please?' I ask him.

'She means *a latte* champagne,' Kat insists in a funny accent. 'Can we get another bottle, please?'

'Oi, I can't get drunk,' I tell her with a laugh. 'I'm not even sure I'm sober from the last time, given that it was only hours ago, and I definitely don't want to spend my birthday drunk.'

'Speaking of your birthday, any wild plans?' Kat asks.

'Just seeing my dad,' I reply. 'I always see him on my birthday. I'd normally see my friends too but, I don't know, it's just not happening this year.'

'What do you mean?' Kat asks.

'Well.'

I glance over at Liam before I say his sister's name. He's pretty engrossed in his pancakes and I don't think he's even listening to us; he's more interested in his food and whether people are staring at the three of us or not. No one is staring. I'm also not saying anything bad about his sister, so it's fine.

'Rachael said, with this being the day after her wedding, she needed the day to just enjoy being married, so could we all celebrate my birthday in the next week or so,' I explain.

'That bitch,' Kat says.

'Who's a bitch?' Liam asks, suddenly interested. Thankfully he didn't hear.

'Your sister,' she tells him.

Never mind.

'Oh, yeah, totally,' he agrees. 'What's she done now?'

'She won't let Poppy celebrate her birthday because it's her wedding day Boxing Day,' Kat replies.

I know what she means.

'What about Sally and Lindsey?' Liam says. 'Can't you just go out with them?'

'Well, they agreed it would be better to wait, so...'

My voice trails off. Yep, I realise how pathetic I

sound right now. I can't even scramble a couple of my friends on my birthday.

'Right, stuff them,' Kat insists. 'We're going out for a drink tonight.'

'Yes!' Liam cheers. 'Let's have a few drinks, get weird, keep the party from last night going.'

'Sorry, babe, no boys allowed,' Kat tells him, patting him on the shoulder.

Liam's face falls.

'Oh, please don't feel like you have to take me out for pity drinks,' I insist. 'Honestly, it's fine.'

'It's not pity drinks,' Kat insists. 'I had a lot of fun with you last night. You're one wild lady when you get going.'

She says this right as our waiter places the bottle of champagne down on the table.

'Oh, yeah,' Liam tells him, with a knowing nod.

The waiter nods back, as though he's impressed, while he tops up our glasses.

Kat takes a sip and sighs.

'Worth it,' she says. 'It always tastes better when it's free.'

Glancing around the busy dining room, I notice Sally, Lindsey and their husbands walking through the tables. They find a spot and sit together as a four-some. See – I'm not even invited to eat breakfast with them.

'Okay, tonight,' I say to Kat. 'It's on, let's do it.'

'Fabulous,' she replies. 'Let's see what trouble we can get into tonight.'

'Great,' I say.

I glance around the room again. Still no sign of Fred.

Whatever kind of trouble we may or may not get into tonight (I don't think I have another night like last night in me), it would be really nice to bump into him again. Sadly, I don't think that's going to happen, do you? Still, it's nice to feel like I have a friend again, one who actually wants to spend my birthday with me.

At least I can say I came away from the singles table with something.

7

'Hello, Dad,' I say brightly as he opens his front door. His smile widens when he claps eyes on me.

'Sloshed already, at 1 p.m.?' he immediately replies.

My eyes widen, like a rabbit caught in the headlights, or a daughter being caught drunk by her dad, I suppose.

'I'm not sloshed,' I insist with a scoff, which actually makes me sound like I've had a few more than I have – which was only a couple of glasses over breakfast. Yep, I realise that sounds bad. 'I had two glasses of champagne with my pancakes this morning. It *is* my birthday. And, anyway, I'm not drunk. Why would you think I was drunk?'

My dad just laughs at me for a moment before nodding down at my body.

'Your jumper is on inside out,' he replies.

I glance down and, sure enough, the exposed seams from the inside of the jumper give me away.

'Ah,' I reply.

'Come on, come in then,' Dad laughs. 'You lush.'

My dad has this cool and classy Charles Dance vibe about him – honestly, you would never guess that I have a share of his DNA. He's so well-spoken, whereas I seemed to gravitate towards the same Lancashire accent my mum always joked she was cursed with. I don't think she actually believed that, but I suppose when you work in a sometimes-snobby industry like the legal profession, there will always be people quick to judge you on your regional dialect. Mum was brilliant though. If anyone ever made her feel bad about the way she spoke, she would ramp up the accent and start affectionately (but completely sarcastically) calling everyone 'duck'.

'If I'm being honest, I'm more hungover than I am drunk,' I confess as I follow Dad into the lounge.

The room looks fantastic, with pink balloons and 'birthday girl' banners all over. The coffee table is laid out with my birthday lunch – the same lunch we have every year – and he's even baked me a cake. Birthday lunch is always crisp sandwiches, glass bottles of Coca-Cola and homemade cake and there's a reason for it.

After I was born, when my mum was finally in the mood to eat something, all she wanted was a crisp sandwich and a Coke. My dad went out and got her everything she needed (I think he felt so guilty for missing my birth that he would have gone out and got her a Bentley if she'd asked for it) and she said it was the best thing she'd ever eaten. It became sort of a tradition that we would always have it for lunch on my birthday, and after Mum passed away it felt even more important to uphold the tradition.

And then there's the cake. Mum would always bake me the most incredible birthday cakes. Elaborate things, with tiers and fancy icing – sometimes she would take requests, and I would give her the most ridiculous ideas, like asking for it to be entirely gold, or to incorporate a strange ingredient like bacon, but she loved the challenge, and she always absolutely smashed it. My dad has always been hopeless at baking but when my first birthday came around after Mum died, and I walked in here and saw that he had baked me a cake, I couldn't stop crying.

'Come on, it's not that bad,' he joked, making light of my reaction, and to be honest it was a little over baked, and the frosting was messy, but the fact that he had tried somehow broke my heart and mended it at the same time. It's been four years since we lost her, and my dad has kept making me birthday cakes – he's getting quite good at it now. I can tell just by glancing at the chocolate cake he's made this year that it's his best effort yet.

'Ah, the wedding of the century – after the last wedding of the century,' Dad jokes. 'How was it?'

'Meh. Ups and downs,' I reply. 'It was a lot more fun than the other girls' weddings. I made a new friend, she was a blast – we wound up sneaking off to a different New Year's Eve party, which was amazing.'

'An apple that hasn't fallen far from the tree,' Dad says with a smile. 'That sounds like something your mum would have done. So, what were the downs?'

'It's just weddings, I guess. They always make me

think back to my own, which makes me think about my divorce, and everything that happened with Zac. Anything that makes me think of Zac always knocks the wind out of my sails.'

'You really loved him, didn't you?'

Dad gives me a sympathetic smile.

'I think what scares me the most is: was he the love of my life? It certainly felt that way, and I haven't met anyone since who I've felt even close to that way about. What if everyone gets one love of their life, and Zac was mine, and I blew it?'

My dad sighs.

'Sorry, that was really insensitive of me,' I say quickly. 'I know Mum was yours and...'

Mum's death was so sudden. One of those horrible stories you hear about where someone goes out in their car and is in the wrong place at the wrong time. If I'm being honest, it's probably one of the reasons I still haven't learned to drive. It doesn't make much sense – I suppose these things rarely do – because I'm fine in cars with other people driving, but the thought of going out in one alone makes me feel sick.

'Well, maybe we get more than one,' Dad suggests as he hands me my sandwich.

I kick off my shoes and get comfortable on the sofa.

'There's something I've been meaning to tell you. I wasn't going to do it today but it feels like the right time...'

He pauses. It can't be for more than a few seconds but it's enough time for me to float the idea of Dad having every possible illness, disease and disorder I can think of.

'I've met someone,' he says with a smile.

My jaw drops. I'm more shocked than I would have been if he'd given me bad news – although obviously still so relieved he didn't. Not just because of my naturally pessimistic nature, but because I've never heard anything so unbelievable in my life. How? How is this possible?

'You've met someone?' I reply. 'How? Where? Where do you even meet people?'

Dad laughs.

'Her name is Dora. I met her online,' he says with a pride that is so very clearly for his ever-improving technological skills, as he calls them.

'Did she ask you for your bank account details?' I only half joke.

Again, he just laughs at me.

'Don't be daft, it was on a website for widows and widowers to connect. I have actually met her,' he insists. 'She helped me make that cake.'

I glare at my birthday cake. The birthday cake my mum always used to make for me. Now my dad is making them with his new secret girlfriend that he met online. It's just one of those gut reactions, a first thought that pops into my head, but the idea of someone replacing my mum practically winds me. I am happy for my dad, of course I am, it's been four years since we lost Mum. Why shouldn't he live his life? I suppose it just reminds me that my mum isn't coming back.

'My point is, don't get so caught up in this idea of there being just one right person for everyone,' he says. 'You need to move on.'

Dad, reading the room, doesn't say much else about Dora, and I don't want to ask any questions, not right now. I don't want him to know that I'm kind of freaked out about it.

'Says the man who hasn't really been in Mum's

office since the day she died,' I remind him with a smile.

'These days it's mostly just because I don't know what to do with everything,' he replies. 'But, okay, I'll make you a deal. How about we both make every effort to look forward, instead of back? I'll sort out your mum's office, and you do whatever it is you need to do, but no more being sad at weddings, okay?'

'Yes, Dad,' I say, like a kid who has just been caught doing something she shouldn't.

I'm not sure what's less likely to happen, me moving on or my dad clearing out Mum's old office. Then again, it sounds like he's been making sneaky moves of his own. I'm low-key horrified at the idea of him using dating sites, not because he's older, or even because he's my dad, it's because my brief stint on Matcher left me horrified. I received so many unsolicited dick pics it was months before I even considered dating again. Grim.

'Goodness, I can't believe my little girl is thirty-one,' he says with a sigh. 'Or that she's had a sandwich in her hand for more than five minutes without eating it.'

'Sorry,' I say quickly. I take a big, meaningful bite. 'It's great, thank you.'

'Just let me know if you want some cake before or after your presents,' he adds.

The sandwich is great, and the cake does look amazing, even if he did have help which I'm starting to suspect he wasn't going to disclose, but there's a feeling deep in my stomach throwing off my appetite. I know that my dad is right. I need to stop looking into the past, stop dwelling on my divorce, and start living for the future. I felt like that's what I was trying to do last night, with Fred, until we somehow lost each other between the two parties. But if I can hit it off with Fred, I can hit it off with anyone. And if my sixty-year-old dad can find love, then maybe there's hope for us all. I just hope I can do it without an app.

8

'I just found out my dad has a girlfriend,' I blurt out of nowhere.

'Oh, boy,' Kat replies. She turns to the barman. 'Can we get two more of these, please?'

We're currently sitting at the bar in Bar None – one of those ultra-trendy cocktail places that seem to be constantly springing up, where everyone is cool and the drinks seem to take twenty minutes to mix, so I guess it makes sense she orders our next round now.

I had assumed I would be spending the latter half of my birthday at home, alone, probably eating a takeaway and watching a trashy movie, so to be all dressed up and sitting in a bar sipping mojitos with Kat is more than a pleasant surprise. It feels good to have someone to talk to as well, especially given the news I received from my dad today.

'I'm a child of divorce,' Kat says in a voice that has clearly said it a thousand times. It obviously doesn't bother her any more. 'I was like eleven when it happened, so more of my memories of my parents are of them separated than together. They were both remarried by the time I turned fourteen which means that, for my rebellious teenage years, I had four parents on my case about everything. I do remember my mum and dad arguing a lot, before they split, so it was easier to see how much happier everyone was by the time they were with other people. And even though I had two sets of parents, I got two lots of a whole load of other stuff – Christmases, birthdays, Easter eggs. I'm just gutted I was out of the Tooth Fairy years; I would have cleaned up.'

I laugh.

'It sounds as if it was all for the best,' I say. 'Sometimes divorces are inevitable.'

'So, your parents divorced too?'

'Erm, no, actually, I'm divorced,' I admit. I still hate telling people. I think the only reason I'm embarrassed by it is because I'm still young. I hate that *they* were right, those people who said Zac and I were too young to tie the knot. No one likes to think of themselves as being young and stupid, even though we all were at some point, I suppose.

'Oh, wow, really?' Kat replies, interested but in no way judging. She isn't even reacting like it's a big deal but, I suppose given that she's lived through it and it's all worked out for the best, it isn't.

'Yeah, but I guess it's not something to get into on my birthday,' I say with a laugh.

'No, of course not,' she replies. 'So is your mum...'

Kat's voice trails off. I get it. People are never sure how to ask.

'She passed away,' I tell her. 'She was in a car accident. Wrong place, wrong time kind of thing. It's going to sound strange, but you kind of remind me of her. You do what you want, you say what you think. You don't take any rubbish from anyone, which I always really admired about my mum, but I've never quite been able to get there myself.'

'She sounds like she was a seriously cool lady,' Kay says with a smile.

'She was,' I reply. 'It's been years, it's not like my dad is rushing into anything, I just had no idea he was using a dating app!'

'Which one?' Kat asks curiously. 'I have generous parameters; I could have seen his profile.'

Oh, God, imagine! The only thing worse than the idea of me dating a friend's brother would be a friend dating my dad.

'It was an app for widows and widowers,' I tell her.

'Ah, right, okay,' she replies. 'I've not resorted to that one yet.'

I laugh but Kat raises her eyebrows, as though to suggest there may have been one or two strange choices she's given a go in an attempt to find love.

'I don't want to get all therapist on you or anything,' Kat starts. 'Especially not on your birthday, and definitely not in a bar. But how do you feel about it?'

'It's a weird one,' I reply. 'He's my dad. I love him. I want him to be happy. I guess it's just hard for me to think about him with someone else. Not because he's my dad, although no one likes to think of their parents as having any romantic feelings, no matter how old they are, but it's more to do with the fact that, well, it feels like this woman is taking my mum's place. Not like she's trying to or anything, just, simply, she's occupying the space where my mum used to be, and I know she's not coming back to fill that gap but...'

I sigh.

'I think holes can be filled by all sorts,' Kat says. I raise my eyebrows and she cackles. 'No, come on, I'm being serious for once. The hole your mum left in your hearts and the chair she left at the table are different things. The chair signifies her loss, but your dad having someone else to sit with him doesn't change the way you feel, or replace your mum, but if it makes him happy...'

'It sounds like she does,' I say. 'She helped him bake my birthday cake. I guess because Mum used to do that, it just freaked me out a bit.'

'Was it good cake?' Kat asks.

I can't help but laugh.

'Yes, it was really good,' I tell her.

'Sometimes that's enough,' she says with a shrug.

'If life is short, then take good cake where you can get it, that's what I say.'

I smile at her.

'You would actually make a really good therapist,' I say.

'I'm just talking semi-philosophical tipsy shit,' she insists, sipping her drink and batting her hand.

'You're talking sense,' I tell her. 'And you supply drinks – that makes a world of difference. I think more people would go in for therapy if cocktails were involved. Then again, I imagine more people would need it.'

'I'll stick with being your own personal therapist,' Kat says with a smile. 'Seriously, though, I know what it's like, when all your friends outgrow you, you've got stuff going on, and no one to talk to. So, if you ever need anything, or to talk – I'm your friend. Call me.'

I may have only known Kat for little more than a day, but I couldn't be happier to have found friendship with her. She seems like a good person – and a really fun one too. I meant it when I said she reminded me of my mum, they've got that same energy, and it's one that supercharges me.

People are right when they say: when you know, you know. I don't think love at first sight only applies to romantic relationships, I think you can apply it to friendships too.

Then again, I've *known* before, and look where that got me.

9

Things between me and the girls have been feeling a bit off for a while now. On the one hand, I get it, our lives are moving in different directions, but on the other hand, surely that's no reason we can't still be friends?

I am trying to come to terms with the fact that maybe there isn't always going to be a place for me with them in their social activities, but when Kat invited herself along to the couples' cooking class, the idea of turning up with her was too tempting to resist. Just for once, I didn't want to resign myself to being the sad single friend, I wanted to join in – even though, technically, it was an activity I wouldn't usually want to join in with. It's the principle of the matter.

Of course, what sounds fantastic in theory (and after a few drinks) isn't always as satisfying in practice, and now that I'm standing here with Kat in tow, my friends and their significant others all staring at us, I actually feel worse than ever. I thought this was going to be great; a way to be included, keeping the numbers up and even in a positively feminist way. Everyone looks so annoyed though, so it's clearly not playing out like I'd hoped.

'Kat?' Kevin blurts. 'What are you doing here?'

I forget that Kat and Kevin are cousins – probably because they're not in any way alike.

'I'm with Poppy,' she announces.

'Ohhh,' he replies, as though he's just had some big realisation. 'We all had our suspicions...'

'Poppy, what are you doing?' Rachael asks, her face contorted with bemusement. 'I thought you had a date.'

'Well, I just, er...'

'She really wanted to come,' Kat interrupts me. 'So I said I'd come with her.'

'Is there a problem here?' a short, redheaded woman asks us in hushed tones.

We're in one of the kitchen classrooms at the local college, and I wouldn't exactly say we were making a scene, but it seems like we're already in trouble with the teacher.

The room reminds me of every food tech classroom I've ever been in. Multiple workstations are dotted around, each with its own sink, hob and oven. Imagine an indoor version of *The Great British Bake Off*, just with a secondary school vibe that somehow makes you panic about having PE later, and without the hilarious hosts.

'No, no. No problem,' I insist, embarrassed.

'Okay, well, if you get your aprons on, we're ready to start,' our teacher replies.

'Poppy, why are you acting out like this?' Sally asks, calling me out in front of the gang. 'Don't think we didn't notice you go AWOL from the wedding, and now you're turning up here with her? And I see you haven't brought my shoes, like you said you would when I texted you only a couple of hours ago!'

'I forgot your shoes at my dad's,' I lie. I never did find them again at the wedding, so my plan is to buy her a new pair and hope she doesn't notice. I'd never hear the end of it.

'Is *she* making you do this stuff?' Rachael asks, shooting Kat a dirty look.

Kat cackles with laughter.

'I just don't understand why you would bring some random girl to this,' Sally says. She is beyond bemused. I hate the way they're all looking at me, even the husbands. They're not saying anything (would they even dare?!) but I can tell they're judging me too.

'Because I want to be included,' I insist. 'And I'm not letting my social life be dictated by what you all seem to think is my inability to find a man. So why wouldn't I bring a girl?'

I feel good about myself, for finding my voice, for sticking up for myself and defending my (what they seem to think is an) alternative lifestyle.

'Okay couples, we're going to start by warming up our ovens and ourselves,' the class leader starts. 'So, fire up your ovens to 200 degrees centigrade and then sensually massage each other's hands. Big, meaningful strokes, look into each other's eyes…'

Oh. So that's why I wouldn't bring a random girl

to couples' cooking class. It isn't just about the cooking, it's about the couples too. Oh, now I get why everyone is looking at me like that. Yep, this is weird.

Rachael's phone starts ringing, breaking the awkward silence.

'This number has called me three times now, I'd better see who it is,' she announces. 'Hello?'

Rachael listens for a few moments before her eyes dart in my direction.

'Right, I see,' she says. She listens a few more seconds. 'Okay, one moment please… Poppy, it's for you.'

'For *me*?' I reply.

'It's a man called Fred who apparently – in a move that has made me very angry and concerned for my data – got my number from the hotel, to contact you. He says he has your shoes. How does he have your shoes?'

'*My* shoes?' Sally chimes in angrily. 'The ones she said were at her dad's?'

Rachael laughs, but it isn't an amused laugh, it's an angry one. Her cheeks flush and her jaw tightens.

'I see,' she says before turning back to me. 'Apparently you took them off when you were trying to convince Liam – my brother Liam, I assume – to jump in the hotel pool naked. He also wants a word with you.'

Rachael meaningfully holds out her phone for me to take and, honestly, she looks so angry, I daren't refuse.

I reach out, wondering whether this might be some kind of trap, but take the phone from her and hold it to my ear. Everyone is watching me. Only Kat is smiling.

'Erm, hello?' I say.

'Poppy, hello,' Fred says. I can hear his smile down the phone. 'Sorry, did I just land you in it?'

'That's okay,' I reply. 'What can I do for you?'

God, I sound so awkward, and ridiculous.

'I lost you at the party and I couldn't find you the next day,' he replies. 'I had your shoes but, also, I wondered, erm… would you like to go for dinner with me this evening?'

'Oh,' is about all I can say.

'I did try to call earlier, but I had to get someone at the hotel to tell me whose wedding it was, give me their number, and your friend didn't answer… I know it's a bit short notice… If you'd rather…'

'Oh, no, that's fine,' I say – again, so awkward, but

everyone is still listening to my half of the conversation.

'Okay,' Fred says with a laugh. 'How about I meet you at Salvo's at half seven?'

'Yep, sounds good,' I reply. 'See you then.'

'See you?' Rachael repeats back to me as I hand her phone back. 'You're going to see this random man?'

'I'm going to get Sally's shoes back, aren't I?' I point out.

'Places, people, places,' the class leader insists for our benefit.

'This isn't over,' Sally warns me. Lindsey just shoots me a look. She's always been the quiet one, but I've always been able to read her eyes.

I can't believe they're all so mad at me, just for letting my hair down a bit, for the first time in ages.

'So, you're seeing Fit Fred again,' Kat eventually whispers to me when I take my place next to her behind our counter.

'He asked me on a date,' I confess. 'I'm meeting him at half seven.'

Kat's eyes light up for me. Now that's a friend.

'It's half six now,' she replies. 'We need to go and

get you ready. What say we just slink out of here now, hope no one notices? Unless you want to rub my neck while I broil something?'

'Ooh, tempting,' I joke. 'But, yes, let's go. I don't think we're wanted here and it's clearly about to get weird. Anyway, I need different clothes, make-up and personality.'

'I'll give you one out of three,' Kat replies through a laugh. 'If this is a date, you need to wear something sexier. Who knows, maybe this time you won't lose him at the end of the night?'

I just smile. Wouldn't that be nice?

10

Salvo's – a gorgeous little Italian restaurant in town – is one of my favourite places to eat. I don't think I ever met an Italian I didn't like (the food or the people) and this place has the best of everything. Salvo, the owner, is the life and soul of the place. He's here working every night, even though I'm sure he doesn't need to, to the point where he's sort of a celebrity. Everyone who has been here more than once knows him, and while he treats everyone who walks through the doors like a member of his family, he can't possibly remember everyone.

Still, after being greeted by Salvo himself, I was shown to a table where Fred was already sitting waiting for me. I'm all flustered, after dashing home to throw on my cleanest little black dress, and the first pair of heels I could find both of. I piled on more make-up, attempting that 'taking it from day to night' thing beauty bloggers talk about, but I feel like I'm sweating it all off already anyway. It's been about thirty seconds since I sat down, and about twenty-nine seconds since everything beyond our table just faded from my attention. It's a small, round table, perfect for an intimate dinner for two. There's a lit candle in the centre of the table but that's about all I take in. I can't take my eyes off Fred.

'I'll be back shortly with your menus,' Salvo says. 'And you look like a couple who would appreciate a garlic pizza bread.'

We both freeze for a second or two, when Salvo refers to us as a couple, but quickly soften again.

'Hi,' Fred says with a smile.

'Hi,' I reply.

God, he looks good. I don't know how buzzed I was on New Year's Eve, but I feel like I had no right to be as confident as I was. I should have been terrified. I'm nervous now – even armed with the knowledge he at least likes me enough to invite me out for dinner – but Fred is so clearly out of my league.

He's wearing a crisp white shirt that somehow looks like it's the exact right size for his body; from his broad shoulders to his slim waist, it fits him to perfection. His hair is neat and his beard looks so perfect he has to have brushed it. His aftershave smells deliciously intoxicating and his eyes are mesmerising. I feel like he's putting me under some kind of spell. But that's what it feels like, when you get that instant connection with someone, isn't it? And I haven't felt it in so long. I just hope and pray that we still get along as well as we did on New Year's Eve. Don't get me wrong, I am happy for myself, and I'm not trying to immediately ruin this by overthinking it, but surely this whole situation is too good to be true?

'I want to say you're not an easy girl to find, but it was surprisingly easy to track you down,' he says. 'And don't worry, I have your shoes in my car.'

'Yeah, I reckon my friend Rachael is going to be writing a very strongly worded email. Subject: GDPR,' I joke. 'And then another one to me. Subject: Going AWOL at wedding.'

'I just had so much fun with you and your friends that night,' Fred says. He smiles nervously. 'And I feel like we had such a spark, I knew I had to see you again.'

I take a sharp breath that hopefully isn't as noticeable as it seems.

'There's just one thing though,' Fred starts, and that's when I know it's coming. Some story, some fact – some*thing* that confirms my worst suspicions. That this is, of course, too good to be true.

'Oh?' I say as casually as I can which, it turns out, is not all that casual. When I say it, I sound like I'm taking air in, rather than letting it out.

'That guy that you met at the party,' he starts. 'He's not me. Well, no, it was me, but it wasn't me-me.'

He's getting flustered so he pauses for a second. Then he laughs.

'Sorry, this isn't coming out right,' he says. 'Let me try this again. The version you met of me at the party is not the fairest representation of me as a person. I'm not really that much fun usually, which sounds lame, but I'm actually quite boring.'

'I'm boring too,' I say excitedly. 'The night of the

party – that wasn't anything like me either. I never do anything like that. I kept saying as much to myself in my head. I was so nervous coming here tonight, thinking you were expecting a bit of a wild child when the truth is my life is not exciting at all.'

Fred laughs.

I feel my Apple watch vibrating on my wrist. I dart my eyes back and forth, in a way that hopefully Fred doesn't notice. It's just my dad calling. I'll just ring him back later. I can't wait to talk to him, actually, to tell him I was on a date, to show him that my love life is just as active as his, thank you very much.

'Other than your boring sounding job, I thought you were a bit of a party girl,' Fred admits. 'I was worried you were going to find out I was dull and want nothing to do with me.'

I giggle like a shy little girl. Thank God he knows I'm not cool now.

'So, we're both boring,' I say – and I sound so happy which, given what I just said, is so bizarre.

Fred places his hand on the table, in front of him, next to the large rounded bottle with the candle in it. You can hardly see the bottle underneath. The candle has been lit so many times that the wax has melted down the sides repeatedly, different coloured candles over years and years, which not only looks beautiful but it makes me wonder about all the couples it has sat between. I wonder if any of them have been as perfect for each other as me and Fred?

I place my hand in his and he holds it so lightly it makes me shiver.

'Both boring,' he says contentedly. 'But honestly, if we have as much fun as we had on New Year's Eve, boring is exactly what I want. I'm sick of the dating game, all the who texts who first, what did this person mean when they used this emoji, how many days do I have to wait to text again and so on. I want my next relationship to be with the one. The person I spend the rest of my life with. I just want easy.'

'Easy is my middle name,' I announce, a little too enthusiastically, right as Salvo places our menus down in front of us.

'I'll be back with your pizza bread,' he says, stifling a laugh.

Fred laughs at me and it makes me feel alive. Not only that, but the fact he's being so open about what he wants is one hell of a turn on. Normally I'd be trying to read between the lines, or trying not to scare men off by – God forbid – caring too much and seeming too interested.

'Well, easy is exactly what I'm looking for,' he replies.

I notice my watch vibrating again. It's Dad *again.*

'I'm so sorry, my dad has just tried to call me, I hate to be rude, but do you mind if I just check my phone quickly? He's called twice, I'm just a bit worried about him,' I say.

I feel awful asking, when things are going so well but, you know, it's my dad.

'Oh, no, absolutely,' Fred insists. 'Please, do what you need to do, make sure he's okay.'

Gosh, he's perfect.

I actually have four missed calls from Dad – and he's calling again.

Fred looks concerned as he notices.

'Answer it, make sure he's okay,' he says encouragingly.

I mouth the words 'thank you' at him as I answer.

'Hello?' I say quickly.

'Poppy, darling, sorry to bother you,' he says. 'Can you talk?'

He's using the tone of voice he usually uses when

he calls about something like, I don't know, accidentally changing the source on the TV and not knowing how to change it back, no matter how many times I show him which button it is.

'Erm, not really at the moment,' I say. 'Is everything okay, though?'

'Nothing to panic about,' he reassures me. 'I have some good news and some bad news. And then some more good news, and some more bad news. Inspired by your words, I've just been cleaning your mum's office.'

I'll bet he's found something and then broken it, or fixed something and then lost it, but whatever it is, it doesn't sound like something to interrupt my date with.

'I'm actually on a date at the moment, Dad, so is it okay if I call you back later?' I ask, my words growing close together as I go on, in that way people always talk when they're winding up to ending the call.

'Poppy, you're still married,' he blurts quickly. His tone has changed to something more serious and his voice is much louder. I don't say anything. 'Poppy? Poppy, are you there? I said you're still married.'

'I'll call you back in a moment,' I reply softly.

I knew it. I knew it from the bloody start. Things with Fred were just too good to be true. Tonight was going too well. I mean, come on, the way we met, it's practically Cinderella. I meet a man who is the millennial embodiment of Prince Charming, we meet before midnight and go our separate ways soon after, and he finds me by returning my shoes. Seriously? This whole thing has been nothing but a fairy tale from start to finish. The universe playing a cruel joke on me. Giving it the old 'here's what you could have won!'

'Shit, is everything okay?' Fred asks me once I'm off the phone. My face must say it all.

'I'm so sorry, it's my dad, he's having trouble breathing,' I reply. 'I need to go to him.'

'Absolutely,' Fred insists as a concerned look takes over his face. 'Is there anything I can do?'

'No, no,' I insist. 'I'm so sorry.'

'Perhaps we can try this again some other time?' he asks. God, he somehow seems both completely understanding and clearly so disappointed, which only makes me feel worse.

As first dates go, this one is definitely a stinker. I

feel bad for lying to him – but I can't exactly tell him the truth, can I? Not after insisting I was oh-so easy. Still being married isn't easy, is it? I can't still be married, surely? I got divorced. I remember it well. It was one of the hardest times of my life – what on earth is my dad talking about?

Anyway, it's not technically a lie, because if my dad has ruined my date for no good reason, he really will be having trouble breathing when I get my hands on him.

11

24 JANUARY 2006

I'm convinced that there's a moment in every teenage girl's life where her life feels just like a romance movie. It doesn't matter who you are, how cool or uncool you are, what you look like – you will get your moment. My moment is tonight.

I couldn't believe my luck when Eric Lawrence – or El, as all his friends called him – asked me to go out with him. El is easily the most popular boy in the whole school, not just in year 10, which upsets the year 11 boys no end. Until recently he was going out with the most popular girl, Aimee Stephens – or evil cow, as most of the kids at my school call her – but they broke up when he caught her kissing a year 11 behind the school substation. This was a doubly stupid move if you ask me, because they literally show us videos in school, of kids getting fried playing near powerlines and substations, so dry humping against one seems kind of idiotic, but also because you would have to be crazy to cheat on El, he's perfect.

I've always fancied him, but I think things really came to a head in year 7, when he was cast as the lead in *Bugsy Malone*, and he was just beyond cool. I played one of the down-and-outs (there are no small roles, just small actors; at least that's what Mrs Bottomley, our music teacher, says) so I wasn't expecting to grab his attention so suddenly, until he accidentally splurged me in the eye (it makes sense if you've ever seen *Bugsy Malone*) and felt so guilty about it, he helped me to the school nurse himself. Mrs Bottomley had been pretty tight with the props, so the splurge guns were just disguised cans of shaving cream, and it stung like a bitch.

It's not like this made El fall in love with me or anything but at least he knew that I was alive. Flash-forward to yesterday, I'm sitting in the quad with my friends, and El just walks up to me and asks me if I want to go on a date with him. Sally almost spat out her orange juice, Rachael looked so jealous she might faint, and Lindsey slapped me a high-five the second he walked off, although she probably should have waited a few more seconds, in case he turned around. But boys like El don't turn around, do they? They're so sure of themselves, they don't need to.

He invited me to the cinema, so here I am, with my ticket to see some terrifying looking film called *Cry Wolf* – a movie that El selected. I would never usually see something that looked so scary, especially not in the dark and silent setting of the cinema. I'm hoping it will be kind of romantic, though – perhaps that's why he chose it? Maybe he's hoping I'll snuggle up to him on the back row or something. See what I mean? It's like something out of a romance movie.

The buzz of the foyer calms down as people filter through to different screens. Gosh, where is he? I shift on the spot awkwardly, my feet sticking to the cinema carpet a little.

My phone rings so I take it from my bag. It's Lindsey.

'Hello?' I answer.

'Hi, can you ring me back please, I don't have credit,' she says quickly.

'I'm at the cinema,' I remind her. 'I'm waiting for El.'

'Call me back,' she insists. 'It's important.'

I'm not exactly credit rich myself right now, but it does sound important.

'Okay, what's up?' I say when she answers.

'I'm at Frankie & Benny's,' she replies.

'I'm wasting my credit on that bit of hot gossip?' I reply with a giggle.

'No, listen, El is here,' she says. 'He's with Aimee, on a date, looks like they're back together.'

'Oh,' I say. 'Erm, okay.'

I don't know what else to say. My face is boiling up with a mixture of anger and embarrassment. I feel like an idiot. Why did I actually think this was happening? Why?

'I'm so sorry, Poppy, he's clearly a dick,' Lindsey says.

'Lindsey Matthews, language,' I hear her mum tell her off in the background.

'I'll let you go if you're with your "'rents," I reply. 'But thanks for telling me.'

'Sorry again,' she says.

Well, that's that, then. I've been stood up. At least no one but Lindsey knows I even turned up – maybe I could pretend I didn't? How would anyone know?'

'Poppy Walker,' I hear a boy screech.

Oh, God, it's Aaron Taylor from school. Shit and he's with his friends. Amazing, fantastic, wonderful! So much for no one knowing, *everyone* is going to know now.

'What you doing here?' he asks me.

'Erm, it's a cinema,' I reply. 'So take a guess.'

'Oooh, all right,' he replies. 'What you here on your own for?'

'Piss off, Aaron,' Zac Hunt chimes in. 'Hi, Poppy.'

'Hi, Zac,' I say with a smile.

I've known Zac all the way through school, since nursery. He's cute but he doesn't say much.

'Come on, Hunt, or we won't have time to play air hockey before the film,' Aaron says. 'Loser is buying the popcorn.'

'Yeah, I'll catch you up,' Zac says, hanging back, hovering next to me. He waits until it's just the two of us. 'What are you seeing?'

'I was just going, actually,' I tell him.

'What did you see?' he asks instead.

Ugh, I know he's just trying to be friendly, but he's killing me here.

'I was going to see *Cry Wolf* but, erm, I'm not now,' I say.

'I'd heard a rumour you were here with El,' he replies, looking around for him.

'You heard a rumour?' I repeat back to him.

'Okay, I heard him ask you in the quad,' he says, shifting his weight back and forth between his feet.

'Well, he's stood me up, he's back with Aimee, so, yep, that's the situation, so I'm going home, and if we could keep this between us... yeah... thanks.'

Wow, I'm just so cool, why on earth would anyone stand me up?

'What a tosser,' Zac says. He actually looks quite mad on my behalf.

'Yeah, it's not a very nice thing to do,' I say with a sigh. 'Anyway, I'm going home, before anyone else sees me.'

'It isn't, I just mean, like, he's crazy for standing you up,' he clarifies.

'Oh,' is about all I can say.

'Yeah,' he says awkwardly. 'So...'

Zac turns around to walk away but does a full 360 until he's facing me again. I can't help but laugh.

'I'll watch the film with you, if you like?' he suggests.

'Do you like scary films?' I ask, when I should just be screaming 'yes' because not only is he cuter and evidentially far nicer than El, but he's also actually here. Zac has a warm smile, long-ish messy Orlando Bloom-type hair (who doesn't love an Orlando Bloom type?) and his eyes just somehow say a thousand words without him even trying. I suppose I always just wrote him off as quiet – maybe he's just shy, but aren't we all, when we're fifteen? – but finally chatting to him, I can tell there's so much more going on in there.

'No, I hate them,' he replies with a smile. 'But I'd watch this one with you. Unless you'd rather watch *Jarhead* with that lot.'

I glance over at the arcade, where Aaron and the gang are pretending to shoot each other with the guns.

'I'm not a fan of horror movies but I somehow prefer them to war movies,' I say. 'They're fractionally less scary for being fictional, whereas war is always...'

'War?' he offers with a smile. 'Don't worry, we can keep each other safe. I'll just go tell my friends and grab a ticket.'

'Okay, cool,' I reply, trying to keep my big dumb grin under wraps. 'I'll get us some popcorn. Sweet or salty?'

'I love both,' he says. 'I usually get a mix.'

My smile drops off to nothing but shock.

'Oh my gosh, so do I,' I tell him. 'My friends think it's minging.'

'Nah, it's the best,' he says with a smile. 'Back in a minute.'

As I head to the food bit to get our popcorn, I can't mask my smile. Not only has Zac saved me from the unliveable embarrassment of turning up for my first date ever and being stood up, but there's way more of a spark between us anyway.

See, it's like I said, every teenage girl gets her romance movie moment sooner or later. I'm so happy mine is with Zac.

12

After walking out on what was frankly the best date anyone has ever had, by the time I get to my dad's I'm feeling more emotions than I can wrangle. Angry, upset, confused – my God, am I confused right now. I *am* divorced. Been there, done that, got the T-shirt (or the decree absolute, at least) – I distinctly remember signing the paperwork, keeping my game face on until I went to the toilets, hiding myself away in a cubicle before allowing myself to cry. Bloody hell, my own mum represented me, and she was the best solicitor in town – and she billed me accordingly!

The door is off the latch, so I walk straight into the living room where I find my dad waiting for me with buttery toast and sweet tea – the traditional Walker family treatment for shock.

'Sit down,' my dad instructs, skipping the niceties. 'I need to explain this now.'

I sit down as I'm told but I don't say a word. I'm so freaked out right now.

'I shouldn't have dropped it on you over the phone,' he continues before puffing air from his cheeks. 'I have some good news and some bad news. Times two.'

Dad seems calm considering he's the one I get my naturally stressed nature from. Then again, when Mum died, he temporarily morphed into someone strong, systematic and supportive. He must have been going through hell, but he always stayed strong around me. Both my parents have always been the absolute best. I'm really lucky in that respect.

'Oh God, just tell me,' I insist, bracing, ready for the hit of bad news.

'The good news is that I finally took your advice and started sorting your mum's office out,' he says proudly.

'Dad, you're supposed to give the bad news first,

so the good news makes it better,' I insist, verging on angrily.

'Right, yes, sorry darling,' he says, shifting from Charles Dance to more of a Hugh Grant type. 'The bad news is that your mum never quite finished your divorce.'

The way he says 'never quite finished' is so gentle I almost don't feel it. It takes me a moment to really take on board what he's saying.

'Wait, she didn't do my divorce for me?' I double check. 'Because she said she did. And she definitely gave us all the paperwork. She took me for a drink, remember, to comfort me when it finally went through.'

I remember that night well. Good old Mum. She didn't just take me for a drink, she took me to The Birdcage, the only gay bar in town, not just because they do the best cocktails but because she kept telling me I was smart, beautiful and that any man would be lucky to have me, and she didn't want men trying to pick me up while we were hanging out. I'm pretty sure she was joking about that last part but that night out with her certainly made me feel better.

Mum really was a wildcard but when she was in work mode, she was a different person.

'Mum was brilliant,' I remind him. 'There's no way she'd make a mistake like that. That doesn't sound like Mum at all.'

'That's the thing,' Dad says softly. 'It wasn't a mistake.'

Okay, that *does* sound like Mum.

'What?' I shriek.

'I found this, printed out in her drawer,' he explains, handing me a small wad of papers. 'There's actually a few different versions. I suppose she didn't know how to tell you. Then she never got the chance.'

I snatch the letters a little too keenly and dart my eyes back and forth across them frantically.

'This is insane,' I blurt.

They all start with basically the same sentiment: I've made a mistake and I don't know how to tell you. Each letter varies in approach, but the bottom line is always the same: you're not divorced.

'I just...'

My voice trails off. I'm speechless.

'It reads to me like your mum was so sure you

and Zac would regret getting divorced, and so confident you would end up back together, that she thought she was doing you a favour. It seems as though, as time went on, and it seemed like it wasn't going to happen, she kept editing the same letter, trying to find a way to tell you, and never quite found the right way in time.'

I can hear a sort of embarrassed sympathy in my dad's voice. Still, I check.

'Did you know?' I ask.

'I didn't,' he replies. 'Your mum says as much at the end of each letter. They're all signed off: "Your dad knows nothing about this. Love you, Pops. Mum."'

It's so like my crazy mum to do something so insane but I never thought she'd go as far as to risk her job – a job she loved so much – for my relationship. Still, I'd be lying if I said I didn't take some bizarre comfort from these letters, regardless of what they say, it's almost as though I'm hearing her voice from beyond the grave, which sounds gross, I know, but when you've lost your mum, you take what you can get sometimes. It's nice to be called Pops again. Only two people have ever called me Pops: Mum and Zac.

Mum and Zac genuinely loved each other. Zac didn't have much family growing up, and family members, including his parents, passed away, and his family got smaller, meaning Zac didn't really have many people left, not that he was close with, but at that point he was firmly a part of our family. Mum was devastated when we split, I think she saw him as one of her kids, in a non-weird way. I'm not surprised she was holding out hope of us getting back together again.

'I didn't want to worry you before I knew the facts. I've got it all worked out, love. The good news is that your Auntie Joan says she can sort it all out for you, you just need to sign some paperwork.'

Auntie Joan works at the firm my mum used to work at. She isn't my actual auntie, just a close friend of my mum's, although we don't see all that much of her since Mum passed away, obviously. She's a solicitor too, so if anyone can sort it, Joan can. I don't sigh with relief quite yet, though.

'You said "the good news",' I point out. 'Why do I get the feeling you're going to follow it with bad news again?'

'The bad news is Zac needs to sign it too,' he

replies. I open my mouth to say something, although I have no idea what. I just gawp at him for a split second before he continues. 'I looked on all the social media thingamajiggies and whatnots and I looked through countless Zac Hunts but none of them were your Zac Hunt.'

It's so odd, to hear him referred to as my Zac. It's been a long time since he was mine.

'Okay…' is about all I can say.

'It was the funniest thing, though. I figured I'd give it a go, searching him on Google, and I actually got a hit in the news.'

'The news?' I squeak.

'Only local news, and not for anything bad,' he reassures me. 'So, if I can get this the right way around this time, the *bad* news is that Zac is seemingly uncontactable and you need him to sign papers. The *good* news is that this article says where he'll be and when.'

'Thanks for ending on good news,' I say pointlessly. 'So, where is he?'

The thought of seeing Zac again, especially to get him to sign divorce papers that he thinks he's already signed, is a concept that is beyond mortifying.

Dad practically winces as he hands me another piece of paper. I'm expecting an address or something but what he hands me instead is a printout of a news article.

Action star's daughter to tie knot in Tarness.

What am I even looking at here?

'Sonny Strong's daughter is set to tie the knot in Tarness,' I read aloud. 'The action star's only child, influencer Lilac Strong, who he shares with former centrefold Cherry Ryan, is set to wed in the newly refurbished Castle Tarness. The castle, on an island in Loch Tarness… blah blah blah… oh my God! With beefed up security for her big day with fiancé Zachary Hunt, a thirty-one-year-old musician from Lancashire…'

My voice tapers off. That's him. That's Zac.

'I can't believe he's getting married again,' I say softly. 'I often wondered if he would – if he *had*.'

I'd usually tell myself that I doubted it. Well, not that it's a competition, but when you're not quite over someone it makes it all the more pathetic if they're moving on. I hate the thought of him moving on.

'Poppy, darling, listen to me,' Dad starts softly but seriously. 'You need to get him to sign these papers and send them to me before he can get married. He'll commit bigamy if you don't. I've tried everything I can think of to contact him – I even tried his old phone number with no luck. Your only option is to go there.'

'Loch Tarness?' I reply. 'In Scotland?'

'It's the only way,' Dad insists. 'I couldn't find any way to contact him. You have to go there, before it's too late.'

'Oh, right, okay, so I'm just supposed to nip up to Scotland, march up to my ex who I haven't seen or heard from in years, and ask him for the divorce he thinks he's already been through? That simple?'

'See in the article, where it says security has been beefed up around the town?' he points out. 'So possibly not that simple, but I don't see what choice you have. Oh, darling, come here.'

My dad opens his arms and beckons me over. I sit next to him on the sofa and hug him tightly.

'Bloody Mum,' I say quietly. 'Always thinking she knew best.'

'Well, usually she did,' he replies. 'Why don't you

stay here tonight? We can watch an old Western, like we used to do when you couldn't sleep, and we'll figure out what you need to do?'

'That'd be good,' I say with a sigh.

I have no idea what I'm supposed to do, or what I'm going to do, but I can tell you what I'm not doing. There's no way in hell I'm going to Scotland, tracking down my ex at his own wedding, to tell him we're still married. No way. Not a chance. Can you think of anything more embarrassing than that?

13

It turns out there is something more embarrassing than driving hundreds of miles to confront your ex with the news that you're still married days before his wedding, and that is your dad offering to drive you there to do it. I'm a thirty-one-year-old woman, with one parent who has already landed me in this mess by trying to help, so the last thing I need is my dad holding my hand.

That said, I am a big baby who never learned to drive, and with no trains in the part of the Scottish Highlands where Loch Tarness is, I do in fact need someone to drive me.

You can always rely on your friends in a time like

this, unless your friends are my friends, who have so blatantly started a group chat without you, because ours has gone suspiciously quiet. But it turns out I do have one person still in my corner, and I couldn't think of anyone better suited for going on this weird adventure with.

'I am absolutely buzzing you called me – no, gave me the honour, in fact, of driving you on this mission,' Kat says as she cruises up yet another narrow road lined with trees, with one hand on the steering wheel and a coffee in the other. 'Genuinely, it's just so nice to meet another handful.'

'What do you mean?' I ask as I warm my hands on my own drink. It's starting to go cold, which either means I've had it for a while or it really is as freezing cold as it feels here.

We just stopped at what was described to us by the man working there as the last petrol station for 'a ways away' so Kat filled up her orange Mini Cooper, we grabbed a couple of coffees and we got back on our way. I thought it was cold back home but the winter hits differently up here. I'm so glad I went along with Kat's top road trip tip that, if you're driving through the night, the best thing to wear is your warmest pair of pyjamas and a big coat. I feel so toasty.

'Someone else as crazy as I am,' she says.

'I'm not crazy,' I insist. 'Honestly, I never do anything like this.'

'Do you know how many times you've said that to me since we met?' she says with a laugh.

'It's true!'

'Yeah, that's what I always say too. And it's definitely what I'd say if I were driving to Scotland to tell my ex he can't get married because he's still married to me,' she adds. 'Which is also big-time handful behaviour, by the way.'

'I'm not going to stop him,' I point out. 'I'm going to get him to sign this paperwork and then we will be divorced. So no need to tell anyone else anything. I'm not here to mess up his relationship.'

Kat practically chokes on her swig of coffee.

'God, I would be,' she says. 'I'm a firm believer that exes should cease to be once it's over.'

'To be honest, it has felt like Zac has ceased to be since we split,' I reply. 'He just disappeared. And it's not like usual, where your ex sort of exists in your peripheral vision, and you occasionally spot them in the supermarket, bump into them through mutual friends, or get to watch their new life without you, playing out on Facebook. Zac really did just vanish.'

'Sounds like the perfect ex,' she replies.

'Apart from the old still being married thing, yeah, I guess,' I remind her.

'There is that,' she replies. 'But don't you think when you see him all the old feelings will come flooding back? What if you want him again?'

I think for a second. It's pretty safe to say that when Zac and I split it broke my heart. I do still think of him often, and I can't help but measure every guy I meet against him.

'I'm here to divorce him, not get back with him,' I remind her. 'Brownie's honour.'

Kat takes her eyes off the road for a moment to glance at me. She narrows her eyes.

'That sounds fake, but okay,' she replies. 'But just so you know, the reason I like my exes to cease to exist is because I've never seen an ex again without sleeping with them.'

'Even if they were about to get married?' I ask in disbelief.

'Only because the situation has never arisen,' she

insists with a shrug. 'But if you say we're here for closure and paperwork, I'll believe you.'

'Well, we are old friends,' I tell her with a smile.

When I stop and think about the fact that I've known Kat for less than a week, it makes this already very weird situation feel even weirder but, honestly, I feel like she's been more of a friend to me in this past week than the other three have in the past year. I barely had to explain my situation to her before she was insisting she would drive me to Scotland to help me fix it. That's the kind of person I need in my life.

'There is that,' she says. 'I wouldn't drive to the arsehole of nowhere for anyone else. Where are we, by the way?'

'You know, I don't think we're too far away,' I reply.

It's early afternoon now. We've been on the road pretty much through the night and according to the satnav, which has served us well so far, we're only ten minutes away from our destination. Our destination is a town and not an exact place, because I realised quite quickly that it was going to be a race against time to get to Zac before he tied the knot again, so we just bagged up some things, shoved them in the car and hit the road. We have no real idea where we're going, other than to a castle in the middle of a loch, and we have no clue where we're going to sleep tonight.

As far as I'm concerned, the plan is to find Zac, get the papers signed, and get the hell out of here. If we could leave today, I'd be delighted, even if we only get as far back down south as Edinburgh and check into a Travelodge there – hell, we could even call it a holiday if we did that, because lord knows I need one. Things have been pretty full-on with work. Even if my job sounds boring, it's actually quite hectic and challenging, and with it being the family business I haven't taken much time off. The plus side to this is that now, when I need time off last minute, it isn't hard to swing it with my dad, and lucky for me Kat is between jobs at the moment so she is free as a bird to do whatever.

'What are you thinking about?' Kat asks.

'Just work,' I reply.

'That explains why you look so constipated,' she says. 'It's not a sexy job, is it?'

'It's not supposed to be sexy,' I insist.

'Do you think that's why your date with Fit Fred went south?'

Is she serious?

'It went south because I found out I was married,' I remind her.

'Hmm,' she replies. 'I'm just saying, if it was Jake Gyllenhaal, and I found out he was married, it wouldn't put an end to the date. Do you know what would? If I found out he framed pictures for a living.'

'I don't—'

'But it sounds like you do,' she interrupts me. 'I'm not trying to be harsh, I'm just trying to do you a favour. Next fella you're interested in, lie about your job, and watch what kind of reaction you get.'

I just laugh.

'Oh, yeah, okay, when the next person is interested in me, because that happens all the time, I'll lie about my job,' I say sarcastically.

'Just try it,' she insists. 'Ooh, look, civilisation. Of sorts.'

I peep at Kat's phone and see that we're finally in Tarness, a small town somewhere in the Scottish Highlands. Pretty high up in them. To be honest, it feels more like we're nowhere than somewhere.

There are bits of snow at the edges of the roads. I think I read somewhere that there's a ski resort nearby, so there must be loads of snow somewhere. There are a few shops that make up the main town, tiny as it is, but most of the buildings appear to be holiday lets. It seems like one of those places where no one really lives, unless they work here, otherwise it's all just tourists. Not that many tourists though. We're more in the territory of *The Shining* than *Chalet Girl*.

It's only as we turn a corner that my impression of this place changes. This particular road is abuzz with people. Paparazzi, security, fans hoping to get a peep at Sonny Strong, wearing T-shirts and holding signs with his name and face all over them. Some of them are wearing *Not Dead Yet* T-shirts. *Not Dead Yet* is the popular movie franchise that Sonny has been starring in for years. They're really awful action flicks. I think I saw the first one or two but they weren't really for me, and while the first few were grounded in reality, I hear they've grown more ridiculous over the years. The first flicks had enemies like billionaire weapons manufacturers and miscellaneous foreign secret agents infiltrating MI5 and things like that. In more recent years, Sonny's character, Jack McVey, has been fighting things like aliens. Just the most absurd stuff. Still, people love it, so much so that fans are gathered here in the middle of nowhere just to get a glimpse of the man himself.

It turns out everyone is fussing around a large dock, which must be where people going to and from the island get on and off the boat. I wonder, given the fact that there's a crowd and security, whether there might be a boat getting in soon.

I can just about see the island in the distance. Right bang in the centre of it is a castle – *the* castle – the one he's getting married in. It looks nothing short of spectacular, even from afar, it's really something.

'Well, even if he does get off that boat, I'm not going to be able to get near him, am I?' I say.

'No, but you know what that means, don't you?'

'What?' I reply.

'It just means we need to get our own boat, and get it over there ourselves.'

One look at Kat confirms she's serious.

'Come on, let's park up,' she insists. 'And go find a boat.'

With no better suggestions and no other options,

I have no choice but to humour Kat but, come on, us on a boat? This is going to end in tears. Then again, if it sinks and I wind up at the bottom of the loch, at least mine and Zac's marriage really will be over. Right now, it certainly seems like the only way I'm going to be able to sort this.

14

14 FEBRUARY 2006

Teachers can be so lame sometimes. It isn't all teachers, all the time, but when one of them gets something in their head and they make a big, stupid deal out of it, it drives me mad.

I should be in double maths right now and, don't get me wrong, I'm not exactly sad to be missing double maths, but the reason we've been pulled from our lessons is because we've all been called for a special assembly, and the reason for this assembly is so stupid, I can't even be arsed to sit through it.

Mrs Pollock, the food tech teacher who somehow makes a lesson cooking pizza even more boring than physics, has whipped everyone into a panic because some year 9, who went abroad for Christmas, has been wearing these sparkly plastic bracelets she bought there, so Mrs Pollock has decided shag bands are clearly back, and we need to do something about it.

Seriously, I think a 'shag band resurgence assembly' is such a pathetic waste of everyone's time. Well, they were never really a thing, were they? The colourful plastic bracelets were real – I used to wear loads of them, when they were cool, back in 2004 – but that stupid urban legend, about how if a boy broke one of your bracelets, you had to get with him (the colour of the band dictated how far you had to go), was never actually true. It wasn't true then and it isn't true now. It's definitely not worth an assembly, but here we are.

It's non-uniform day too so, as if it's not bad enough we have to sit on the floor in the hall, I have to do it in my own clothes instead of my geeky uniform. I love non-uniform days because they feel like a chance to show people the real me. I'm wearing jean shorts with black leggings underneath, a vest top, two layers of pearl beads, and loads of bracelets (*not* shag bands, though). We're allowed to wear more make-up on non-uniform days so, in addition to my usual Dream Matte Mousse, I've got loads of black eyeliner on my top and bottom lids, and I've layered on my mascara to make my lashes nice and big and thick, not that you can always see them properly because I've super backcombed my hair and my big, thick fringe is swept to one side; I've tried to fix it in place with my flower headband but these fringes have a mind of their own.

We're currently lined up outside the hall, being let in, a class at a time. We have to stand in silence, obviously, because we just do. There's lots of stuff we just have to do that I don't see the point in, like these dumb assemblies, or watching plays about heroin addicts, or having our ties down to our waist, even though we all know the cooler the person, the shorter the tie.

'Poppy Walker, what's that?' my form teacher, Mr Grant asks me.

I realise he's looking at the pink Jane Norman bag in my hand. My trainers are poking out of the top of it, because God forbid we're allowed to wear trainers to school, so on PE days I have to stuff them in a second bag with my kit.

'My PE kit, sir,' I tell him. What else does he think it's going to be?

'What are you doing with it?' he asks me.

'PE,' I say, stating the obvious.

'Don't cheek me, Poppy Walker,' he says.

'Sir, I wasn't,' I insist. I wasn't. What does he want from me?

'I want you to take your kit and put it in your locker,' he tells me. 'And then you've got two choices: you can come back for this assembly like the mature young woman you're supposed to be, or you can take yourself off to isolation and see how far your cheek gets you in there.'

I feel my cheeks flush red. This is so embarrassing. I didn't even do anything! I just answered his question! I swear the teachers at this school are power mad.

'That was well tight,' Sally whispers to me when Mr Grant is out of earshot.

'I don't get what his problem is,' I reply. 'I'll take this to my locker before I get in trouble for something else I didn't do.'

I leave my place in the line to go to my locker, which is at the other end of the school. Well, good, because I don't want to sit through this stupid assembly anyway. My plan is to walk as slow as humanly possible, armed with the excuse that Mr Grant sent me to my locker in case anyone stops me and asks what I'm doing in the corridor after the bell, when we're supposed to be in a special assembly.

As soon as I reach my locker, I place my hands inside for a moment, flip open my Razr phone and send a text to Zac.

OMG Grant is been a ryt dick 2day x

I need to rant to someone. I just hope Zac has his phone on silent in the assembly. I don't want him getting in trouble too.

I'm about to flip my phone closed and head back when I feel it vibrate in my hand. It's a reply already.

He sux. Where R U? x

@ my locker. WBU? X

I wait a few seconds for a reply, but nothing comes through. I'll wait a little longer, see how long I can get away with it, because I am fully addicted to Zac. We've been spending a lot of time together, ever since he rescued me at the cinema. We hang out at school, we hang out after school, and whenever we're not together we're either texting or on MSN Messenger. The problem is that I fancy him so much, and sometimes I think he fancies me too, but we just hang out. He did hold my hand for a bit inside the cinema, but now I'm wondering if it was just because it was a scary film, because he hasn't done it since. There have been a few moments, when it's just been the two of us, when it's seemed like the right kind of time to kiss, but I am terrified of kissing him, and he's either too scared to kiss me or he just doesn't want to, and it's the fact he might not want to that puts me off. I keep thinking I'll text him, or ask him on MSN, because dropping hints about having a crush on someone in my Myspace bulletins isn't working as well as I hoped it would.

'Hi,' Zac says as he approaches me.

The corridor is otherwise empty, so I jump out of my skin.

'Oh my God, Zac, what are you doing? Why aren't you in the assembly?' I ask him.

'I had the dentist today,' he reminds me. I remember him mentioning it last night now. 'I had a filling – I still can't feel my bottom lip properly, look.'

Zac flicks himself in the lip. I laugh.

'Well, Grant started on me for no reason,' I tell him. 'I guess he was annoyed I had my PE kit on me, but I didn't have time to put it in my locker and I didn't want to be late or I'd get detention. But he thought I was being cheeky, so he told me to go to isolation or come back with a better attitude. He's the one with the attitude problem, not me. If we're both late to the assembly, maybe we can sit together? We can laugh at Mrs Pollock saying things like "oral sex" and "penetration".'

So, so cringey.

'We could,' Zac replies. 'Or we could twag it.'

'I wish,' I reply. 'I've never dared skip a lesson.'

'It's not technically a lesson,' he reminds me. 'And everyone thinks I'm at the dentist. If Grant notices you're not here, he'll think you have actually gone to isolation. And it's not like we need to go – do you promise that you don't let boys snap your shag bands?'

I laugh.

'I promise that no boys get to break my shag bands,' I reply. 'Not in 2004 or now.'

'See, we're fine,' he says. 'So...'

'So, where shall we go?' I ask him. 'If we get caught, we'll be in so much trouble.'

Zac steps out from behind the lockers and peers up and down the corridor.

'I don't want to freak you out, but Buttner is coming,' he tells me.

Mr Buettner – or Buttner as we all call him – is the deputy head, and he's somehow even scarier than the actual head.

'In here, Pops.'

Zac opens the door to a supply cupboard and steps in before pulling me inside after him. It's pitch black in here but, right on cue, we both take out our phones and flip them open to get the light from the screens. It's only a small cupboard and all the walls are lined with shelves, all covered in textbooks that were probably printed before we were born. They've all got such a distinctive smell. Being in this tiny room with so many of them isn't very nice. Being stood so close to Zac is though. In this little space, our bodies are almost touching. If either of us moves a muscle, our clothes just about brush one another. I barely feel it, but it makes me think about wanting to kiss him again. I swear, that's pretty much all I think about these days – if I fail my GCSEs, that will be why.

'What if he catches us in here?' I whisper, scared but excited too.

'He won't,' Zac whispers back. 'Everyone is in the assembly so no one will be getting any books. Buttner will be headed for the smokers' staff room.'

'He smells worse than these books,' I say with a quiet giggle.

Zac laughs.

'You smell really nice,' he tells me.

'Thanks,' I reply. 'It's probably my Impulse. I accidentally sprayed it in my hair this morning.'

Oh my God, I'm such a loser, why did I tell him that? Probably because I'm nervous and I can't ever think of anything cool to say.

Zac leans forward and places his head just next to mine. He takes a big sniff of my hair.

'Yep, that's the smell,' he says, practically whispering into my ear.

As Zac slowly moves his face away from mine, I

don't know what comes over me, but the urge to kiss him overwhelms me, and the fear just vanishes. I put my lips on his and I snog him – which is something I haven't done before and, I have to say, I'm really impressed that I seem to be doing it right because Zac snogs me back. Eventually, we separate, and the fear I had about kissing him comes flooding back. Uh-oh. Was that the right thing to do?

'Okay, I definitely felt that,' he says, touching his lip lightly with his fingertips. But then he smiles and as the fear starts to fade again, I get my words out while I still can.

'I really like you,' I tell him. 'More than friends.'

'I really like you more than friends too,' he replies. 'I was going to ask you to be my girlfriend but then I saw a Q&A you did on Myspace where you said you had a crush on someone, so I backed off.'

'I have a crush on *you*,' I point out. 'I should have just told you, but I was scared. I'll definitely be your girlfriend.'

Shit, he didn't actually ask though, did he? He said he was going to.

'Okay,' he says, through a sort of giggle-meets-snort.

'Okay,' I reply, sounding equally as geeky. 'Do you want to kiss again?'

'Okay,' he replies.

And just like that, after weeks of worrying, wondering what would happen, I suddenly have a boyfriend, but not just any boyfriend, Zac Hunt. I can't wait to tell the girls; they know how crazy I am about him. Even my mum knows that I fancy him – I had to tell her, to try to get an extra mobile top-up, but she said he sounded like a nice boy. He is though – he's such a nice boy. Not like all the other smelly, horrible, annoying boys at this school. And now he's mine and I can't believe it. All I need to do now is everything I can to not mess this up. Suddenly I'm not so worried though. With Zac I get the feeling everything is going to be as easy as my first time kissing. And now I can't wait to do it again.

15

I'm not sure exactly what sort of boat I had in my head when Kat suggested that was our best bet for getting to the island. I don't really know boats but, I guess, something like a small fishing boat, or a little motorboat, perhaps? It's a small ferry that usually transports people back and forth – that would have been perfect. But, no, that's not what we're hiring.

I say hiring... We tightened up our coats and popped into the office where you can usually buy tickets for the ferry tours and hire boats for fishing or whatever, to see what we could do, but they're not currently letting people do that, because of the wedding being on the island and all the extra security and what have you. Kat, not seeing this as, in any way, a stumbling block, thanked the man for his time and then led me outside and down the shore a little to a seemingly abandoned rowboat.

'We'll just borrow this,' she says, rather casually, given the fact that we have no idea what we're doing.

'There was a display in the office, with facts all about the loch,' I tell her. 'It said that at its deepest point it was pushing 200 metres deep.'

Kat just shrugs.

'So what?' she says.

'Two hundred metres,' I say again, extra emphasis on every word.

'What if it were only twenty metres?' she says. 'It makes no difference. That's still fucking loads. If you can swim, you can swim. If you can't, well, you're screwed in two metres of water, right?'

I massage my temples. I can't argue with that.

I'm starting to think that, as lovely as Kat is, when she described herself as a handful, she wasn't wrong. She really does remind me of my mum. My mum would have been super down for 'borrowing' a boat.

'Give me a hand to push it into the water, will you?' Kat says, stretching with all the seriousness of an Olympic athlete. 'We'll make sure there's nothing wrong with it and if it all seems fine, we'll just nip into some loos, get dressed and head over while the coast is clear.'

I'm not so sure about this one. Still, I make moves to help her.

'Wait,' I say quickly. 'It looks like there's a motor-boat heading over this way from the island, see?'

Kat narrows her eyes to get a better look.

'It does look like it's coming this way,' she says. 'Come on, let's hide in the bushes until we know we're safe.'

Kat hurries off. I swear, she must have done this, or at least similar, before. I don't know if that makes her a great person to have around in a situation like this, or if perhaps she's just going to get me into more scrapes.

I stare out at the boat. It's far enough away that I can't make out any detail at all, but I'm fixated on trying to work out who is onboard. Imagine if Zac was on that boat right now. Suddenly, the thought of seeing him again really freaks me out. Not just because it's been years and years, or because I'm in my pyjamas, but because of why I'm here. We're not bumping into each other in M&S or reconnecting in a Facebook Messenger window, I've basically stalked him here, which is creepy enough, but to tell him that we're still married too – that's just horrifying. Not that I've had much time to think any of this through since Dad dropped the news on me, not properly, but it's just hit me that, while I know what I need to tell Zac, I have no idea how I'm actually going to say it. Do I open with pleasantries and then hit him with it? Will that soften the blow a little? I certainly shouldn't do it like my dad did, a confusing barrage of good and bad news, that ultimately only seemed like bad.

I need to get in the bushes with Kat, quickly, because...

'Poppy?' a familiar voice says from the side of me. 'Shit, Pops, is that you?'

I know that it's Zac before I even turn to look at him. Not that I can turn to look at him right now. I can't move, I can't speak, I can't do anything. I'm not even sure that I'm breathing. I'd be practically playing dead right now, if I weren't on my feet.

'Pops?' he says again.

I mean, he's definitely seen me. He's standing feet

away from me and I'm just here, alone, in a clearing by the loch, not only looking like an absolute creep, but we've been driving all night, I'm not wearing much make-up, I'm tired, I'm scruffy, I'm in my bloody pyjamas, for crying out loud – when I'd imagined how this would go, repeatedly on the drive up here, I was always dolled-up when I approached him. In some ways, blurting the truth might even make this less awkward, but I just don't know how to say it.

I finally force myself to look left, to where he's standing. I feel my eyes widen, as I take in just how much he's changed. He somehow looks taller but I think perhaps it's just because he's started going to the gym – well, he actually looks like he's been going for a while. The scruffy guitarist I married is long gone. His long brown indie-boy haircut is no more, in favour of a short, neat cut. He reminds me a lot of Sebastian Stan, which he didn't used to; it's as though cutting away his hair has revealed this whole new version of him. Well, that and a few other factors.

He's wearing a dark blue suit that fits his body to perfection, like it was made for him (which it probably was, given the flash-looking Rolex I notice on his wrist as he runs a hand through his hair).

It's Zac – my Zac – run through some Prince Charming machine. But as different as he looks, just looking into his eyes, and hearing his voice, is like that feeling you get after a holiday, when you've had a great time and you don't want to leave, but the second you walk through your door you just feel so good because you're home.

I can't believe he looks this good – so good – and here I am in my pyjamas. So much for questioning whether old feelings would come flooding back when I saw him. I'm drowning in them. Kat was right, 200 metres of icy cold loch water or less than two metres of ex, if it's going to pull you under, it doesn't make a difference.

I remember, when we were first getting together, I was absolutely petrified to kiss him. My God, I would kiss him in a heartbeat now. Well, if he wasn't about to get married, obviously. Mustn't forget that key detail.

'Pops, what are you doing here?' he asks as he slowly approaches me.

I can hear footsteps approaching, coming from behind him, and I panic.

'We're still married,' I whisper quickly.

'Zachary?' a voice calls out. 'Zachary? Oh…'

Her tone changes when she sees him standing here with me.

I vaguely know of Lilac Strong, just from random pictures on Instagram, TikToks and occasional Tweets I never really pay much attention to. She only really gained followers in the first place because of who her dad is, but these days she puts out a constant stream of content, largely sponsored stuff. She's much smaller in real life than I imagined her being. She can't be much over five foot. Zac, on the other hand, is 6'2", so he towers above her. At 5'8" I feel like a giant, closer to Zac's height than Lilac's. She's petite with a sharp, stylish bob. Her hair is dyed a soft lilac – of course – and most of what she wears has elements of different purples, as though it's her trademark.

'Zachary, who the *hell* is *this*?' she snaps, her tone shifting into something much angrier. She looks me up and down and her hostile expression intensifies.

'This is Poppy,' he says not all that confidently.

'Er, and who the hell is Poppy?' she asks. 'Someone you're clearly used to having sneaky conversations with in the woods. And in her nightwear, no less.'

We're cloaked by trees, but I'm not entirely sure that constitutes the woods. I'm banged to rights as far as the pyjamas go, although they are fleecy plaid ones, so not exactly sexy lingerie. This is a pretty nuclear reaction for something so seemingly innocent – imagine if she knew the truth.

'She's my cousin,' Zac says, thinking fast.

'Your cousin?' she replies.

'Yeah, my cousin,' he says again.

We're joined by none other than Sonny Strong, flanked by two burly bodyguards and his wife, Cherry Ryan.

'What's going on?' Sonny asks. 'Who's this?'

'It's Zachary's cousin,' Lilac tells her dad.

'What? I thought you said you didn't have much family,' Sonny replies. He isn't suspicious though, he's pleasantly surprised. 'You're here for the wedding?'

'Well, it would be weird if she wasn't,' Zac says with a laugh, clearly tipping me off to play along.

'Of course I am,' I eventually say.

'Wherever you're staying, I'll pay the bill, but you're coming to stay in the castle with us,' Sonny insists. 'There's always room for family.'

A rustling sound precedes Kat scrambling out of the bushes, clearly not wanting to miss out on an invitation to the wedding, but her appearing from nowhere, her pyjamas covered in bits of tree, only makes this whole thing seem even weirder.

'Hi, hello, I'm here,' she says, brushing herself down, steadying herself on her feet.

'Okay, who is this?' Lilac asks.

'Our other cousin,' I say quickly.

'So, all three of you are cousins then?' Sonny confirms.

Shit, why did I say that? I guess we have to go with it now.

'Yep,' Zac says.

I can tell from the subtle way he glances at me and then looks away again that he's wondering why I said that too. Obviously, I should have pretended Kat was my sister but, funnily enough, I've never been in this situation before.

It's interesting that I can still interpret the hidden

meaning in Zac's facial expressions. I panic, briefly, when I assume Lilac can do the same, but thankfully she's not picking up on it.

'What were you doing in that bush?' Cherry chimes in.

'Oh, just having a wee,' Kat replies.

'I'm Poppy, this is Kat,' I say, making the introductions, because obviously Zac has never met Kat before, and Kat needs to stop talking about peeing in the bushes.

'More family,' Sonny says with a smile. 'It's bloody freezing out here. Come on, everyone back to the castle, we'll sort these ladies a room and then we'll do the introductions properly.'

'Yes, definitely,' Lilac echoes. 'It will be good to finally meet some of Zachary's relatives.'

I can't put my finger on why it is exactly, but I get the impression she doesn't quite mean that.

The boat that has been approaching for a little while finally stops next to us.

'This is the boat we use to get back and forth,' Sonny explains. 'The other is a decoy.'

'Very smart,' I say.

'I'm looking forward to getting to know you both,'

he says.

'Me too,' Lilac adds, a lot softer this time. 'Okay, on the boat.'

I glance at Kat who looks genuinely overjoyed by all of this. We hang back a moment while the others board the boat.

'This is a nightmare,' I whisper to her.

'No, this is brilliant,' she insists. 'We get to stay in the castle.'

'But now we have to stay here,' I remind her.

'Which means you can get your papers signed easily,' she adds.

'But also that I have to watch my ex get married and pretend to be his cousin all week,' I say.

'Ohhh,' Kat replies. 'Okay, yeah, I guess that's awkward. But just look at it this way: we get to stay in the castle with a movie star.'

Kat is genuinely buzzing about all of this but I can't share her excitement. For me, this is torture. At least she's right about one thing though, at least now it will be much easier to get Zac to sign the papers. It shouldn't be too hard to get him on his own for a chat. Well, we are cousins, after all.

16

'Okay, I know you're kind of going through it, and you're in a real mess of a situation, you've got a job to do and all that. But, can we just acknowledge how sick this is?'

Castle Tarness is like nothing I've ever seen before – not in real life, at least. The best way to describe how it looks is like every castle you've ever seen in epic fantasy movies and TV shows. Not like Edinburgh Castle which, gorgeous as it is, reminds me of a cross between my middle school and the prison in *Bad Girls* from some angles. Castle Tarness is a castle-castle, with towers, battlements, archers' slits – the works. I'm telling you, it's a good job we were invited inside, there would be no way on earth we would be able to get in otherwise.

It's big – in fact, it's huge. Imagine having your wedding in a place like this. Just hiring it out for all your family and friends, all hanging out on a private island, in an amazing castle, what an absolute dream. I had my wedding reception in a function room of a three-star hotel, so it was far from bougie, to say the least.

Inside the castle is stunning too. From what we've seen, which so far is only from the door we entered through, to our room, which an actual butler showed us to (total butler stereotype: older man, black suit, black tie, stiff upper lip), it's very castle-y. A mixture of cold, exposed stone and dated soft furnishings, but it really looks the part. You wouldn't want any of it in your living room but here it looks just right.

The butler, whose name we didn't catch, because Sonny just called him 'buddy', first showed us to a small living room. Inside, there were couple of chesterfield sofas, a mahogany desk, and stone staircase, which is apparently 'the turret staircase', at the top of which was the door to our bedroom and another door to our bathroom. We peeped inside the bathroom first and were delighted to be greeted by a large copper bath. I can't wait to try that later.

'It is gorgeous in here,' I admit, taking in the beautiful bedroom.

'It's the silver lining,' she insists through a grin. I'm very much getting the feeling this Kat (like most cats) always lands on her feet. 'Sonny is kind of hot, right?'

'Absolutely not,' I say quickly. 'He's married.'

'Being married doesn't change how hot someone is,' Kat claps back. 'You're married and you're still hot. Sometimes it makes people hotter.'

'He's, like, sixty,' I point out. 'At least. Maybe older. You can't possibly fancy him.'

Kat is lying on the double bed that we're having to share. I guess people think we're cousins, and I suppose it's not like we haven't shared a bed before, during our brief friendship.

She stretches out like a starfish.

'Have you seen that scene in *Not Dead Yet 5* where he punches the train?' she asks, biting her lip.

My face scrunches up with confusion.

'He punches a train?' I ask. 'Why?'

'To stop it,' she says, like it's the most normal

thing in the world. 'Anyway, come on, what's the plan?'

'The plan is to get Zac on his own, explain, have him sign the papers and get them sent off ASAP,' I reply.

'Are we staying for the wedding?' she asks. I think that's what she's the most interested in.

'Not if I can help it,' I reply.

'Sounds like someone is still hung up on her ex,' Kat sings. 'I won't rule out sabotaging the whole thing just yet. I've got a few ideas for it. God, that Lilac is a bit intense, isn't she? When she caught you and Zac together, her face went as purple as her hair.'

'We did seem pretty suspicious, to be fair,' I reply. 'I can't really blame her.'

'She seems like the type to rip a sword from the wall and skewer you with it,' Kat says.

There is what I would describe as far too much weaponry on the walls of the hallways for a wedding. When I think about the weddings I've been to over the years, my own included, I'm relieved there were no swords or bows and arrows to hand – especially at

Sally's wedding, because I spent pretty much that whole day thinking about shooting her.

'Well, hopefully she never knows the truth,' I reply.

'Let's hope not. She's got big psycho girl energy,' Kat says with a bit of a laugh, like it's kind of funny, but it's also scarily true. 'I've got your back though.'

There's a knock at the door. A woman in a traditional maid's outfit (could easily be an Ann Summers one too) takes a step inside. She's an older woman with a face so serious I'm starting to wonder if I've made her mad, despite the two of us meeting for the first time right now.

'Dinner is served,' she announces in a Scottish accent so strong it takes all my concentration to follow what she's saying. 'Mr Strong requests your company in the dining room.'

'For Mr Strong, anything,' Kat says with a wiggle of her eyebrows that only I can see.

'Are you dressing for dinner?' the maid asks.

'We are dressed,' Kat says with a smile. 'But I just need to pop to the lav. Poppy is ready though.'

We're dressed in the sense that we're wearing one

of only a few outfits we've got with us. Kat's pyjama advice may not have ultimately been all that good, but I am glad she talked me into packing a dress. She said I should bring something dressy in case we needed to go to a bar, drink of bunch of drinks and have a Scotsman shag us silly until we forgot all about our problems – yes, that's a direct quote, and I like to think she wasn't intending for it to be the same Scotsman.

The maid pulls a face and jerks her head, signalling for me to follow her downstairs for dinner.

Well, one thing's for sure, this is going to be interesting...

17

Is there anything more embarrassing than being the last person to walk into a room full of people? It turns out there is. It's being the first one to arrive.

I really am the first one, and the only one too. Kat decided, just before dinner, that she couldn't resist trying the bath – something she told me via text as I headed downstairs – but she did assure me she'd be down in time to eat.

The dining room is a tall, gorgeous room with plain stone walls but it's so cold in here. Literally, it's freezing, and so empty and soulless too. Don't get me wrong, it looks rich in history, and it's all fascinating to look at, but it doesn't feel like a proper dining room. There's a long wooden table that runs down the centre of the room, with a bright red runner on the top of it. The table is set with stunning silverware for far more people than I was expecting, so God knows who is coming tonight.

The focal point of the room, if you don't count the creepy suit of armour that bizarrely somehow follows you with its eyeholes as you move around the room, is a stone fireplace, exposed on both sides. I've walked around it a few times now, partially for something to do but mostly to keep warm, and it really is something.

The loud creaking sound of the door snaps me from my thoughts. A tall, muscular man walks through it.

'Hello,' he says brightly in an east-coast American accent.

I'd guess he's in his thirties, maybe – young-looking early forties, tops. He's wearing jeans and a tight black T-shirt, even though it's so cold in here. He walks with so much confidence it almost looks painful – or that could just be his gigantic thighs rubbing together while he walks.

'Hi,' I reply.

'It's cool in here, huh?' he says.

'It's very chilly,' I reply – I don't think I could sound more English if I tried.

'I meant cool, like rad,' he says with a laugh. 'But if you're cold I can light the fire for you?'

'Sorry, thanks,' I say. It's so like me to embarrass myself in front of someone so hot. And even more English of me to be apologising for basically nothing already.

I watch as he messes with the fireplace, filling it with logs before lighting it, the flames growing quite quickly.

'Hey, check this out,' he says.

As the man plunges his arm through the lit flame, holds it a second or two, and then pulls it back out, I can't help but scream.

'Oh my God,' I blurt.

'Cool, huh?' he says with a laugh. Then he realises I'm understandably freaked out. 'Shit, sorry, I was just trying to impress you. I'm Farrell, the stunt double.'

I puff air from my cheeks.

'Do weddings usually need a stunt double?' I ask.

'Weddings don't,' he replies. 'But movies do. I'm Sonny's stunt double in the *Not Dead Yet* movies.'

I must make a face.

'I know, I'm a lot younger than him, but everyone always says we're a dead ringer for one another,' he replies.

Now that I think about it, Farrell does look a bit like a younger, fitter Sonny Strong.

'What are you, the babe of the movie?' he asks.

I'm floored by what I think might be a compliment.

'No, I'm the cousin of the wedding,' I say, confusingly. 'I'm the cousin of the *groom*, at the wedding. There's a movie?'

'Sonny will tell you all about it, don't worry,' he says. 'He'll be mad if I steal his thunder. I could fix you a drink though?'

'That would be lovely, thank you,' I reply. 'I'm Poppy, by the way.'

'Poppy. Cute name,' he says. 'For what it's worth, you could definitely be in the movies. What is it you do?'

Oh, God, my shitty framing company answer. I

can't tell him that, he's going to take it on face value, and think I'm a loser, like everyone else does.

'Do you really think so?' I reply, ignoring his question. 'I don't think I'd make a very good actress. A stunt double, perhaps. I am always tripping and falling.'

Farrell laughs.

'That's basically the job. Get hurt, jump off shit, set yourself on fire, on set, and at weddings, to impress beautiful ladies.'

I blush. Hopefully I can style it out as a reaction to the heat from the fire, which feels glorious. It's really taken the harsh edge off the room.

'So, drink?' he says.

I think I've safely dodged the occupation question for now.

'Whatever you're having,' I reply, because I think it makes me sound cool.

'That'll be a bourbon,' he says. 'Coming right up.'

Urgh. I really don't like bourbon but I don't want to look uncool, so I don't say anything.

I watch Farrell head over to a drinks cabinet across from the fireplace. He grabs two square glasses and adds ice from a hidden freezer before splashing bourbon in to the glasses.

'You can't do that here, mate,' Sonny says as he approaches us, clocking the bottle in Farrell's hand. 'You want a hard drink, it's Scotch whisky. You want a soft drink, it's Irn Bru.'

His wife Cherry laughs in a way that suggests she doesn't actually understand what Sonny is saying, just that she knows she should laugh at her husband's jokes.

'Oh, honey,' she says.

Sonny's cockney geezer accent and Cherry's strong Texan accent sound miles apart – which they are, obviously, but you know what I mean. It's almost as though, without their celebrity status in common, they never would have ended up in the same room, never mind married. I have a lot of time for odd pairings though, and they've been together a long time so they're clearly doing something right.

'Cherry, you've gotta be with me on this one?' Farrell asks her.

'Leave me out of this one, boys,' she replies. 'Always been more of a wine girl.'

'I'm surrounded by girls,' Sonny concludes. 'Poppy, was it?'

I nod.

'Well, Poppy, how about I pour you a Scotch to go with that bourbon, you close your eyes, and tell me which one is best, how's about that?' Sonny suggests.

Oh, brilliant, I'm going to have two drinks I don't like. It's still just the four of us – perhaps I'll be able to subtly ditch them before the other guests arrive.

'Sure,' I say with an impressive but entirely put on enthusiasm.

'Just don't get drunk before dinner,' Farrell says with a laugh. 'I'll have to carry you to bed.'

'Steady on, geezer, you've just met the girl,' Sonny jokes.

'Oh, because she said she falls a lot,' Farrell quickly insists. He turns to me. 'Sorry, I meant to your own bed, obviously.'

'That's okay,' I reply with a smile.

Cherry loses interest and takes her seat at the table, quickly engrossing herself in something on her phone, something I imagine she does often, when the boys are being boys. Sonny heads over to the bar to pour me a drink.

'Okay, eyes closed,' he instructs me.

I do as I'm told.

'Farrell, mate, put your hands over her eyes, I don't want her siding with you just because you're handsome.'

There's something so undeniably charming about Sonny. He always comes across as a bit of a tool in the media, a caricature of a cockney, ramping up his accent for the cameras because it's such a huge part of his identity, but I really like how friendly and playful he is, and I love his relationship with Farrell, his stuntman. I wonder how many actors are so close with their doubles? Still, there's no denying the fact that Farrell and Sonny essentially playing the same person in movies is some big-time camera trickery or CGI or something, because Sonny definitely looks old enough to be Farrell's dad.

Farrell dutifully slips his hands over my eyes from behind me. He does it so gently it almost tickles.

'I don't want to rub your make-up off,' he says thoughtfully.

'You give her black eyes, she'll give you black eyes,' Sonny jokes. 'Okay, try this.'

I hold out my hands until I feel a glass handed to me. I hold it carefully in both hands as I raise it to my lips and take a sip. Vile. Absolutely vile.

'Next,' I say, trying to hide the disgust in my voice. Well, as someone who only ever drinks the sweetest drinks, this is what I'd imagine drinking petrol is like.

'Number two, coming in, open up wide,' Sonny says as he switches the glass in my hands.

I feel Farrell's hands lightly shift before settling again as I sip from glass number two. Fuck me, that one is even worse. Like licking a razor blade covered in battery acid – I imagine, because I do that as often as I usually drink whisky.

'So?' Sonny prompts.

'Oh boy, yes, okay,' I say, trying to hide the rasp in my voice. I feel like my tonsils are never going to forgive me – if they make it through the night, that is. 'It's got to be the first one.'

Either the first one was the least horrible or it took a layer of skin off the inside of my mouth, making the second one seem worse, but either way, I clearly have no real opinion to give here, so best to just say one and get it over with.

Farrell quickly removes his hands.

'Yes!' he says. 'Correct answer, come here!'

Farrell grabs me by the waist and twirls me around, and for a moment my life is like a movie, until I realise the room has filled with guests while I was blindfolded.

'Am I missing the fun already?' Kat asks.

The next person I notice is Zac. He's standing with Lilac, an arm around her waist, and he doesn't look happy with me at all.

Lilac springs into welcoming mode, now she knows I'm not the kind of girl to steal her man in the woods.

'Poppy, Kat, come and sit at the top of the table with us, family all sit at the top of the table,' she says.

'I'm basically family,' Farrell tells me. 'How about you sit next to me?'

'I'd like that,' I tell him.

Zac shoots daggers into me.

'Zachary, you sit here next to me,' Lilac insists. 'Poppy, Kat, you sit opposite us.'

It's interesting that Lilac calls Zac Zachary, because that's not actually his name. Zac is Zac, short for nothing. I suppose she just likes the way it sounds, maybe? More grown up? I don't know. To me, it just seems weird.

Kat and I sit directly opposite Lilac and Zac at the long table. Farrell sits to my right, opposite Cherry, and then we've got Sonny at the head of the table on the end. I have no idea who all these other people are, but I don't suppose it matters.

'I'm so glad Zachary is going to have some people at the wedding,' Lilac says. 'People who aren't just, you know, my people too.'

'You've invited half of *Heat* magazine,' Sonny points out. 'And I saw you'd sent out a few last-minute invitations today, so that's the other half of *Heat* magazine, and a good chunk of the *Daily Scoop* too. I told you, there's a heavy snow warning, anyone who isn't here now probably won't be able to get here, babe.'

'It's just a few more super close friends,' Lilac tells me and Kat with a bat of her hand. 'Remmy Keating, who plays for, erm, either Man City or Man United, but they're basically the same thing, right? Grace and Mary, the two sisters who were on *Love Island* last year, oh, and I know he's your least favourite actor, Dad, but my agent is going to see if

Freddie Bianchi might come, seeing as she's trying to get me in to his next movie.'

'He's the one who makes the mom porn?' Farrell chimes in, without a hint of judgement.

'Ooh, the *Edge of Eden* movies,' Kat says, now that we're onto her specialist subject. 'Those movies would make a *Fifty Shades* fan blush.'

'What do you want to be in those movies for?' Sonny asks her. 'Be in one of mine. I've told you.'

'Right, but your movies aren't cool, Dad, no offence,' Lilac replies. Her dad's face drops. 'I mean, like, they're not cool for me, because you're my dad. That's blatant necrophilism.'

'Nepotism,' Zac corrects her.

'What?' Lilac replies.

'Nepotism,' he says again. 'That's the word you meant.'

'Oh,' she says, looking visibly puzzled. 'What does what I said mean?'

'So, are you working on anything at the moment?' I ask Sonny, nipping that topic of conversation in the bud.

'We're just about to shoot,' he tells me. '*Not Dead Yet 9*. We're shooting some of it here.'

'Here?' I say. That can't be right.

'Yeah, after the wedding,' he says. 'Well, we've already got this place hired anyway, and it's the perfect location for the new flick.'

'So, what's the big, bad enemy in this one?' Kat asks.

'Get ready for this,' Sonny says, leaning forward in his seat and lowering his voice just a little. 'The Loch Ness Monster.'

I feel my bottom jaw physically fall away from the top.

'The Loch Ness Monster?' I repeat back to him.

'Yep,' he says proudly. 'No one is going to expect that.'

'You're filming it here?' Kat says. 'Isn't this Loch *Tar*ness?'

'It's basically the same thing,' Sonny replies.

It really isn't.

'Anyway, it's my production company, Deadlad Films,' Sonny continues. 'Do you know how much more it costs to film at Loch Ness? Fucking hell, you'd think they did have a monster there. Then it'd save us some money on the VFX.'

The villains in the *Not Dead Yet* movies have been

getting sillier over the years, but the Loch Ness Monster is just ridiculous.

'The first scene takes place at a wedding, here at the castle,' Farrell says. 'The monster sticks one of its tentacles in through one of the windows, into the ceremony room, spears it through the bride. Sonny's character, Jack McVey, is there, because it's his niece, and he swings in on one of the high curtains and tries to save her – and I'm the one who does the swinging, obviously.'

Farrell sounds genuinely jazzed that he's going to be swinging through a big room on a curtain like a jacked George of the Jungle.

'But I don't save her,' Sonny says. 'So, the rest of the movie is me trying to kill the Loch Ness Monster, to avenge my niece. Great, right?'

'I'm so here for it,' Kat says.

'Ah, the food is here,' Sonny announces, clocking the waitstaff entering the room with trollies. 'I thought it might be nice to try some local cuisine. Traditional haggis with neeps and tatties.'

I've never actually tried haggis, but the idea of it puts me off just a little. Still, I grab my fork and tuck in to my vegetables. They're delicious, at least.

As I eat, even though I'm looking down at my plate, I can feel Zac staring at me. Somewhere around the time I told him we were still married, I noticed his jaw tighten, and it hasn't loosened since. He must have so many questions. I need to get him on his own, sooner rather than later, to try to explain to him. He must be terrified, never mind absolutely fuming with me.

'You never told me what you did for a living,' Farrell pipes up once we're all settled in to eating.

Shit.

'I, erm...'

'She's not really supposed to tell you,' Kat chimes in. She lowers her voice. 'She's an agent for MI6.'

I don't know if I choke on my neeps or my tatties but it takes a big gulp of table water to stop me coughing.

'Kat,' I say under my breath.

'I know, I know, it's supposed to be a secret,' she says. 'The Secret Service. But that's what she does.'

'Wow, is that what you do too?' Lilac asks Kat.

'No, I don't work, I married well, he passed away, it was a whole thing but, basically, I don't need to work,' she says rather casually. I definitely get the feeling she does this all the time.

'Incredible, MI6?' Farrell says. 'I'd love to talk to you about it. I realise there's only so much you can say, so it would only be about the job generally, but I'm really wanting to play James Bond, so anything you can tell me. I want to be ready for next time they audition.'

'James Bond's stunt double?' I reply.

'No, *the* James Bond,' he says.

'They'll never let an American do it,' Sonny tells me. 'They wouldn't even let me audition. No one born within the sound of Bow Bells gets a look in, so they're certainly not going to give it to a Yank. No offence, mate.'

'Yeah, but just wait until Poppy gives me all the intel,' Farrell replies, touching his temple with his index finger.

'So, Poppy, obviously you're always quite busy, being an international spy,' Zac says, finally breaking his silence towards me, only just masking how ridiculous he finds this. 'How have you been, otherwise?'

'Erm, yeah, good,' I reply. 'Business is obviously

booming, always spy stuff going on, friends are all doing good – they're all married now.'

'Rachael finally married some poor bloke on New Year's Eve,' Kat informs him.

I watch as Zac's eyebrows raise ever so slightly. Obviously, he knows Sally, Lindsey and Rachael from the good old days, but he has no idea who Kat is.

'That's great for them,' he replies genuinely. 'It must be six years since I saw them all last. Say hi for me.'

'Of course,' I say with a smile.

'How are Martin and Ellie?' Zac asks. 'Sally's parents.'

He quickly adds that on to the end because Martin and Ellie are my parents, but to mention them would only raise more questions about how someone with not very much family suddenly seems to have a whole bunch of relatives he never mentioned. It's already pretty dodgy that Kat and I are apparently both his cousins, as well as being cousins ourselves, not to mention the fact that none of us look even remotely related.

'Martin is doing great,' I tell him. 'His business is

doing really well; he seems really happy. We, erm, we lost Ellie. Car accident. Four years ago.'

I can barely get the words out. Zac's face falls.

'Oh my God, Pops, I'm so sorry,' he says, dangerously close to breaking character but, for a few seconds, I don't even think he cares. 'That must have been so horrible for... for Sally, after everything she's been through.'

'Yeah, it was really hard for her,' I reply. 'But she had her dad and they helped each other through.'

'I wish I'd known,' he says right as Lilac gives him a hard shove with her elbow.

'Erm, this is our wedding week, we're supposed to be happy,' she says angrily. 'Not talking about Sally's dead mum who died four years ago.'

Her words punch me in the stomach.

Zac looks deeply uncomfortable. Kat, who I exchanged life stories with on the long drive up here, grits her teeth.

'Sally's mum was important to our family,' she eventually says, in a surprisingly calm way. That's quite a measured response for Kat. She's been, so far, so nuclear during our short friendship.

'Come on, Lilac, let the cousins catch up a bit,'

Sonny says. 'The rest of the weekend is going to be all about you.'

'That's true,' she says with a contented smile. 'Zachary too, obviously.'

'Obviously,' Kat replies. I get the feeling she doesn't like Lilac. I'm not sure I do either.

Lilac and Cherry start chatting about all things wedding while Sonny and Farrell talk about what's most important to them: *Not Dead Yet 9: Jack McVey vs The Loch Ness Monster*.

'Remember those drinks you used to make?' Zac asks me. 'Reckon you could show me how to make one now?'

'Erm, yes,' I reply, trying to mask the fact I have no idea what he's talking about.

We walk around the fireplace, up to the drinks cabinet. Zac passes me a glass and I reach for the neatest bottle, which just so happens to be rum. As I fuss around pouring it, I notice Zac subtly unfold a piece of paper in front us. It says: *Meet me on the jetty at midnight*.

I nod gently.

'This message will self-destruct in five seconds,' I

joke quietly. Zac doesn't say anything, so I quickly wipe the smile from my face.

I reach inside the hidden fridge for a mixer. I top the rum up with Coke and add a few ice cubes. I'm pretty happy with it until I realise that, if anyone asks what this special drink I make is, the drink being a rum and Coke isn't going to cut it.

I notice a shelf at the back of the bottles where there are a series of fancy syrups for making cocktails. One of them is vanilla, so I pour a generous glug into the glass.

'There you go, cuz,' I tell him, handing it over.

We make our way back to the table, just in time to catch Kat telling another tall tale.

'...but it's like I told the police, I can't cause someone to have a heart attack, can I? It's not like we were up to anything at the time because, if we were, hmm, maybe I could...'

She flashes a cheeky smile and her audience laughs. Christ, I can't believe she's doing a dead husband bit, and I really can't believe she told everyone I'm a secret bloody agent. I appreciate that my job may be boring but I'm sure there are a whole other bunch of far more interesting jobs somewhere between running a framing company and being a secret agent – jobs I could do a more convincing job of pretending I'm capable of.

Lilac eyeballs Zac's drink.

'Go on then, let's try this special drink,' she says.

Zac, who hasn't even tried his drink, offers her his glass.

Lilac takes a sip. Then another one.

'Oh, wow,' she blurts. 'This is actually really nice.'

'Give it here,' Sonny demands. He takes a sip too. 'It's a bit sweeter than my usual tipple but that's bloody good, that is. You came up with this?'

I nod. Yep, just now, with zero to little thought.

Cherry takes a sip next.

'My kind of drink,' she says. 'What do you call this concoction?'

'We call it a Messy Divorce, don't we?' Kat chimes in.

I shoot her a look.

'Yep, that's what we call it,' I play along. 'No idea why.'

'Well, I see a lot of Messy Divorces in this coming week,' Sonny says with a smile. 'Shaken, not stirred, right?'

He winks at me. I just smile.

So, obviously I'm going to need to spend the night googling MI-fucking-6, to try to do a vaguely convincing job of pretending I work for them. But before I worry about that, I need to worry about something more important: my meeting with Zac at midnight. We've spent many a time outside together, late at night, but this is different, isn't it? It isn't for fun, it won't be romantic, it's a secret meeting about how the hell we're supposed to get divorced before he gets married again.

Suddenly, trying to pass myself off as a secret agent seems much more straightforward in comparison.

18

18 AUGUST 2012

'Where do you think we'll be in ten years' time?' I ask Zac.

'Here,' he says.

'What, lying on the grass in my back garden?' I say with a laugh. 'Just kissing and looking at the stars?'

To be fair, we do spend a lot of time outside, late at night, staring up at the sky. When we left the cinema after our first date, everyone was talking about this fireball in the sky. I don't know if some people had seen something, or it had just been a rumour all along, but it turned into a bit of a short-lived urban legend, so we went and sat in the town square, in the cold January air, and stared up into the night sky for a while. We didn't see a fireball, but we did end up holding hands. Fireballs sound cool, I'll bet it would be sick to see one, and it's a once in a lifetime kind of thing but, discovering that spark with Zac, that's forever. Honestly, these last six years together have been perfect. I think there's an expectation that you'll grow out of your relationship with your school sweetheart, but we never have. Our feelings have only ever grown stronger.

'Not specifically here in the garden,' he says with a laugh. 'I think your parents might object, if we just set up a camp in their back garden.'

'I don't know, if we do it while they're in Wales for the weekend,' I suggest playfully. 'We're already throwing a house party. What's a bit more trouble?'

'Ah, but I'm going to help you tidy up, so much so that the house is going to be cleaner than it was when your parents left it,' he says with a smile. 'But, seeing as how they told you that you were not under any circumstances to throw a party, they'll probably be suspicious if the place is too tidy, so I'll help you mess it up again, just enough to throw them off.'

'Boyfriend of the year,' I say with a smile.

'Yep, I'm pretty perfect,' he jokes. 'The marriage proposals just flood in left, right and centre.'

'Well, I'll be sure to get mine in there for consideration,' I say through a chuckle.

'Do you want to get married?' Zac asks, his tone suddenly a little more serious.

I quickly jolt my head up and stare at him, my eyes wide with surprise.

'Oh, I'm not asking, not right now, don't panic,' he insists.

'Phew,' I joke playfully, resting my head back down on him, now I know I can relax again.

I mean, I say phew, but, thinking about it, I don't really mean it, I'm not freaked out at all. The idea of being married to Zac sounds like a wonderful thing. I'd love to be his wife – now I'm almost disappointed he isn't actually asking.

'I just mean, one day, is marriage something you want?' he asks. 'Or kids?'

'I'm not quite sure about kids yet,' I admit. 'I think I still feel like one myself most of the time. Example being, I'm twenty-one, and I'm throwing a house party while my parents are away for their anniversary. I do like the idea of marriage, though.'

'I do too,' he says. 'In ten years' time, in my head, I see us married, a family, if that's what you want.'

'Well, 2022 is a long way away,' I point out. 'But I would love to be married to you by then so... I guess... when you want to ask me, know that I probably won't say no. Just, you know, not tonight.'

I'm reiterating that I'm freaked out about him even asking right now but I'm not. I'm really, really not.

I lean in and plant my lips on his. We kiss for a moment, on our blanket on the lawn, before things start heating up a little. Zac lies back and my body naturally gravitates until I'm on top of him. It's a warm summer night, pretty much silent, apart from the quiet thump of music from the party indoors. I could not be more in love with him and this is just one of those perfect romantic moments that you can never quite believe actually happen to real people.

Suddenly the music gets louder.

'Poppy, this is a top night,' Sally says as she staggers down the garden. 'What are you two doing, hmm?'

She says this with a knowing tone but, whatever

she thinks she was disturbing, she's still happy to do so.

'Shift up,' she says, plonking down on the blanket next to us. 'Rachael is destroying your bathroom, her Lambrini is making a comeback. Lindsey may well be destroying your bed, because she's in there with Mike, or Mick, something like that? The one who's training to be a doctor.'

'Paul?' I reply.

'That's the one,' she says. 'I knew it was something like that.'

I love Sally when she's drunk. I like to think I know how to have fun, but Sally is wild.

She snuggles up to me and rests her head on my arm. In less than minute, she's fast asleep.

'See, we're like a weird little family already,' Zac jokes.

'We are,' I reply. 'And I couldn't be happier.'

19

The castle (nope, I didn't think I'd be starting any sentences with that this day, week, month, year either) is so abuzz with guests and staff during the day that it's actually quite creepy at night. So creepy that I walk down the stairs keeping an eye out for God knows what; it's pushing midnight but everyone seems to be in bed, which only makes it seem scarier.

I'm not saying I believe in ghosts, because that would be silly, right? But I'm not *not* saying that either. When it comes to the supernatural, I'm somewhat of an agnostic, just keeping my mind open enough so that, if ghosts are real, they don't feel like I've disrespected them, and therefore don't feel the need to prove anything to me. It's amazing, the weird things that pop into your head when you're sneaking out through the castle gates at midnight, hugging your own body through your coat to try to protect yourself from the chill of the cold night air.

I wander down the path and along a little to find the jetty. I can see Zac standing there alone, underneath one of the lights, so I make my way down there.

As I get nearer to him, I psych myself up for the major bollocking I'm about to receive for turning up here, and for dropping the bad news on him. I almost wish I'd had more to drink with dinner but, then again, turning up to the secret meeting drunk could only make things worse. I'll bet Zac is going to erupt with questions the second he clocks me. I just hope I can answer them all, and that he's not totally fuming with me. Of course, I'd fully understand if he was. Who wouldn't be with their ex turning up at their wedding, breaking the news to them that they're still married?

'Zac,' I whisper quietly. He's looking out at the water. I can't get over how flat and still it is. The calm before the storm.

Zac turns around and walks over to me purposefully. For a split second, my warped little mind contemplates whether he's going to push me in the loch and hope I don't come back up. But instead of murdering me, Zac grabs me and hugs me. He squeezes me so tightly and for a moment his arms transport me back in time, back to happier times, before our divorce, when I felt so safe and so content with him. I feel the relaxation creeping through every inch of my body. I can't even feel the cold any more. All I feel is home and safe and exactly where I should be, until he eventually releases me and holds me at arm's length, then I'm straight back to reality, freezing my tits off next to a loch, in the dark, about to tell the man I so painfully divorced once that we need to do it all over again.

'Pops, I'm so sorry about your mum,' he says. 'I can't believe it. I can't believe you had to go through that, that I wasn't there – I wish you'd told me.'

'Well, you disappeared after the split,' I remind him. 'I couldn't have contacted you if I'd wanted to.'

'I was working in London so much I decided to move there,' he says. 'Did you want to contact me?'

There's a nervous curiosity in his voice but I'm not answering that.

'I would have invited you to the funeral, if I could have,' I reply. 'Mum worshipped you.'

'And I loved her,' he replies. 'She was like a mum to me. And your dad – how's he doing?'

'He's much better these days,' I reply. 'Actually, I just found out he's dating again.'

'Really?' Zac replies with a smile.

'Yep. He's using apps.'

Zac laughs.

'Look, about us—'

'Hang on a sec,' Zac stops me. 'Before we get on to that, get in the boat.'

I stare at him, puzzled, then notice the rowboat next to us. I snort.

'Yeah, right,' I reply.

'I'm serious,' he replies. 'This castle, this island – there are people everywhere, all the time, lurking, sneaking. There's no privacy. The only way I can guarantee we can talk about *that* safely is in this boat.'

'You don't row,' I point out.

'I do,' he insists.

'What, really?' I reply. I can't hide my surprise. It must be part of the new and improved *Zachary Hunt*.

'Yeah, well, I row at the gym,' he says.

I scoff.

'That doesn't count.'

'Pops, would you just get in the frigging boat, please?' he replies sharply.

'Fine, fine, I'll just get in the boat, in the water that's two hundred metres deep, with the man who only rows at the gym,' I say under my breath.

Zac offers me a hand and helps me in before joining me. He takes a position between the oars and grabs one with each hand. He looks unsure of himself, which isn't what we love to see, but I'm here now. Sink or swim.

He only rows us out until we're slightly offshore, which I'm fine with, but it almost doesn't seem worth it.

'Foolproof,' I tease.

'You say that, but no one can sneak up on us,' he replies. 'If anyone approaches us, we'll see them before they hear anything. No need to head for Norway. I thought MI6 would have known that.'

Now he's teasing me.

'Who is the girl you brought with you?' he asks, bemused.

'That's Kat,' I tell him. 'She's my friend.'

'She doesn't seem like someone Rachael would get on with.'

'Well, funny you should say that,' I start with a smile. 'She's actually her cousin-in-law. And you're right they don't get on. To be honest, I don't get on with Rachael and the girls so well these days either.'

'That surprises me,' he says. 'You lot were always thick as thieves.'

'So were you and I,' I remind him with a slight smile.

'Fair point,' he replies.

Zac breathes warm air into his hands before rubbing them together.

'So, the reason you're here,' he starts. 'Are we really still married?'

'Yep,' I reply. 'Sorry.'

'How does that even happen?' he asks.

'Keeping in mind how much you said you love my mum,' I start. I can tell from Zac's eyes that he's connected the dots already. 'Dad found some letters she wrote in her office. The general sentiment was that she was so sure we were going to get back together that she thought she was doing us a favour by not actually filing our divorce or whatever. She died before she could come clean.'

'God, that's so your mum,' he says with a smile.

'I'm going to level with you, I thought you'd be more upset, more angry.'

'Well, yes, of course I'm upset, and angry, but come on, Pops, it's Ellie. She always had the best intentions. What's the point in being mad at her?' he says. 'Plus, I assume you know what needs to be done to fix it?'

'Yep, good old Dad,' I reply.

Zac smiles.

'Always the sensible one,' he says.

'That's him. He's had Auntie Joan draw up the paperwork, all we need to do is sign it, then send it, and you can get married as planned,' I tell him. 'The only tricky bits being that we need two witnesses to sign it too, and we need to scan and send it. I don't imagine we can do any of that here?'

'You'd be right,' he replies. 'But we can do it in town, we just need to think of a reason to sneak away.'

'Sneak away,' I say with a laugh. 'Wow, I feel like I'm having an affair with my husband.'

Zac allows himself to laugh, even though this is a way bigger deal for him than it is for me, given that he's supposed to be getting married in a matter of days.

'Don't get me wrong, I'm not happy about any of this, but if there's a plan to fix it, no point in me being mad,' he says. 'I'm sorry for blurting out that you were my cousin, I didn't know what else to say. If you want to come up with a reason to leave before the big day, you're welcome to, but you're equally welcome to stay, too. There's always room at the wedding for my two favourite cousins.'

'Thanks,' I say through a smile. 'Now can you get me back to dry land, please?'

'Yes, miss,' he replies. 'Or, erm, missus.'

As Zac rows us the few feet back to the jetty, I can't help but feel a heavy weight in my heart. He may look different, seem different, he may even sound slightly different, having spent so much time around a fiancée who clearly went to a very nice private school where she learned to talk 'proper', despite clearly not being the most intelligent. Okay, maybe that's mean, just because she muddled a few words, I guess I'm still smarting from the way she dismissed the conversation about my mum dying.

But Zac is still the same person inside, and the qualities that made me fall for him in the first place still shine through. I'm the CEO of overthinking, always have been, always will be. The slightest thing can seem like the end of the world and the mildest inconvenience can make me feel like I want to punch a hole through something (although I don't because breaking the bones in my hand would be a whole new stress to contend with), but Zac isn't like that at all, he's so chilled out, so balanced, a total Mr Brightside. We were so good for each other, balancing one another out. I would light a fire under him when he was too chilled out – when he wouldn't be worried at all but perhaps should be, just a little – and when I was freaking out, he would calm me down, whether it was with his reassuring words or by simply lying me down, switching on the fancy star lights we used to have in our bedroom, and putting on one of his chillout playlists. We really were perfect for each other.

A thought hits me like lightning, allowing my

ghost agnostic brain to wonder: is something spooky going on here? Are strings being pulled by a higher power? Is someone or something not of this world trying to send me a message? Could this be my mum, matchmaking from the other side? Now that the thought has simmered in my head for a few seconds, it seems highly unlikely, but it's made me think. Has fate or coincidence brought me here to try to get Zac back?

Nah, it's like I said to Kat, I'm here to get a divorce, not back together. And Zac seems like he's keen to get it sorted too, so that's that. We'll get it sorted and then I'll get out of here. Kat's stories may be ridiculous, but she has given me the ultimate Get Out of Wedding Free card. I can simply state 'MI6 stuff', and be on my way. That's what I'm going to need to do, as soon as I can, because one thing I'm sure of is that there's no way I can watch Zac marry someone else.

20

Breakfast is in the same room as dinner was, except there's a breakfast buffet all laid out on the side for guests to help themselves, so no forced local delicacies today, thankfully.

'I am going to absolute town on this,' Kat told me as she loaded up her plate when we first came down. She even went back for seconds.

A full Scottish breakfast is like a full English, but potentially even better. There are eggs, bacon, beans, mushrooms, tomatoes – all the usual things you would expect to see. But then there are the bonus items. The sausages, for example, aren't like the cylindrical ones I'm used to, they're more like square slices of sausage meat. There's also black pudding, which I'm actually quite fond of, as well as fried potato cakes, or tattie scones, as the server called them. I'm a big fan.

Sort of like a hotel, breakfast is served during a window of time, and everyone eats together. I'm still overwhelmed by all the people here, most of whom haven't been introduced to me, but that suits me just fine. It's fewer people I have to lie to.

'Wow, that's insane,' Farrell says. We've been chatting for a while now and he seems captivated by my stories. 'It's insane that assassins would dress up as clowns and attend a kids' party, just to take out a target.'

All I can say is: thank God Farrell hasn't seen any of *Killing Eve*. I wonder how much I can coast on the three seasons I've watched.

'It's a tough job, but someone has it do it,' I reply with a casual shrug.

Oh, I did not just say that. That's so corny. A secret agent would never say that, surely?

'Wow, I'm so impressed,' he replies and he really

sounds like he means it. 'It's so rare I meet someone with a more interesting job than mine.'

'You definitely have the coolest job in this room,' I tell him.

'Cooler than Sonny?' he replies. 'Do you think?'

'Of course,' I insist. 'Because his job has limits. You do all the things he won't do, no matter how dangerous it is. Without you, his movies would be nothing.'

'Man, you're quite the cheerleader,' he replies with a smile. 'Can you just follow me around saying nice things? When you're not fighting Russian assassins, that is.'

'Sure,' I tell him, smiling back.

'I guess Lilac's job is cool,' he continues. 'She basically gets paid for nothing. And Zac is a big-time session guitarist – although you'll know that, obviously – that's a pretty sweet gig.'

I didn't know Zac was a big-time session guitarist. When we were married, he was a barman playing occasional gigs, usually for nothing more than free drinks or exposure, and then right before we split, he had just landed himself a sort of trial period, working in a studio in London. I smile for a moment, knowing that he's bagged his dream job, but it quickly falls away when I think about how unimpressive I seem in comparison.

'Morning,' Zac says, sitting down opposite us. 'Morning, Kat.'

Kat has been sitting next to me, chatting to the person on her left, but when Zac speaks to her it pulls her back to our conversation.

'Morning, dude,' Farrell replies. 'Actually, I have a question for you both.'

'Oh?' I say. What could he possibly have to ask me *and* Zac?

I feel Kat scoot up closer to me, to make sure she can hear our conversation over all the chitchat in the room.

'Yeah. Don't tell Sonny, because he'll flip if he knows, but I stepped outside last night for a sneaky cigarette,' he starts, and I already know where this is going. 'Did I see the two of you in a boat?'

'In a boat?' Kat says with a squeak. We've definitely got her attention now.

'Yes, you did,' I reply quickly, my logic being that,

if we had something to hide, we'd be trying to hide it right now, instead of telling the truth.

'Yes, we're all keen rowers in our family,' Zac says, taking the reins. 'We like to have races. Poppy was always the cox.'

'I've heard that said before,' Kat jokes under her breath.

'Really?' Farrell replies.

'Yep,' Zac says, as convincingly as he can. 'It's a Hunt family tradition.'

Farrell opens his mouth to speak but we're interrupted by the sound of Kat sniggering. We all look at her.

'Is Lilac taking your name?' she asks Zac.

'Yes,' he replies. 'Why?'

'Lilac Hunt?' she says to him. 'It doesn't exactly roll off the tongue, does it?'

'Oi, it's a beautiful name,' I insist. 'Anyway, we were talking about rowing.'

I can't believe I'm dragging the conversation back to my lie, but the subject was taking a real turn.

'Yeah,' Farrell replies, also getting the conversation back on track. 'I love rowing. I'm pretty good at it. Maybe we could race?'

Oh, God, now I wish we could go back to Kat making fun of people's names.

'Maybe,' Zac replies.

Let's hope that's the last of that. Well, I doubt they'll be competing on rowing machines and, if they do, I don't fancy Zac's chances against a stunt man.

'So, what do you all do here for fun during the day?' Kat asks curiously.

'Games,' Farrell replies.

'Forced fun,' Zac says at the same time.

Farrell shoots him a look.

'I'm just not really into the games,' Zac tells us. 'Lilac's family always play this game called Find and Sneak – it's one of those games you only played growing up if you lived in mansions. We couldn't have played it in our house.'

Zac purses his lips. I think he was talking about our house, as in the tired three-bed semi we lived in when we got married, but Farrell is too busy hoovering down a gigantic plate of scrambled eggs to notice.

'I think Sonny wants to have a sort of Highland games event,' Farrell says. 'That will be more your style, Zac. Maybe we could fit our boat race in after?'

'Maybe,' Zac says once again. I can tell he wants absolutely no part of it.

'Good morning, campers,' Sonny announces brightly. 'How's everyone doing today?'

Sonny is the star of the show, no matter where he goes or what he does. The second he walks into a room, it's all eyes on him, both because people are interested in him, but also because he commands it.

'Poppy, can I borrow you, darling?' he says, which takes me aback, because no one ever believes the most important person in the room wants to talk to them, do they?

'Sure,' I reply, semi-reluctantly abandoning the last of my breakfast. I say semi because I am actually intrigued by what Sonny could want to talk to me about, and I've definitely eaten way more than I should have. If I were a cox today, I'd sink the boat.

He ushers me across to the other side of the room, next to the pastries – would it be weird to grab one? Of course it would. I won't do that.

'Between you and me,' he says, lowering his voice, hardly moving his lips as he speaks, lest anyone be lipreading him right now. 'Something strange is going on in this castle.'

'Strange?' I reply. 'How do you mean?'

'Look, I'm not saying it's ghosts,' he starts.

Oh, God, fuck it, I need that pastry now.

'I'm not ruling anything out,' he continues. 'But something is going on. Strange things keep happening and they're getting worse. Last night, for example, after everyone went to bed, someone, or something, came into our bedroom.'

It's on the tip of my tongue to ask him if it was the Loch Ness Monster – or the Loch Tarness Monster, at least.

'How do you know?' I ask curiously.

'They took the wedding rings,' he replies. 'Lilac's ring, which was my late mum's ring, worth a bloody fortune, and then the ring Zac chose for himself – also worth a fortune – both gone. Lilac will go mad when she realises, so I need to get them back ASAP.'

Oh, shit. This is actually serious.

'Who do you think it was?' I ask him.

'I was hoping the family MI6 agent might help me work that out,' he says with a hopeful smile, crossing his fingers and waving them in front of me.

Double shit.

'Erm, yeah,' I say. 'Of course. Well, I mean, what are you after?'

Wow, I sound *so* professional.

'The only people with access to the family wing are, obviously, the family – me, Cherry, Lilac and Zac – obviously none of us would have taken them because, you know, they're already ours. That just leaves two members of staff,' he explains. 'Part of the deal is that we have absolute privacy. Staff not only signed nondisclosure agreements, but agreed to stay on the island for the whole wedding, so if one of them has taken the rings, they won't have had chance to get away with it. I was hoping you'd interrogate them with me. I have some experience, from my movies, but waterboarding them feels a bit heavy-handed at this stage.'

Sonny laughs wildly.

At this stage, yeah, *probably*. I keep my sarcasm to myself.

'Right.'

'I thought, you know, you have more real experience than me,' he says. 'You could talk to them.'

'Yeah, okay, sure,' I reply, although I'm deeply, deeply uncomfortable with this.

It's hard to say who is the least qualified for this job: me or Sonny. I think I'm going to back myself, in this instance, as being the right person for the job. At least I don't know how to waterboard anyone.

This should be interesting.

21

There are two people who do the housekeeping in the family wing of the castle: Sophie and Sophia. Sophie is a fifty-something English woman. Sophia is a twenty-something Italian. Sonny refers to them as the Sophs, and never seems to quite get a handle on which one is which.

We're currently standing in one of the old stone corridors (but aren't they all) where Sophia is pushing a trolley stacked with toiletries. I swear, these are nicer than the ones we have in our bathroom.

'I was just looking for you, babe,' Sonny tells her.

'Do you want my hands?' she replies.

She's obviously just muddling up a fairly common phrase, but Sonny's eyes light up.

'Mate, do I,' he says. He turns to me, to give me a geezer nudge, but he can tell from the look on my face that I'm not having any of it.

I'm not here to help him Me Too a maid, I'm here to help him find the missing wedding jewellery – I'm barely here to do that, I'm just going along with Kat's stupid lie.

Sophia doesn't get his joke, and for that I'm grateful.

'Some jewellery has gone missing from the family room,' he finally says.

It sounds like the family room is some sort of shared space between Sonny and Cherry's room and Zac and Lilac's.

'Oh, no,' Sophia says. 'I know nothing about that. I clean bathrooms and kitchens; I don't clean rooms.'

'What do you reckon?' Sonny asks me. 'Is she telling the truth?'

Sophia looks at me, anxiously waiting to see if I clear her name.

Honestly, how the hell should I know? Neither Daniel Craig as James Bond nor as Benoit Blanc in

Knives Out could figure this one out from such limited information, surely?

Honestly, I just feel so deeply uncomfortable with this, I just want it to end.

'She doesn't seem like she's lying to me,' I reply. 'Her micro-expressions aren't indicative of lying.'

A little something I picked up from *Lie to Me*. Isn't it amazing, how much you can learn from just watching TV?

'Okay, you can go, for now,' Sonny tells her. 'But I'm watching you.'

Sophia frowns.

'Where's the other one?' he asks her. I cringe.

'Sophie?' she replies. 'She's in your bed.'

'Chance would be a fine thing,' Sonny says under his breath. 'Come on, you.'

He nods for me to follow him. This is like the world's worst buddy cop movie – incidentally, something Sonny would probably star in.

When we arrive in Sonny's bedroom, he suddenly remembers that Sophie is the one closer to his age. He pulls a face, like he regrets his joke about wanting her in his bed.

'Oi,' he calls out. 'We need a word with you.'

'What on earth is the matter, Mr Strong?' she replies, putting down the pillowcase she's currently stuffing, hurrying around the bed to greet us.

Sophie seems both dutiful and polite – hardly a jewel thief.

'Someone has stolen some jewellery from the family room, and we think it's you,' he says plainly.

My eyebrows shoot up to the turrets.

'Well, I've never been so offended in my life,' she says. 'In all my years in the job, not once have I stolen, not once have I even been accused.'

'Well, it wasn't the other one,' Sonny tells her. 'She checked out. So you're looking pretty guilty right now. Would you agree to letting us search you and your room?'

'Oh, Mr Strong, absolutely not,' she shrieks.

Sonny turns to me.

'That's her banged to rights,' he says quietly, although she can still hear. 'Only guilty people have something to hide. Hmm, that would make a great movie title.'

Oh, yeah, Sonny, get right on that, when you're finally done flogging the *Not Dead Yet* horse.

'She probably just doesn't want anybody going

through her things,' I tell him. 'And she obviously doesn't want us patting her down – no one would want that.'

Sonny narrows his eyes.

I really can't see it, that either of these women would have crept into Sonny's room during the night and stolen two wedding rings – especially given the fact that no one can leave until after the wedding, when obviously it would be noticed that they were missing. I know, I'm not actually a secret agent, but that just seems like common sense to me. Sophia and Sophie are clearly just trying to do their jobs here. It's the right thing to do, to use my stupid lie, to nip this in the bud.

'Look, okay, I shouldn't be showing you this, but there's a super-secret MI6 technique for instantly telling if someone is lying or not. But we're not supposed to do it off the job, ethically, but how about I do it now, so that Sophie can get back to work?' I suggest.

'If you wouldn't mind,' Sonny says with a sigh of relief.

'Sophie, do you mind?' I ask.

'Erm, okay,' she replies. I don't think she has a clue what I'm on about. Neither do I, to be fair.

I take Sophie's hand in mine and examine it. Next, I hold it, as though I'm shaking her hand, but I extend my index finger to her wrist and press it lightly.

'Do you know anything about the missing jewellery?' I ask her slowly.

'No,' she replies in a similar tone. I'm not sure she's buying it, but Sonny is lapping it up.

'Yep, telling the truth,' I confirm to Sonny. 'Come on, let's leave her to it.'

'Sorry about that, Sophia,' he says, getting her name wrong. 'It's just, y'know, it's the rings for the wedding. They're a big deal.'

Sophie grits her teeth.

'That's okay, Mr Strong,' she says, not exactly selling the sentiment, but who can blame her. 'Perhaps look a little closer to home.'

Sonny and I make our way back out to the hallway.

'Well, now I feel awful,' Sonny says. 'But things just seem to be going wrong for this wedding, left, right and centre. Liles is my little girl, y'know? I just want to make it perfect, and now the rings are missing. And it was her who proposed to Zac, so she didn't even get a ring in the first place.'

'That's okay, I understand,' I tell him. Well, I kind of do. I get wanting to do the best for your family. Not so much blindly accusing the people who clean up after you, but still.

I don't know why I'm surprised that Lilac was the one who proposed to Zac, it is 2022 after all. But it definitely makes me think about when he proposed to me.

'Could you do me one more favour, please?' Sonny asks.

'What's that?' I ask.

'Tonight, when everyone goes to bed, just walk the halls, keep an eye out, use your skills to see if anyone is lurking around after dark, doing anything weird,' he says.

'Erm...'

'Please,' he says.

'Yeah, okay, I'll have a look around, see what I can see,' I reply.

'You're a diamond,' he replies. 'I'm so lucky to be merging my lot with such a beautiful family.'

I smile.

'Right, let's go get on with the fun stuff,' Sonny says. 'But first, I need some breakfast.'

Yay, this must be the forced fun Zac was talking about. I only need to stick it out a little longer, until Zac and I can sneak off to the mainland to get the papers signed and sent.

Until then, I just have to play along, whatever the games may be.

22

31 OCTOBER 2014

More often than once in a blue moon, but still rare enough to be special, Halloween falling on a Friday or a Saturday night is one hell of a magical thing.

When you're little, Halloween is awesome, obviously, but it's always a pretty similar affair. You get dressed up, go trick or treating, eat sweets, play games, have a spooky dinner, eat more sweets. I've always loved Halloween. I used to try to stay up late on Halloween when I was a kid. It all started when my mum told me that, supposedly, if you ate an apple, brushed your hair and looked in the mirror on Halloween night, you would see the face of the man you were going to marry. I never quite managed it

'Wait, do you have to pick all those up now?' Sally asks.

'Yeah, that's why I was late,' she explains. 'I gave my flatmate a demo.'

'I am not pissed enough for this,' Sally says with a sigh.

'I'll grab us some more drinks,' I laugh. 'Ciders all round?'

As I push my way through the overcrowded house (you've got to feel sorry for whosever house this is because it's going to be such a mess) something catches my eye. Is that... is that? No!

'Zac?' I blurt.

'I'm not Zac,' he says. 'I'm, well, I'm Groot, aren't I?'

'I can see that,' I reply. 'But I thought we were going to be Gamora and Star-Lord – he's a cool guy, in his jacket, with his Walkman. And here you are, Groot, the giant tree fella.'

'I'm not really a cool guy though, am I?' he says with a laugh. 'Let's not pretend otherwise.'

I roll my eyes. I should have insisted he get ready with me, but he said he was running late. I think I understand why now.

'At least you've smashed it,' I admit. 'Lindsey is here as the ice bucket challenge, you need to see it to believe it, I'm just going to grab some—'

'Can I talk to you?' he asks, not really listening, suddenly so serious.

'Erm, okay,' I say nervously.

'Let's find somewhere upstairs,' he suggests as he leads me up the staircase.

My heart is pounding, and not only because I nearly fall back down the stairs trying to step over the Smurf and the vampire kissing on the top step.

'Empty,' Zac says as he opens one of the doors. 'Here will do.'

I follow Zac in to the empty bedroom. He pushes me back against a wardrobe and starts kissing me. I'm all for it, for about five seconds, until I stop him.

'I'm not shagging you in a random room at a house party,' I tell him. 'What if someone walks in?'

'That was one time,' he teases as he kisses my neck. 'But don't worry, I've not brought you here to shag you.'

Zac runs his hands down my body, his lips following them, until he's down on the floor in front of me.

'Oi, come on, I'm serious,' I say. 'That's definitely shagging adjacent.'

Zac only needs to move back a little before I realise he's down on one knee, looking up at me, with a small black box in his hands.

'Poppy Walker,' he starts, and I can't breathe. 'You're the most amazing woman I've ever met in my life. You're not only perfect for me but you are perfect in every way. I know Halloween is your favourite night of the year, so I wanted to make this one extra special. Would you please make the happiest man in the world and would you... I mean... will you marry me?'

He finally opens the box to reveal a ring I've seen before. We saw it in a shop window, months ago, and I casually but genuinely admired it. A white gold band with a neat little diamond held in place by swirls of rose gold.

'Yes,' I practically scream. 'Yes, yes, yes.'

'Yes?' he repeats back to me, almost in disbelief.

'Yes,' I squeal again. 'Okay, screw it, now you can shag me in a stranger's bedroom. You only get engaged once.'

'Okay,' he says casually.

Zac pounces on me, grabbing me, throwing me back onto the bed.

'Is everything okay?' a zombie asks, bursting through the door.

Oh, God.

'Yep, sorry, everything is fine,' I babble.

'It's just we heard screaming,' the zombie explains. 'We thought someone was being attacked.'

'I'm fine,' I insist. 'He just asked me to marry him.'

'Oh, no way,' the zombie replies. He's suddenly a very smiley zombie. 'I thought shouting "yes" was a bit unusual for an attack, but you've got to make sure, right?'

'I really appreciate it, thank you,' I tell him sincerely.

Still, he hovers in the doorway and I shift awkwardly under Zac.

'Oh, sorry,' the zombie apologises. 'I'll leave you to it. Congratulations.'

'Thank you,' I call after him cheerily. 'Such a polite zombie.'

'I can't believe we're engaged,' Zac says, kissing me again.

'I can't believe you asked me dressed as bloody Groot,' I reply.

'I told you, I'm not a cool guy, I'm a nerd,' he says. 'I just wanted to make sure you knew what you were getting yourself into.'

'Oh, I do,' I insist. 'And I can't wait to spend the rest of my life with you.'

23

I don't know much about Highland games so, to know what I was getting myself into, I watched a few YouTube videos earlier. It all sounded really interesting, I was actually really excited to get to witness it, first-hand, in Scotland. It doesn't get more authentic than that, does it?

Unfortunately, that still hasn't happened, because what I'm watching here, right now, is not what I expected it to be, given the videos I watched earlier.

It all started out pretty strong. Sonny orchestrated the whole thing, or had someone do it for him, at least, so we had a genuine piper and traditional Scottish dancers, just like they do in real Highland games. We even had a big crowd of spectators of various people from the wedding party, most of whom I don't know and haven't spoken to, but I very much get the vibe that, when you're as famous as the Strong family, you just always have a bunch of people around you.

Unfortunately, it's January and we're on an island in the middle of a loch so it's absolutely *freezing*. Only Sonny and Farrell wanted to take part, obviously, and Zac was sort of forced into it by Lilac. This isn't his thing, even if he does have muscles now, I know he'd much rather fight them on the FIFA field than the frozen solid patch of grass we're currently standing on.

It hasn't exactly been a legit Highland games, going by what I watched online, although I'm no expert either, clearly. No one was allowed to do the hammer throw, because we didn't have the right shoes to do it safely, and I swear a few of the games have been totally made up by Sonny.

The crowd of spectators has shrunk at an alarming rate. Almost everyone has lost interest. Farrell might be the only one still into it and that's probably just because he's winning.

Unbelievably, it hasn't even been that much fun to watch. No one is good enough or bad enough at anything to make it interesting or amusing. I've mostly found myself staring out across the loch. It's amazing how flat and still the water is. It's like glass, like a mirror, reflecting an exact copy of all the trees that frame it on all sides. It really is beautiful here. You've got to respect a place that looks beautiful even when the weather is bad.

It's all been building to this moment, the final event, the caber toss.

It's a one-on-one event. Sonny, so sure he would make it to the final, stated that the two players with the most points would go head-to-head in an all-or-nothing battle. Of course, as expected, Farrell won every single event, Zac came a distant second and Sonny, well, it turns out he clearly does none of his own stunts because, despite an impressive set of vanity muscles, he's not all that strong or athletic. He seems genuinely furious to be in last place. That means he's out.

'Right, okay,' Sonny says. He marches over to us and, although nothing detectable happens, he develops a sudden limp. I'd be tempted to say he's putting it on because he goes from looking like there's a stone in his shoe to (an absolutely shocking) young Forrest Gump impression in a matter of seconds. It seems like he borrows from the screen just as much as I do when I'm bullshitting. He *must* be bullshitting. Call me cynical, as I so often am, but I doubt he's hurt himself at all; I think he probably thought he and Farrell were pretty well matched, given the fact they're almost like one thing on set, and I think he's feeling a little embarrassed to be in last place. Well, maybe not embarrassed, more like pissed off. He can't even stand to stay here and watch who does win.

'It's an old injury, from the set of *NDY 5*,' he explains. 'I'm supposed to elevate it immediately when it flares up.'

'Aw, Dad, watch the final at least,' Lilac says. 'You're the host.'

'Everyone has gone in anyway,' Sonny points out. 'Basically, lads, just see who can throw the caber the furthest. Come on, Cherry.'

Sonny is right, pretty much everyone else has already gone in, due to it being freezing. Even the dancers have called it a day but the piper, incredibly, even with his bare legs, is still here, waiting to play for the winner.

'I'm not even that bothered to finish if Sonny is going in,' Zac admits.

It's just him, Lilac, Farrell, me, Kat and the piper out here now.

'Lilac, I didn't realise you were marrying a chicken,' Farrell points out. He moves his arms in a way that I imagine is supposed to be like a chicken, but isn't at all.

'I'm not a chicken,' Zac insists. 'I'm freezing.'

'A frozen chicken,' Farrell says with a laugh.

'He's hot but he's not funny,' Kat whispers to me.

'I can easily throw the thingy further than you,' Farrell tells him. 'Come on, be a man, throw it.'

'You can't chicken out now, Zachary,' Lilac tells him, patting him on the arm in the most condescending way. 'Just finish the game, fair and square.'

'Bloody hell, okay, fine,' Zac says, giving in.

'I'll go first,' Farrell suggests. 'Show you how it's done.'

Farrell, unsurprisingly, picks up the caber with ease. With one big swoop, he throws it as far as he can, which, also unsurprisingly, is pretty far.

'Top that,' he says proudly.

Zac rolls his eyes.

'Let's just get this over with,' he says.

'Come on, baby, you can do it,' Lilac calls out.

This only seems to make Zac appear even more annoyed that he's having to do it.

'Jesus Christ,' he says as he picks up the caber, which must be three times his height, at least.

Zac's face turns purple and his arms tremble, but he does it. He throws the caber.

Probably less than half the distance Farrell does, though.

'Ha,' Farrell announces. 'The champion – as if it were in any doubt.'

I shouldn't say anything, should I? I'm only here because I have to be. I shouldn't get involved.

'Never mind, Zachary,' Lilac says, not all that convincingly.

'In your face, Zachary,' Farrell teases him, copying Lilac's accent as he says Zac's sort-of name.

Nope, I can't do it, I can't keep my mouth shut.

'Erm, excuse me,' I say, walking closer.

'Come to congratulate the hero?' Farrell asks me.

'Not exactly,' I say. 'It's just, I was watching a few

videos earlier, and the aim of the caber toss isn't actually to see who can throw it the furthest. It's to see who can throw it the straightest, essentially. I'm no expert but, based on your throws, it was Zac who did that. It doesn't matter that it didn't go far, just that it flipped straight, if, er, you know what I mean.'

'That's not true, is it?' Farrell says. 'You're just trying to make your cousin feel better. Is she making this up?'

Farrell turns to the piper, as though he's going to be the authority on all things Scottish. Thus far, he's kept his mouth shut – except to blow his bagpipes, obviously.

'No, the lassie is right,' the piper says. 'It's the only thing I've heard all day that has actually been right.'

'Wait, so, I won?' Zac asks me, puzzled.

'You won,' I tell him.

Zac's eyes widen with a combination of disbelief and joy. He runs over to me, grabs me and hugs me tightly. I know it's just because I'm the one who delivered the news, but still, my God, I've missed his touch, which I know is a creepy-stalky, bunny-boiling ex-wife thing to say, but I don't mean it like that, it's more of a nostalgia thing.

Lilac physically pulls Zac from my arms.

'Baby, oh my God, I'm so proud of you,' she says as she jumps into his arms.

'Whatever,' Farrell says as he heads for the castle.

I look over at Kat. Knowing the truth, she can see how strange and awkward this all is.

'Poppy, come with me,' she says.

Kat leads me over to the piper.

'My friend wants to know if you wear anything under the kilt,' she tells him.

Oh my God, her friend is me, and I absolutely do not want to know that.

'If your friend is so brave, why doesn't she have a look and find out for herself?' the piper replies with a cheeky smile.

'Okay, sorry, we're going now,' I tell him. 'But thank you, so much, it's a beautiful sound, it really is.'

I drag Kat back to the castle.

'I can't believe you just did that,' I tell her. 'That was so awkward.'

'More, or less awkward than all that shit with Zac just now?' she replies, proving her point.

'Fair enough,' I tell her.

It's a rare day when sexually harassing a man who is just trying to do his job is less awkward than hugging your cousin, isn't it?

24

'Thanks for coming with me,' I whisper to Kat.

There's something about sneaking around in the dark late at night that forces you to whisper.

'Oh, you're welcome,' she replies. 'Now this is my kind of fun.'

Of course it is.

'I still can't believe you told them I worked for MI6,' I say. 'What the hell do I know about being a spy?'

'Fit Farrell clearly finds it sexy,' she points out. 'So, you're welcome. But not only is it a sexy job, it's a highly confidential one. Anyone asks you any questions you can't answer, you just say it's classified. Simple.'

I laugh to myself quietly. I suppose she's got a point.

'Well, it's landed us Scooby Doo duties,' I remind her. 'This is so weird, hanging out in these cold hallways at night, suits of armour everywhere, paintings of dead people with eyes that follow you wherever you go. And I don't know if it's a good or a bad thing, but we haven't seen a soul yet.'

I'm starting to wish I'd never agreed to patrol the castle for Sonny. It's so cold and dark and creepy. To keep a sort of authentic aesthetic, the lights on the walls are shaped like traditional candles and every so often they even flicker like the real deal. I'm not sure whether this is intentional mood lighting, dodgy old electrics, or the 'something spooky' Sonny warned me about.

The reason I'm finding us skulking through the castle at night so very Scooby Doo-esque isn't just because we're investigating somewhere creepy, but also because these old castle corridors remind me of that old style of animation, where characters would be running and it would seem like they were on a treadmill with a background that barely changes, just the same loop of corridor with the same pictures and the same sculptures. It's exactly like that here. It must be so easy to get lost – and so easy to hide too. It makes me wonder if we really are alone, or if someone – this potential jewellery thief – could be watching us.

'It's a good thing that we haven't crossed paths with anyone,' Kat says. 'It sounds as though Sonny thinks someone is sabotaging the wedding, so you'd expect to see something going on... unless... *unless*... Poppy! Are you sabotaging this wedding?'

I've never seen my new best friend brimming with so much pride.

'Of course not,' I insist, raising my voice slightly, before quickly lowering it again. 'I cannot stress enough the fact that I have absolutely not come to steal my ex from his wedding. Anyway, it sounds like the sabotage started before we got here – or I would have blamed you.'

'Thanks,' she replies, taking a compliment where I didn't intend one. 'So, what's it like seeing him again after all these years?'

'Torture,' I admit. 'The old feelings are still just

right there, front and centre. I still look at him and just see the perfect person for me. The love of my life. Seeing him so happy, watching him getting ready to marry someone else – it's like my own personal nightmare.'

'You're keeping a decent lid on it,' Kat says with a half-smile.

'That's because I'm a woman on a mission,' I tell her. 'I have to get these papers signed, so we can both get on with our lives – who knows, maybe on a deeper level I could sense that I never had real closure? I'm hoping this divorce sets me free too.'

'You're so mature,' she tells me.

'Thanks,' I reply, still whispering. 'Oh my God, duck!'

Kat and I huddle behind a large wooden chest of drawers when we realise someone is on the move. It's Lilac.

'Whose room is that she's leaving?' Kat whispers.

'It's Farrell's room,' I reply. 'What is she doing creeping out of Farrell's room at midnight?'

She hurries away quickly, in the direction of the family wing. Farrell closes the door behind her.

'Perhaps they're running a scam together,' she

says. 'Stealing the jewellery, selling it, going halves on the profits. It's a victimless crime, if the insurance pay up.'

'Wow, that's quite the theory,' I say with a smile.

'I know,' she replies. 'I thought you were supposed to be the super spy.'

'I'm more used to framing people,' I joke.

My phone vibrates in my pocket, causing me to jump out of my skin.

'Jesus Christ, it's just a message,' I say. 'Wow, it's from Fred.'

'Fred?' she replies.

'The one I went on the almost date with,' I remind her. 'He's asked me if I want to go on another.'

'Oh, Fit Fred, the giant of a hottie from the wedding,' she replies. 'Wow, after you walked out on the date, and he knew your real job, that surprises me. I'd ruled that guy right out.'

'Thanks, hun,' I say sarcastically.

'What are you going to say?' she asks.

'I can't say yes, not yet at least,' I tell her. 'All he kept saying was how he was just looking for something straightforward, no drama. If I have to tell him

I'm here and explain why, then he's going to think I'm a mess.'

'Mess shouldn't put people off,' Kat says. 'And you are cleaning it up.'

'True,' I reply. 'I think I'll just tell him I'm away for work at the moment.'

'You kind of are,' Kat says with a laugh. 'Shit, Farrell's on the move.'

It's pure luck that the chest of drawers we're hiding behind isn't in the direction Farrell is walking, otherwise he would almost certainly see us, and what would I tell him? How much weird shit can I realistically explain away as spy stuff?

'Where do you think he's going?' I whisper.

'I know where you wish he was going,' she whispers back. 'Your bed.'

'You mean *our* bed,' I remind her.

'I'm game if you are,' she jokes. 'Seriously though, you do fancy him, don't you?'

'A little bit,' I admit. 'But I've got a lot going on.'

'Well, get a lot more going on – with him,' Kat insists. 'You're the only reason I'm not cracking on to him.'

'I've never had such a good friend,' I say sarcastically.

'Look, all I'm saying is that you've got options,' she tells me, talking at a more normal volume now she's sure we're alone. 'There's Fred, there's Farrell, there's whoever the hell you want.'

'Zac,' I say quickly.

'I knew it,' she replies excitedly. 'Let's—'

I quickly place my hand over her mouth and gesture with my eyes down the corridor. She widens her eyes in acknowledgement, realising that I'm not saying I want Zac, but that I can see him.

I peep over the top of the chest of drawers we're still hiding behind. He looks puzzled as he glances up and down the corridor. Then he looks at me. Right at me. He stares into my eyes.

'Shit,' I say quietly.

'What?' Kat whispers, popping her head up. 'Shit, I think he can see us.'

'I can hear you too,' Zac points out as he approaches us. 'What the hell are you doing here?'

'What are we doing here? What are you doing here?' I ask him, assuming some sort of high ground I have absolutely no right to.

'Lilac was just down here getting a drink and she said she could hear someone,' he says. 'I told her I'd take a look.'

'Ah,' I say. I finally stand up. 'That was probably us. It's nothing weird, though. Sonny asked me to do it, to keep an eye out for anything suspicious.'

'That's absolutely something weird,' Zac points out.

'Nice pyjamas,' Kat tells him.

I don't think I've ever seen Zac in pyjamas but here he is, standing in front of us, in the tartan works.

'They came with the castle,' he insists, a little embarrassed. 'I don't wear them outside, though.'

'Oh, our cousin is sassy,' Kat says through a big grin. 'Come on, Poppy, let's get to bed. We need to craft the perfect reply to Fred.'

I feel like she's saying this for Zac's benefit, even if it's true. His ears prick up for a second before he quickly lets go of it.

'Secret service is over for the night then?' Zac teases.

'Yep, standing down,' I reply. 'See you in the morning.'

'Try to keep out of trouble,' he tells us.

Kat waits until Zac has gone before she speaks again.

'I can definitely see what you see in him,' she tells me. 'Even in those dorky PJs, he's pretty fit, and he's funny too.'

'You're not helping,' I tell her. 'I'm supposed to be divorcing him.'

'Sorry, let's focus on Fred,' she says. 'And I really will help you craft a reply to him, come on.'

As Kat and I head back to our room, I try to keep my mind on Fred. He seemed great – lots of men seem great, though, it's just none of them ever really measure up to Zac.

How the hell do you get over the love of your life? I suppose I'll start small, by actually divorcing him, and then take it from there.

25

If you grew up in a humongous house (but let's face it, how many of us actually did?) then you'll know all about Find and Sneak. If you didn't, then I'll explain it to you, as it's just been explained to me. Basically, the group splits up into two teams who both start at opposite ends of the house (or castle, in this case). Each individual on a team starts in a different room. The sneakers have to try to make their way through the house to the other team's base. The finders have to try to spot them. If a finder sees a sneaker and shouts out 'found you' while they still have eyes on them, then that person is out.

I'm on the sneaking team, so I just have to get to

the other side of the castle without anyone seeing me. It's huge, so it should be simple enough. Then again, this lot play all the time, and I'm a newbie.

'Hi, Poppy, can I borrow you?' Lilac asks me as we're gearing up to start.

I hope Zac didn't tell her about catching me and Kat hiding outside Farrell's room last night. Not only because it's weird, and because her dad doesn't want her knowing about the rings going missing, but because, well, to be honest, Zac said she was getting a drink, but she was absolutely in Farrell's room with him. I can't help but wonder why. I doubt Kat's jewel conspiracy is true, but it still seems a bit iffy.

'Erm, yeah,' I reply. I step to one side with her. 'What's up?'

'So, this is just between you and me,' she starts, lowering her voice. 'But someone has trashed my wedding dress.'

'What?' I squeak. 'How?'

'Someone has covered it in blood,' she says, widening her eyes for effect, just in case I wasn't picking up on the severity of the situation. 'My beautiful white dress, stained all down the front with red. I got such a shock when I saw it. And it's not the only thing that's happened. Lots of strange things have been going on since we got here. I'm starting to wish we were getting married in a normal hotel. This place is beyond creepy.'

'Does your dad know about this?' I ask.

'He knows some things have been going wrong, but not this,' she replies. 'He would honestly freak the fuck out if he knew about the blood. I know where he bought my dress and they had already measured me for adjustments, so I've just ordered another one with my own money. It will be here the day before the wedding.'

'Thank God you were able to get another,' I say genuinely. I'm surprised she's confiding in me about this.

'Yeah, well, if you throw enough money at a problem,' she says with a smile. 'I was just thinking, with your job, if you could keep an eye out for anything suspicious. See if you can catch anyone red-handed, so to speak. I'd really appreciate it. And if you could not tell anyone.'

Ah, she only wants me for my fake job.

'Your secret is safe with me,' I reply. 'And don't worry, I'll keep an eye out.'

Poor Lilac. Someone really does have it in for her. Obviously, I'm not an actual spy but someone destroying her wedding dress is just despicable. I'll keep my eyes open, for all the good it will do.

'Christina, my bridesmaid, will be arriving later today,' she says excitedly. 'She's always in everyone's business, always knows what's going on, always watching. She's...'

'Perceptive?' I offer.

'I was going to say "a fucking nosey bitch",' she says through a laugh. 'Anyway, we'd better hurry up, the game is about to start.'

Everyone who is playing gathers in the large reception room in the centre of the castle. There must be ten of us on each side. Both Kat and Zac are on my team, but we've all been given our own individual starting point and told to head there now. I am slightly tempted to sneak off and do my own thing somewhere, but what? And where? Everyone else I know is playing this, so I may as well get involved.

I wonder what's easier: finding or sneaking? Surely it's harder, being the sneaker? It sounds so simple, but I get the feeling it's going to be trickier than it looks. I'm starting on one of the upstairs corridors and the aim is to get to the kitchen – I'm sure the staff will love us all running around in there.

So far, it's so easy. I'm just walking slowly along the corridor – another Scooby Doo corridor made of stone with all the usual furnishings. The hardest part is going to be telling one corridor from the next, making sure I'm heading in the right direction. It's really quiet, no sign of anyone, nothing happening. This is actually quite boring. How do these people play this all the time? I get that you need a big space to be able to do it but, the castle is just so big, surely it's easy?

A few more stretches of corridor, a few more turns, and I'm ready to call it a day when I see him, it's Farrell (who is on the other team), at the other end of the corridor. Luckily, I spot him before he spots me. I quickly head back around the corner and start walking quickly, although I have no idea where I'm going to go, and I'm definitely going the wrong way. Suddenly, even though I was just thinking about quitting, I'm feeling quite competitive, and I don't want to be found.

I stumble a little, because of course I do (I'm clearly not used to anything vaguely resembling physical activity), banging my knee on a sideboard. It makes a noise. Not a loud one, but it's enough.

'Shit,' I whisper quietly to myself. So quietly I'm not even sure I say it out loud at all.

'Hello?' I hear Farrell call out. He does this in such a menacing way, practically singing it, as though it's designed to freak out his opponent. It's working. I'm terrified. All I can think about is not getting caught but it's that feeling that clouds my brain, making me panic, preventing me from coming up with any kind of smart strategy.

I go to move again and bang my knee on the exact same piece of sideboard.

I'm just about to turn the air blue when someone grabs my arm and pulls me to the side.

'Shh,' Zac says. 'In here.'

My eyes widen. Behind a bookshelf, there's this weird cut-out in the wall, specifically designed for hiding behind.

Zac pulls me in with him and closes the fake door behind us. There's just enough room for two in here but, now that we're in and the door is closed, it's pitch black.

'Hello?' Farrell sings again. 'Where are you? I know you're here somewhere.'

My heart is pounding so hard and so fast I'm certain Farrell will hear it, and it's not just because this game is exciting and terrifying, but because I'm now squashed in a hole in the wall, with my body pressed up against my not-quite ex-husband's. As though the feeling isn't nostalgic enough (to put it politely) this reminds me so much of our first kiss, back when we were at school, when we hid in a supply cupboard and wound up locking lips.

'I'm getting closer,' Farrell sings, although he actually sounds like he's getting further away.

I feel Zac fidgeting in front of me. Eventually, his iPhone screen lights up our hiding place, just enough for us to see each other. Now it really is like déjà vu.

I notice he's smiling.

'What does this remind you of?' he asks me.

'I was just thinking that,' I reply.

This, whatever it is, feels dangerously close to a moment. Probably just because it is so similar to our very first moment. I quickly change the subject.

'So, how did you find this random hole in the

wall?' I ask.

'The first day we got here, the bloke who showed us to our room told us all about these secret hiding places dotted around the castle,' he whispers. 'No one else was listening but I knew, when we played Find and Sneak, that I'd be able to use them to my advantage.'

'That's very clever,' I whisper back.

Clever and so very, very him. Every now and then, when I look at the new and improved *Zachary*, I see glimpses of my Zac in there, and it makes me as happy as it does sad.

'I'm also the only guest who knows about the service staircase,' he whispers. 'We can be in the kitchen in under two minutes, if we can just get to the staircase without being seen.'

'You might have to go on without me,' I tell him playfully. 'I'm clearly crap at this.'

'I never leave a man behind,' he jokes, still in hushed tones. 'I'm going to peep, see if the coast is clear.'

As Zac slowly opens the hidden door, the light pours in. I squint until my eyes adjust.

Zac peeps out before stepping out completely. He

doesn't speak, he just holds out his hand. I hold my own hand up and point to it, to check that's what he wants, to make sure I'm not getting the wrong end of the stick.

He smiles as he nods so I take his hand. I feel fifteen again.

Zac walks me along a corridor to a T-junction. He peers around the corner before ducking back. He gestures with his head for me to peep. Shit, it's Lilac and Farrell, about halfway along the corridor, whispering with one another.

I watch as Zac takes a deep breath. Next thing I know he's picking me up, throwing me over his shoulder, and then running past the end of the corridor where they are. Seconds later, we're through a door and into what I'd guess is the service staircase. With the door closed behind us, he finally laughs as he returns me to my feet.

'Sorry, I didn't know what else to do,' he says. 'If I'd said anything they would have heard me. If I'd dragged you, by the time they clocked me in their peripheral vision they would have seen you behind me. It was our best shot.'

'You're more competitive than you used to be,' I

point out with a smile, to let him know that I'm not mad. I actually found that completely thrilling. I'm not going to tell him that, though. I probably enjoyed it a little more than I should.

'Yeah, well, someone helped me win the Highland games and now I've got a taste for victory,' he replies. 'Thanks, by the way.'

'Ah, I didn't do anything,' I insist. 'The rules are the rules, I just follow them.'

'Then you're a lot more sensible than you used to be,' he points out.

Only because I'm not cool any more.

'Right, show me how we get to this kitchen,' I say. 'Because now I really want to win too.'

'Okay, this way,' Zac says.

He takes me by the hand again. I'm not sure he needs to, any more. He didn't really need to in the first place, did he? Although to ask that might come across as a complaint and I'm definitely not complaining. As much as they sting, just a little, I love these little glimmers of my past life, I just need to make sure I don't get too used to them because, soon enough, we'll be signing the papers and then it really will all be over. *Again.*

26

16 MAY 2015

When you think about the perfect wedding day, what do you imagine? Because if it isn't your new husband and your dad performing a duet of Seal's 'Kiss from a Rose' then, let me tell you, you've got your priorities all wrong.

Some people laughed when we said we wanted karaoke at our wedding reception, but it's turned out to be an absolute smash of an idea.

'They're quite the crowd pleasers,' I say. 'And who knew Dad's voice could go so high?'

'Your dad has a beautiful voice,' Mum replies. 'He just doesn't like to use it in front of people, unless he's had a few, which isn't that often.'

'Maybe we can get a couple more drinks in him,' I suggest. 'Then the two of you can do a duet.'

'I'm thinking the four of us should do an Abba song,' she says. 'But he'll definitely need a few more drinks for that.'

'Which song? "I Do, I Do, I Do, I Do, I Do"?' I say, gently running my hands down my wedding dress.

God, I love this dress. Every part of this wedding has been relatively cheap and cheerful, given that we were insistent we paid for it ourselves, but the one gift my parents wanted to give me was the wedding dress of my dreams. I considered what I wanted, but with so many options, I didn't know where to begin. I don't know what it was, I would try a few on, and I would always feel silly, like a kid playing dress-up in her mum's clothes. It was only when Mum was helping me look at celebrity weddings for inspiration that I spotted Amal Clooney's wedding dress and, even though she and I have nothing in common, I kind of fell in love with it. Granted, there was no way Oscar de la Renta was going to make me a dress, or that I would let my parents spend so much money on me but – I don't know how she did it – Mum found me a dress that looked really similar. It's an ivory off-the-shoulder gown with pearls and beads down the bodice. The train isn't anywhere near as long, but I don't mind. I'd only fall over it.

Mum is a real contradiction of a human, either so serious or so much fun, depending on the setting. Being a solicitor, especially one who deals in family matters, isn't exactly a light-hearted occupation. People usually only ever go to her when they're divorcing, fighting over kids, or fighting over estates when someone dies. She's so good at her job – an absolute professional – but when she finishes work for the day that's her done, and legal hotshot Eleanor Walker disappears and goodtime girl Ellie Walker comes out to play.

She's always been such a fun mum, and yet somehow totally appropriately strict. I think that's the best of both worlds, though. I got to enjoy such a happy childhood, but she never gave me enough slack to go off the rails.

Mum has always made sure I know just how proud she is of me but today is just something else. Her smile is so big, so bright. She's absolutely in her element as the mother of the bride; doing the rounds with the guests, posing for photos, looking absolutely fantastic in her big hat, which she described as 'the biggest she could find'. She's also fulfilling the role of chief bridesmaid, helping me out with whatever I need, even though my three actual bridesmaids, Sally, Rachael and Lindsey are knocking around somewhere. Rachael and Lindsey are having a blast, more than tipsy, as you can imagine, but Sally has another of her increasingly dull boyfriends here with us. His name is Seth, and it sounds like he comes from a rich family – and it sounds like that because Sally keeps telling us so.

'Was that as embarrassing as it felt?' Zac asks as he approaches us.

He looks so good, I swear I sigh every time I remember he's mine. He's wearing a blue suit – one that actually fits him – and although he's discarded his tie at some point, and successfully petitioned to wear his favourite bright blue and yellow trainers instead of shoes, he looks amazing. I don't know if it's because I rarely see him dressed so smart, because it fits him so well, or if I'm just so deliriously happy, but I couldn't love or fancy him any more right now if I tried.

'Darling, you were phenomenal,' my mum tells him.

'I feel like Martin played me,' he replies. 'He told me he was crap, too.'

'I couldn't be prouder to officially be your mother-in-law,' Mum insists.

'I'm just going to say this now,' Zac starts seriously as he places an arm around my waist and pulls me closer, almost like a security blanket. 'Ellie, since my mum died, you really have been like a mum to me, and I can't thank you enough. You and Martin have made feel like a real part of this family. I know how lucky I am.'

'Oh, love,' my mum says, quickly whipping away the single tear that has managed to escape her eye. 'Come here.'

She grabs us both and hugs us tightly.

'I love you both,' she says. 'I'm not just so proud of you but I'm so pleased for you. Sometimes, like with me and Martin, opposites attract, but you two are one another, the same person. The same weird, nerdy, warm, wonderful kind of person. I love you, I love you, I love you.'

'Poppy, seriously?' Sally says, interrupting our lovely moment. 'Karaoke at a wedding? So uncouth.'

Seth, her rich but dull boyfriend of the week, is standing next to her, drinking what looks like a sherry, so I imagine this is for his benefit.

'It's fun,' I tell her. 'Go put your name down.'

'Very funny,' she says.

The two of them wander off.

'God, she's a miserable cow these days,' Mum muses. 'Usually, people lighten up when they get a man.'

I snort with laughter. I love how Mum just says it like it is.

'At least the other two are still a laugh,' I point out.

Rachael and Lindsey are on the karaoke machine now, singing 'Livin' La Vida Loca' and, somehow, they both not only sound like they're singing a completely different song from the one that's playing, but a completely different song from one another, too.

'We're doing Abba,' Mum informs Zac.

'Sounds good,' he says with a smile. 'Someone has already put you down for something, Pops. "True Colours".'

I whip my head to look at my mum.

'Okay, that was me,' she says. 'But you always used to sing it so beautifully in the shower.'

'Everyone sings beautifully in the shower, Mum,' I point out. 'The tiles trick you.'

She laughs.

'Right, I'll go grab a drink, and your dad, and get our names down,' she says. 'Back in a flash.'

'Abba sound good?' I say to him once we're alone.

Zac grabs me and somehow manoeuvres me into a slow dance, even though the only thing to dance to is the sound of my friends murdering Ricky Martin.

'I'm pretty sure you could get me to agree to anything today,' he tells me as he squeezes me. 'I love you, Poppy Hunt.'

'I love you, Zac Hunt,' I reply.

I relax into his arms, more than happy to move to the music with him, even though the music is nothing short of awful. I'm just so happy today, that I couldn't care less. Today is the first day of my new life as a married woman and, despite some people telling us we're too young to tie the knot, and others telling us karaoke at a wedding was a mistake, today really has been perfect. If I'm half as happy as this for every other day of my life, then that's fine by me, I've made it, I've got everything I've ever wanted. You can't get better than that, can you?

27

'I'm here,' Christina sings as she marches into the main castle sitting room. 'Now it's a wedding!'

She flings her arms out by her sides, as if to say 'Ta-da!', before turning to the man dragging her bags behind her.

'I said to my room, you idiot,' she tells him off. 'Why would I want my cases in here?'

Lilac laughs. 'Chrissy, you're so bad,' she says as she runs over to hug her. 'For everyone who doesn't know her, this is Christina, my bestie. Christina, I think you know everyone apart from Poppy and Kat, they're Zac's cousins.'

'God, I've had enough of your family,' Christina

replies.

'What do you mean?' Zac asks with a confused laugh.

'Your bloody gran,' she replies. 'She just does not stop yapping. I tipped the butler to leave her parked up in the corridor for a bit, just to get some peace.'

Zac springs to his feet. 'She made it,' he says through the biggest smile. 'I didn't think she could come.'

He dashes out of the room, eventually returning with the one, the only, Nanny May. Christina may not like her, but I've always loved Nanny May. She loved me too.

'Hello, everyone,' she says brightly.

'Everyone, this is Nanny May,' Zac says. Everyone makes polite introductions. 'She lives in an assisted living home in Rochdale – she told me she didn't think she'd be able to make it.'

'What, because of this thing?' she says, slapping the sides of her wheelchair with her hands. 'No chance, I wanted to surprise you.'

'Well, you've certainly done that,' he tells her through the biggest, cutest smile.

I don't know what I'm thinking, but I'm just so, so

delighted to see Nanny May looking so happy and healthy that I run over to hug her.

'Oh my goodness, Poppy my love, hello,' she beams. 'What on earth are you doing here?'

I stop squeezing her and hang back, shifting awkwardly on the spot. I don't know what to say.

'Oh, you remember cousin Poppy,' Zac says slowly. 'She was just saying how she hadn't seen you in years.'

Nanny May stares at Zac, then at me, then back at Zac.

'Sorry,' she says. 'I'm slowly losing my marbles. Yes, of course I remember cousin Poppy.'

'Pops, if you want to sit with Nanny, over on those sofas, I'll bring her a cup of tea, we can have a family catch-up,' Zac suggests.

'Oh, sounds lovely,' Nanny May replies.

I do as I'm told, pushing her over to the sofas at the other side of the room.

'Poppy, love, what have you got yourself into?' she asks me once we're alone. 'He's telling people you're his cousin?'

She isn't losing her marbles at all. If anything, she's found some.

'It's complicated,' I tell her in hushed tones. 'I hadn't seen him since the split, until recently, when I found out our divorce was never finalised.'

'The two of you should never have broken up,' she tells me. 'You were made for each other. And what happened to you...'

'By the time I realised, it was too late,' I tell her. 'I learned that Zac was about to get married so I had to come here, get him to sign the papers, and then we need to get them sent off before the wedding.'

'Oh, love, I'm sorry,' she says. 'This must be horrible for you. But Nanny is here now, I'll look after you.'

'Thank you,' I say with a smile. 'You see that girl over there, feeling Sonny's bicep? That's Kat. She's my friend but we're pretending she's a cousin too.'

Nanny May just laughs.

'And there's me thinking Zac was boring these days,' she replies.

'Oh, he is,' I insist. 'I can't get over it. It suits him though; he seems more mature, more like he can handle things properly.'

Nanny May reaches out and takes my hand in hers. She rubs it lightly.

'I'm going to have a word with him,' she says. 'Get him to sign the papers so you can go home. It's not right, you being here. Not fair on you at all.'

'God, it's good to see you,' I tell her.

'You too, my love,' she replies. 'How are your mum and dad?'

It never gets easier, no matter how many times I say it.

'Dad's doing great,' I tell her. 'Mum passed away.'

Nanny May does everything she can to hide from me that she's welling up, but I can see it. I can see the sadness building in her eyes.

'You poor love,' she says. 'No one your age should know so much heartache.'

'Hello,' Lilac says, loudly interrupting us. 'So good to finally meet you, Nanny. But can I just borrow Poppy?'

She talks to Nanny May as though she were deaf. Last time I checked, being in a wheelchair wasn't for those who can't hear.

'Oh, haven't you two met before?' I ask. I'm a little surprised. Zac doesn't have much family, but Nanny May is his oldest living family member. Everyone has to pass the vibe check with Nanny May.

'I think their courtship has been too brief for that,' Nanny May suggests politely. 'But we're meeting now.'

'And we can have more of a chat later,' Lilac tells her, patting her on the arm with all the warmth of the castle hallways. 'But I just need to borrow Poppy, just for a sec.'

'Go on, my love,' Nanny May says. 'I'm sure Zac will be back in a minute.'

I'm reluctant to leave a woman who feels like family to me, to go and chat to one who I don't exactly like all that much. I don't know what it is, Lilac is only a couple of years younger than me, but we just seem like polar opposites. I wonder what drove Zac to be with someone who couldn't be less like me – I hope it isn't for that very reason. That would hurt.

'Okay, so, Poppy, this is Christina, my bestie. I was just telling her about the wedding drama,' Lilac brings me up to speed. 'And I told her... about your job.'

It's funny that she whispers the last three words, given the fact that only Christina can hear us, and she knows all about it now.

'You don't look like a secret agent or whatever,' Christina says bluntly.

'No?' I reply. I shift awkwardly on the spot. I always panic in situations like this. Bloody hell, even the way I said no just now, I don't even sound like I believe myself.

'Nope,' she insists. 'You don't seem especially physically fit, which I'd imagine is a necessity, and you seem kind of self-conscious and unsure about yourself. Although perhaps that's just because Lilac and me are here.'

I hope what Christina is getting at is the fact that both she and Lilac are influencers, otherwise it's actually quite mean, and as 'unsure' as I may seem, there's a sword about ten feet away from me and I'm pretty sure I know exactly what I'd do with it right now.

'Well, see, that's what makes me so effective,' I tell her. 'We're supposed to blend in.'

She narrows her eyes suspiciously. 'I never would have had you for the interesting type,' she says. It looks like it physically pains her to say it. 'No offence.'

'Some taken,' I say with a smile.

'Are you single?' she asks me.

'Oh, yeah, I forgot to ask,' Lilac chimes in.

'Yep,' I say reluctantly.

'Kat too?' she continues.

'Kat too,' I say.

'Well, Christina is my bridesmaid, so obviously she'll be at the top table, but you and Kat don't need to worry, because I've got an absolutely banging singles table. Fabrizio Napoletano is going to be on it.'

'Isn't he the one who was on *Love Island* and now he's a serial dater, always shagging some poor random girl on some random reality TV show?' I reply.

'That's him,' Lilac says excitedly. 'Honestly, he's the best.'

'I'd aim for him, if you can,' Christina adds. 'Should hopefully be an easy target.'

'Cheers,' I reply.

'Right, well, I think we're having dinner in a couple of hours, close family and friends only, so it should be more intimate,' Lilac explains. 'In the meantime, if you could try to get to the bottom of this whole wedding sabotage thing? It's really stressing my dad out. Thanks, babe.'

Lilac doesn't give me a chance to reply. She turns to Christina and starts fussing with her long, out-of-a-bottle red hair, telling her how much she loves her new style.

I have no idea what to do about the alleged wedding sabotage. I'm not really qualified to do anything useful, so I suppose I'll just hang out with Nanny May. It will be nice to catch up with someone I care about, to distract myself from all this.

'Have you seen Beth Bonas's hair lately?' Christina asks Lilac.

'Oh my God,' Lilac replies. 'I thought it was a wig. So bad.'

'Isn't it horrible?' Christina replies. 'Like, she's done that on purpose. She seriously thinks she looks good.'

I walk away. Wow, these girls are vile. Why are they so awful? Proper bitchy, mean girls. The kind who, when you hear how they talk about people, you wonder what they say about you behind your back.

I feel my phone vibrating in my pocket. It's Rachael. Erg, I doubt she's calling to see if I want to hang out, she's probably calling to tell me off for, I don't know, basically everything I've done this year so far. All the stuff at the wedding, Sally's shoes, crashing and then bailing on couples' cooking. The longer I leave it, the worse my telling off is going to be. I may as well just get it over with.

'Hello,' I answer brightly.

'Don't you "hello" us,' I hear Sally shout in the background.

'I'm on speaker, I take it?' I reply. 'Is everyone there?'

'Yes, all three of us,' Rachael replies. 'Where are you?'

'What do you mean?' I reply innocently.

'We planned this whole inter*friend*tion – Lindsey even baked – and we popped round to yours and there was no sign of you. Twice. So we figured you were at your dad's, so we went there, and you weren't there either,' she says.

'No,' is all I say. It would be good to know how much he's told them.

'He told us you've gone all the way to Scotland, to see Zac, days before he's getting married, to try and get him to re-sign divorce papers,' she continues.

Great. He's told them everything.

'Tell her she's a fucking idiot,' Sally calls out.

'Sally thinks you should come home right now,' Rachael translates. 'We all do. You being there, it's not going to end well, it's a mistake. This isn't how you do this.'

'If he doesn't do this paperwork, he can't get married,' I point out quietly. 'We're heading in to Tarness in the morning. We need two witnesses who aren't related to us, and there's a fax machine at the holiday cabin park, I already checked, they said they could send papers for us. I've got it all under control.'

'Except you don't,' Rachael replies. 'Because it's Zac. You were a mess after the split, you haven't spoken since – now you're at his wedding? That's not right. That's messed up. You're going to get hurt.'

'I'm fine, honestly, I've got Kat with me,' I say, but that just makes things worse.

'Kat?' Rachael shrieks. 'Kevin's Kat? She's a psychopath.'

'Erm, she's actually being a really great friend to me,' I clap back, careful to keep my voice down, so no one else in this room hears. Thankfully, it's massive. 'She's helping me with my problems, she encourages me, and she doesn't make me feel like shit for being single. Look, I need to go, I'll call you when I get back. Bye.'

I don't give them chance to reply. I just hang up. Look, I know what they're getting at, they think I'm going to spend a few days around Zac and fall madly in love with him again, but they're wrong. I never stopped loving him. My feelings for him never changed, our circumstances did. But I know why I'm here and, ultimately, it's to help him, not to cause trouble, not to hurt myself. This is the right thing to do, I just need to get on with it.

I head back over to Nanny May. She's sitting with Zac, who is pouring cups of tea.

'Can I have one of those, please?' I ask him.

'Of course,' he replies.

I sit down in the chair opposite Nanny May.

'Fancy a proper catch-up?' I ask her.

'I'd love that,' she replies. 'I want to hear all about everything you've been doing since I saw you last.'

It's almost a shame I have nothing too exciting to tell her.

'Well, the family business is booming,' I tell her quietly, because everyone here thinks the family business is MI6. 'I'm running it, now. We make fancy custom frames and ship them all over the world.'

'I'd love to buy one,' Nanny May replies. 'I always knew you'd do amazing things.'

'Me too,' Zac adds as he hands Nanny her tea.

I realise he's smiling at us.

'What?' I ask with a laugh.

'It's just nice to see you two back together, drinking tea, like a day hasn't passed by,' he admits.

He hands me my cup and it looks perfect.

'It's nice to see you two back together, too,' Nanny May says. She has a cheeky glimmer in her eye. 'You know what I mean. In the same room. Talking. Happy. I never thought I'd see the day.'

To be honest, neither did I. Oh, the irony, that it's taken my finding out we need to get a divorce to bring us back together. It makes me feel sad that, as soon as Zac signs those papers, and we send them, that's it. We're done again. I almost feel like it's going to be harder this time, knowing what happens when we part ways. Still, it has to be done. I have to get this sorted, get closure and get on with my life. What other choice do I have?

28

28 AUGUST 2015

'Come on, Pops, I need the loo,' Zac calls through the bathroom door.

You hear all about wedded bliss, but no one ever tells you just how much little things, like only having one bathroom, can really kill the mood sometimes. Not that I'm in the mood right now. I couldn't be less in the mood if I tried.

'All right, I'm coming,' I tell him, irritated that I'm being rushed but, in my defence, I'm having a bad day.

'Thank you,' Zac says as he hurries past me through the doorway.

I quickly move out of his way, careful he doesn't see what's in my hand. I don't want to tell him anything until I know what the situation is.

'Are you okay?' he calls through the door.

'Not exactly,' I reply.

'Is it work?' he calls back. 'One minute.'

I pause while Zac flushes the loo.

I'm definitely not okay, and it's not because of work. I'm worried because I'm late. Yep, that kind of late. And I'm never that kind of late, so I'm panicking.

I've never done a pregnancy test before. I've never needed to, obviously. I wondered, even when I went to buy one at lunch time, why they came in packs of two, then I realised, it's because executing a pregnancy test for the first time is harder than you think it's going to be.

I bought a box of two tests and a large iced caramel latte, and I drank the whole thing on the walk home from the shops so that my bladder would be fully loaded by the time I got in. It was, but holding the test under a steady stream of urine must be a skill that develops with practise, because I totally missed and then, that was that, no pee left to test with. That's why I was glad I had a second test but then I had to go back to the drinking phase and chug glasses of water, ready for take two. Skimming the instructions for tips, and not wanting to make the same mistake again, I noticed that it said you could pee into a container and dip the test in, which sounded far easier, so I decided to do that. Conscious that Zac would be home from work soon, and with no better ideas, I popped the lid off a can of dry shampoo and peed in that before dipping the test in. That's when I heard Zac arrive home and immediately come upstairs to use the loo. So, I placed the cap on the test, stuffed all evidence of tests back into the box, which I then hid in my wash bag in the cupboard, because Zac never has any reason to look in there.

The test is firmly in my hand. In fact, I'm squeezing it pretty tightly, considering what I just did with it.

Zac emerges from the bathroom, so I hide it behind my back.

'Are you pregnant?' he asks me plainly, his expression completely blank.

What the actual hell?

'What?' is all I can say. I opt for calm but, if I was wanting to throw him off, I should have probably reacted with more surprise than that.

'Pops, are you pregnant?' he asks me again.

'Erm, why do you ask?' I reply.

'Because there's a cup of wee on the windowsill in the bathroom,' he says.

Crap, I forgot to get rid of the wee.

'So, either you're pregnant or you have something really weird you need to tell me about.'

'Okay, look, I might be pregnant,' I reply. 'Might. I'm late, so I've done a test.'

I pull it out from behind my back, because there's no point hiding it now, but the second I look down at it I see it, clear as day, those two telltale lines.

'Shit,' I whisper quietly.

'What?' Zac asks as he approaches me. 'What?'

He looks down at the test, but he's none the wiser.

'What do two lines mean?' he asks.

'It means I'm pregnant,' I reply simply.

It's almost as though it happens in slow motion. A tidal wave of realisation washes over Zac and I see his face cycle through the whole spectrum of emotions. It only takes a split second, but it's like watching a spinning wheel, waiting to see what it lands on.

Zac's face erupts into the biggest smile I've ever seen on a person.

'Pops, what?' he says excitedly. 'What? How?'

'I'd imagine that's the reason we're in this mess,' I half joke. 'You not knowing the answer to that question.'

Zac doesn't laugh. His face falls. He takes me by the hands and leads me to the bed where we sit.

'Mess?' he says softly.

'Yeah,' I reply. 'Well, work is just starting to get busy, with the new online stuff we're trying. You don't have anything lined up now that the wedding season is over and the other band members are going back to their other gigs. We've not been married that long, we're only twenty-four. Why aren't you freaked out?'

'Because all I can think about is this tiny version of you that we could have in our lives,' he replies.

'What if it was a tiny version of you?' I joke to break such an uncomfortable moment.

'You can't joke your way out of this one, Mrs Hunt,' he replies with a smile. 'Still not sure if you want to be a mum?'

'I'm just not sure it's for me,' I tell him. 'I'm just scared I won't be any good at it.'

'Pops, listen to me, okay?' Zac takes my face in his hands and looks me in the eye. 'You would make an amazing mum. You're sweet, kind, caring. Any kid would be lucky to have you as a mum. Plus, your mum might just be the best mum on the planet, and you are just like her, so I reckon you'll be just as great as her.'

'That might be the sweetest thing you've ever said to me,' I tell him honestly. 'And you've said a lot of sweet things.'

'Well, it's true,' he replies. 'Look, whatever you want to do, that's what I want to do too. You've got my support, one hundred per cent. Okay?'

I nod.

'You're always so perfect,' I tell him. 'Always saying the right things. A tiny version of you might not be so bad.'

'Just think of all the annoyingly adorable things I

do,' he says. 'Like leaving shoes all over the hallway or toothpaste all over the towels. There could be two of us doing that.'

I laugh.

'You're really selling it to me,' I chuckle.

'Okay, well, picture this,' he starts, clearly about to change strategy. 'Imagine, a few years from now, when your fancy internet ventures are really paying off, and I'm playing session gigs for the stars, and we've got a big house, a massive kitchen with one of those sexy kitchen islands you like – your words, not mine. Imagine baking cookies on Christmas Eve, while me and little Zac junior sit on the stools, and you're constantly telling us not to eat raw dough or the baked cookies until they've cooled and we're just pinching them anyway... Tell me that doesn't sound like a dream?'

I smile. God, that does actually sound quite nice.

'You really think we can do it?' I reply. 'All of it?'

'Of course I do,' he insists.

'And you think I can do it?'

'I don't think anyone could do it better than you.'

I exhale deeply. Am I really going to do this?

'Okay,' I blurt.

'Okay?' he echoes back.

'Yep, okay,' I reply. 'Let's do it. Let's have a bloody baby.'

'Pops, oh my God,' he says excitedly.

Zac grabs me and pushes me back on the bed, hugging me, squeezing me so tightly.

'Okay, okay, enough of that,' I joke. 'That's *definitely* what got us into this mess.'

Zac laughs and smiles and, wow, that look on his face, the happiness, the excitement, and I can even see his love for me in his eyes. It's everything.

'So, what happens now?' he says.

'I've never done this before,' I remind him – of course, he knows that. 'I guess I'm supposed to go to the doctor? Get it confirmed? I guess they'll tell me what to do after that.'

'Let's do it, then, let's get it booked, let's find out,' he says, still buzzing. 'God, I can't believe it. We're going to have a baby.'

Zac lies next to me on the bed. We hold hands and lie there in silence for a few minutes.

My heart is pounding and my head is racing. Shit. I'm going to be a mum. I didn't actually think I wanted to, given how I've always felt in two minds about it, but now that it's happening, and Zac has painted that picture of what life could be like for me, that's it, it's locked in, it's what I want.

I smile to myself as I puff air from my cheeks. I can't wait to tell my mum.

29

As intimate family dinners go, tonight's is a weird one.

There's Sonny and Cherry, of course, then Lilac and Zac. Nanny May is here, as Zac's most important relative, and then there's me and Kat, just to get the numbers up, as Zac's B-team family members. Christina is here, as Lilac's bridesmaid, and then there's Farrell, who seems to be a member of the family, even though he's just Sonny's stunt double. I guess you form a pretty close bond with the man who nearly kills himself to make you look cool. I don't mind, though, I quite like being around him. He's funny and friendly and we need all the nice people we can get. All Lilac and Christina do is bitch about people. People they know, people they don't know, people who didn't come to the wedding, people who are here. It's horrible to listen to. I'm mostly trying to ignore them.

Nanny May has just been telling us all about the activities they have at the assisted living facility where she's been residing for the last few years. Kat – who she is getting on with like they are genuinely related – wants to move to one. It does sound great, with its own pool, cinema and different restaurants. A bit like a cruise ship where people take care of you. Plus, it sounds like she's got lots of friends there – more than I have.

'God, you must be so bored,' Lilac blurts. 'I'd be going out of my mind if that was my life.'

'Lilac,' Zac ticks her off.

'What?' she replies. 'I'm not making fun of her, I'm just being honest.'

'I've had a full and happy life,' Nanny May tells her with a smile. 'I'm happy with my lot now.'

'Nanny May is a brilliant genealogist,' Zac informs her.

'Like Albert Einstein?' Lilac asks.

'That's a genius,' Zac corrects her.

'It's tarot cards and shit like that,' Christina tells her.

'No idea what your logic is there,' Zac replies, bemused. 'Genealogy is the study of family trees and family history.'

'Is your party trick still asking people their names and telling them the meaning?' I ask with a smile.

'It certainly is,' she replies. 'Did I hear this young man's name was Farrell?'

'That's right, ma'am,' he replies.

'Farrell means hero, or man of courage,' she tells him.

'Does it?' he replies, absolutely fascinated. 'I'm a stunt man, you know.'

'Well, there you go,' Nanny May says with a smile. 'You were clearly destined to do that job.'

'Do me,' Sonny says excitedly. 'Sonny Strong.'

'Strong is what it says on the tin,' Nanny May tells him with a smile.

'That's just my stage name,' he tells her. 'My original surname was Craven.'

Nanny May laughs. 'Funnily enough, that means weak or cowardly,' she replies.

'Thank God I changed it,' Sonny replies. 'You can't be an action hero with a weak name.'

'Our family surname is Hunt,' she continues. 'The hunter. If you were to have children, a boy, and you named him after his grandfather, then you would have Sonny Hunt, son of Hunt. It's all a lot of fun to play around with.'

'It sounds kind of lame,' Lilac replies, pulling a face. 'And I'd never name my kid after my dad, that's too confusing, how would I tell them apart?'

'The baby would be the one in the nappies,' Kat points out.

'Do you think you'll have any little Hunts?' Cherry asks, clearly delighted to have found an excuse to ask.

Everyone at our end of the table looks at Lilac for an answer.

'I'm sure we will, but not yet,' Lilac says. 'We're far too young, I at least want to be in my thirties. Mum almost had a baby before me, but it died, long before it was born, but she always says it was a blessing in disguise, she was too young, and she's happy she just has me.'

'Young lady, miscarriage is nothing to be discussed so flippantly,' Nanny May tells her, her voice quivering. Her usual soft, relaxed demeanour has stiffened into something uncomfortable.

'All right, chill out,' Lilac tells her rudely.

'Lilac, leave it,' Zac warns her delicately.

'It's never a blessing in disguise, never,' Nanny May continues. 'Never say that again.'

'Bloody hell,' Christina chimes in. 'Calm down, grandma. She didn't mean anything by it.'

'I didn't,' Lilac insists. 'I just meant, for my mum, it wasn't a tragedy, was it, mum?'

'Let's not talk about it,' Cherry replies.

'You never know who you will upset, saying things like that,' Nanny May tells her. I think she's telling her for her own good. Lilac seems irritated that she's been called out.

'Okay, I get it, it happened to you, and it upsets you, but you don't know everyone's story,' Lilac rants.

'Lilac, come on,' Zac insists. 'Just let it go.'

'No, she can't talk to me like that, not at my wedding,' Lilac says, getting angry, slapping Zac's hands away as he tried to comfort her, to calm her down, to nip this in the bud.

'Okay, okay, stop,' I insist. 'Just stop. Nanny May is saying this to protect me. I had a miscarriage. It was a long time ago, but it reshaped my life and I don't like to think about it, so can we just stop, please?'

'Darling, I'm so sorry,' Cherry says sincerely.

'It's fine,' I tell her.

I sigh. I don't know why but here, now, with these people, at the tail end of dinner, it just feels like the time to open up.

'I didn't mean to get pregnant,' I tell them. 'I didn't even think I wanted kids. I was twenty-four, I hadn't been married long, we were both so immature… but my husband was over the moon when he found out. We talked about it and suddenly, that was it, I wanted this baby. I miscarried not long after. I was devastated. So was my husband. He wanted to try for another one almost right away. I didn't. We had two choices, fill the hole it left or let it break us. We were young, we didn't know how to process our feelings, so we broke. That was it. We divorced.'

Cherry gets up from her seat and walks around the table. She wraps her arms around me. She seems like one of the more genuine branches of the Strong family tree.

'Darlin', I'm sorry,' she says. 'Lilac just got the wrong end of the stick. Lilac, I never meant that I was happy I lost my first, just that I was more than content with you.'

'People need to be clearer,' Lilac says with a shrug. 'And we really need to change the topic of conversation, because this is such a drag.'

I look over at Zac, who looks like he's been punched in the stomach. His jaw is tight and his eyes have glazed over ever so slightly. All the signs are there, that this has really upset him, more than you would expect for a cousin, but only if you're looking at him, which no one else is. Everything I just said is what I've thought about saying to him for years. Neither of us was in the wrong. We were young and grieving and we took separate routes to get over it. I think that's why Mum was so sure we'd get back together. I remember her saying to me at the time that we may have wandered down different paths to recovery but that there was no reason those two paths wouldn't meet up again further down the line. I should have guessed that she was up to something. He quietly rubs his nose as his defences go back up.

'Let's have a dance, loosen up,' Lilac suggests. 'Then tonight is my hen slumber party. Poppy, Kat, you have to come. It will cheer you both up.'

'Oh wow, thanks,' Kat replies.

She's verging on the sarcastic, but no one really picks up on it.

'Yeah, thanks,' I say.

Sounds like hell.

'Right, I'll get some music on,' Lilac says. 'Back in a sec.'

'We don't have to go to this thing, do we?' I whisper to Kat.

'I think we should,' she says. 'It'll be hilarious, plus we can drink more. I haven't been this sober for this long since I was fourteen.'

'Thinking Out Loud' by Ed Sheeran plays through a hidden sound system. I imagine it's hidden because it doesn't match the aesthetic of the castle. I wish they had hidden it better, because the last thing I want to hear right now is mushy music.

'Come on,' Lilac insists to Zac. 'We can practise for our first dance.'

'I'm not really in the mood,' he tells her. I can tell that I've upset him. She doesn't seem to pick up on it, though.

'Come on, grumpy,' she insists, grabbing his hand, dragging him up.

'Let's show these kids how it's done, Cherry,' Sonny tells his wife as he stands up and pulls out her chair for her.

I sigh.

'Would you like to dance with me?' Farrell asks.

I naturally assume he's talking to Kat, because why wouldn't I? But he isn't. He's talking to me.

'Oh, erm, yes, okay,' I babble. Sexy, Poppy. Oh-so cool and sexy.

Farrell offers me his gigantic hand and leads me to the floor space where the other couples are dancing, right alongside Zac and Lilac, which makes me kind of uncomfortable. I'm finding it harder and harder to watch them together, especially as more memories come to the forefront of my mind.

'I'm not very good at this,' Farrell tells me. 'But when in Scotland.'

'I'm rubbish too,' I admit. 'So at least we'll be rubbish together.'

'I can live with that,' he says.

I wrap my arms around Farrell's neck as he places his hands on my waist. We move slowly to the music. I really don't know what I'm doing, but you just move around a bit, don't you?

'I love that your name means courageous,' I tell him. 'So apt for a stuntman.'

'My dad was a stuntman, too,' he tells me. 'So he probably knew what he was doing when he named me. Dad was kind of a crash dummy. Cars and bikes were his speciality. I remember when I was in kindergarten, I told the kids my dad drove cars into walls and my teacher told me to stop being silly, I was so embarrassed. I went home and told my dad what she said. He told me he'd sort it with him. My dad cornered the guy in the school parking lot and smashed a sugar glass bottle over his own head, the teacher was so freaked out, but I remember him apologising to me the next day. Dad didn't tell me about this until I was older. I still miss him, every day.'

I give his neck a sympathetic squeeze.

'I get it,' I tell him. 'I lost my mum.'

'They say my name means courage – I think

Poppy means courage. The things you've been through. You must be one strong lady.'

'I don't know about that,' I say, a little embarrassed. 'We just deal with what we have to, right? Whether it's losing a loved one or going through a tough time. Nanny May once told me Poppy doesn't just refer to the flower, she said it means "the milk of happiness" and, I guess I seem like a sad person, but I strive for happiness. Nothing has beaten me yet.'

'That's such a beautiful sentiment,' he replies. 'You're a beautiful woman. You're making me very happy right now, Poppy. Anyone who thinks your baggage defines you doesn't deserve you.'

There's a look on Farrell's face that practically paralyses me in his arms. I feel a dorky look take hold of my face, the kind I'd imagine briefly appears on a person's face before they're hit by a bus. It isn't a bus that's coming though, it's Farrell.

He leans forward and places his lips on mine. He practically sucks me in, holding me in place. It's a powerful kiss, a great one – one that is totally unexpected.

Eventually he releases me, and I just stare at him for a second.

'Sorry,' he says. 'Couldn't resist. Sometimes you just have to take chances.'

I smile at him, hopefully masking how freaked out I am, but not because it's upset me, because it hasn't. Farrell is gorgeous and he seems like my kind of guy. It's just so unexpected and such strange and awkward timing.

I lean forward and rest my head on his shoulder as we dance. My big dumb smile remains firmly in place until something catches my eye. It's Zac, glaring at me. He's dancing with Lilac, but his attention is firmly fixed on me. I get that he's mad at me, muscling my way into his wedding party, drawing attention to myself, but I'd rather not be here, believe me.

The good news is that this time tomorrow it will all be over. The papers will be signed, faxed, delivered, and I'll no longer be his.

We just need to find an excuse to nip to the mainland tomorrow, before the blizzard hits. No idea how we're going to do that but we'll cross that loch when we come to it.

30

11 OCTOBER 2015

'Can I make you a cup of tea?' Zac asks.

'No thanks,' I tell him. 'I'm absolutely swimming in the stuff.'

'Has your mum been feeding you buttery toast and sweet tea all day?' he says with a smile. 'The Walker family cure for everything.'

I shoot him a look.

'Sorry,' he replies. 'Just trying to make you smile.'

I pull my blanket up to my chin and snuggle down deeper into the sofa.

'Do you want me to get your mum to come back?' he asks.

'Nope,' I reply.

Mum has been with me all day, right up until Zac arrived back from London, saying she would leave us to talk, but the last thing I want to do right now is talk.

'Pops,' he starts, but I don't let him finish. I don't want to. I don't want to hear it right now.

'How was London?' I ask, cutting him off.

'Are you serious right now?' he replies. 'You want to talk about London?'

'Yep,' I say. 'How was the audition?'

'Poppy, we're not talking about my audition right now.'

'Why not?' I say.

I feel strangely numb. I thought I'd be feeling more, I don't know; something. Apparently, this happens sometimes.

'Because there are far more relevant things to talk about,' he reminds me.

I'm not angry at Zac for being in London when I lost our baby, I'm just angry that it happened.

'There's nothing to talk about,' I tell him. 'It's done, I lost it, I fucked up. I don't know what I did.'

Zac, who has been keeping a sort of delicate distance, sits down next to me and wraps his arm around me. Normally he would squeeze me so tightly, but today it's like he's too scared.

'You did nothing wrong,' he tells me. 'I may not know anything about anything in this arena, but I know that much.'

'Just one of those things, that's what the nurse said,' I tell him with a sigh. 'Just some random act of shitness that just had to happen to us – and it had to happen while you weren't here.'

'I wish I hadn't gone,' he says softly.

'It wouldn't have made a difference,' I tell him. 'It was horrible at the hospital, but... I'm home now.'

'How are you feeling?' he asks.

I'm sure he means physically but, my God, every single thing every person is saying and doing feels like fire against my skin.

'I feel horrendous, inside and out, in all ways imaginable,' I tell him, my voice cracking. 'So can we please, please just talk about your audition?'

Zac doesn't say anything. I see him mentally shift gears.

'Okay then, sure,' he says. 'If that's what you want. I think it went well...'

Zac chats away about his trip to London, which is

what he thinks I want, and it's what I asked him to do, but I just completely tune out.

I should be so excited. This is his first potential big break as a session guitarist, auditioning to play with Dylan King from The Burnouts, but I can't absorb a word he's saying. I can't keep my mind on anything.

It's going to take time, that's what a few people have told me, but there's no way to fast-forward this bit, is there? I don't want to talk about it, I don't even want to think about it.

Eventually, I lean in to Zac and rest my head on his chest. I can get through this if I keep him close, not push him away.

Time and love, that's what I need, exactly what the nurse said. It's just one of those things. It's not my fault.

It's *not* my fault.

31

I've always hated hen parties.

I didn't have one, not a proper one, not really. I did have a night out in the week before we tied the knot, but it was arranged by the girls and it was for Zac too. It was just like one of our usual nights out and a lot of fun. There were no penis-shaped straws, no strippers (unless you count what Zac did when we finally got home at 6 a.m.) and no one wore so much as a pink sock. I loved it.

Lilac's hen party isn't much like a hen party either. It's worse. It's like a sleepover at the rich kid's house, when you're eleven, and all she does is basically lord it over you while you sleep on her floor. It's also like every sleepover scene you've ever seen in every movie – so over the top.

We've got cocktails, facemasks, and everyone is wearing silky pink pyjamas and super fluffy slippers. Everyone except me, that is, because no one knew I was coming so, sadly, none for me. I wish I'd been quick thinking, like Kat was when she made her excuses not to come tonight. She was all for it until she had to listen to Lilac and Christina talking about how they were going to hide their supposed friend Lauren in the back of the wedding photos because she's just had a wonky boob job. That was when Kat decided she couldn't stand to be around them any longer tonight. There are only so many excuses you can make, when you're trapped in a castle on an island, so when Kat started making hers, I had kind of hoped it would get me off the hook, or at least be something I could piggyback on. But she said she had bad period pain, so unless I could sell the fact that all cousins in our family had synchronised cycles, I didn't think that one was going to work for me.

So, I've kept my mouth shut, I've had my nails

painted, I've worn the facemask, I've joined in with all the silly games. I've even gritted my teeth and endured it while Lilac bragged about her sex life – something that was beyond excruciating for me, but I've been through worse. I decided it was time to call it a night so, currently, I'm in the bathroom washing the pink glittery gunk off my face. It's definitely past my bedtime.

I dry my face before heading into the corridor on my way back to the bedroom, when I hear Lilac and Christina chatting. I hang back for a second, waiting for them to go, because if I try to make my excuses to them out here, two on one, they'll probably try to convince me to stay. My plan is to grab my bag from the sleepover room and then head for my own bed, hopefully without being seen. No one will miss me if I'm gone, but they'll know I'm leaving, if they see me.

'You need to lighten up,' Christina tells her. 'You're getting married.'

'I know, it's just so awkward, with Farrell being here,' Lilac tells her. 'I know it was months ago, but he will not stop talking about it.'

What will Farrell not stop talking about? I've only known him a matter of days, but my money would be on either something to do with James Bond or his lat muscles. He only seems to talk about his job or his body.

'So you slept with him, big deal,' Christina says. 'I sleep with people all the time.'

What?! Farrell is Lilac's ex? I didn't know that.

'I know, but it's obviously different,' Lilac insists. 'I cheated on Zac with him.'

'Once, months ago, and it didn't mean anything,' Christina seemingly reminds her. 'That's what you said, right?'

'I know,' Lilac replies. 'It's just… shit, we shouldn't be talking about this out here, should we? Let's talk in the bathroom.'

I hurry back, as light on my feet as I can be, until I'm out of sight. I wait for the two of them to head into the bathroom before I head for my own room.

That horrible, horrible cow. She cheated on Zac? Wonderful, gorgeous, brilliant, perfect Zac? My God, listen to me. I can't be going down this road. I need to keep my nose out of this. This is nothing to do with me. I can't get involved… can I? I'm here for a divorce, not to ruin his wedding. Would he even believe me if I did tell him? Would Lilac lie, and say I was making it up? Would Zac believe her and think I was just here to mess things up for him? Shit, I have no idea what I'm supposed to do with this information but, if one thing is for sure, whether it's going to ruin his wedding or not, I can't let it ruin my divorce.

32

It turns out you have to get up pretty early in the morning if you want to be the only ones at breakfast.

Breakfast starts at 7.30 a.m. It's 7.20 now and we're already at the table, just me and Zac, ready to plan how we're going to make our great escape today to head over to the mainland and complete our paperwork. That sounds like such a casual thing, doesn't it? Our paperwork. Such a gentle term for our divorce but how big a deal can it be? We've already done it once, or at least we thought we had. Same difference.

I don't remember the last time we were in a room, just the two of us. Actually, I do, I suppose it's obvious, really. The day we decided to break up. After that there was always a supportive parent or solicitor – or both, in my case.

The stupid and frustrating thing is that, as bad as it feels, being a guest at the love of my life's wedding, it feels good too, just to be around him again. I've missed him.

'First thing first,' Zac starts.

'You say that as though there's going to be a second thing,' I point out.

'There is,' he replies, which terrifies me. 'We need an excuse to go over to the mainland.'

'Well, it's no trouble for me,' I tell him. 'I'm MI6, remember?'

'I'm not going to forget that revelation in a hurry,' he says through a smile. 'Okay, so you're going to work, why am I going?'

'I don't know, a wedding surprise or something?' I suggest.

'But then I'd have to actually have something to show for it,' he points out. 'So unless some tourist tat will suffice…'

As a thought hits me, I start laughing.

'What's so funny?' Zac asks.

'Something just occurred to me and now I'm wondering. Why didn't we just tell everyone the truth?' I say. 'If I had just turned up and said hello, not-quite ex-wife here, our divorce was never finalised due to what we'll call a clerical error. No sense in telling the whole truth on that point. But here I am, I have papers for you to sign, then you'll be officially divorced, and free to get married. Boom.'

'To be honest, it never crossed my mind,' he says. 'Quite the opposite, actually. For one thing, Sonny is always threatening to beat me up, if I ever wrong his daughter, and it doesn't always sound like he's kidding. Secondly, Lilac isn't like you. She has trust issues. One time, she caught me looking at a photo of you on my phone. She didn't see that it was you but she knew you must have been someone special. She made me delete it. And the ironic thing is the fact that—'

'Zachary, there you are,' Lilac says as she marches into the dining room. She looks half asleep, her eyes barely open, her voice still a little croaky. She tightens her dressing gown belt as she approaches us at the table. 'Morning, Poppy. Zachary, something terrible has happened. The cake isn't coming.'

'The wedding cake?' he replies, as though she might be referring to a different cake. 'Why not?'

'They said someone cancelled it,' she replies. 'I woke up to a cancellation, so I called them, and they confirmed it. Apparently, someone called them to cancel it. I'm sure it's just a stupid error or a mix up but… I don't know… I feel like this wedding is cursed.'

Zac jumps up to comfort her. 'Curses aren't real,' he tells her. 'What do you want to do, cake wise?'

'I've sorted it already,' she says. 'I called up that café over on the mainland, asked them if they could bake me a cake, threw a ton of money at them, they said yes. It's ready to collect later today.'

'Oh, okay,' he replies. 'Phew. Well, I can go over and collect it, if you like?'

'Don't be silly,' she says, squeezing him tightly. 'There's a blizzard coming later, it's freezing out there. We'll send staff.'

'I want to go myself,' he tells her. 'That way, I'll know exactly what's going on with it and I won't let anything bad happen to this one.'

'Can you manage it alone?' she asks.

'I'm going over to the mainland to send some work documents,' I tell her. 'I can help him.'

'That's brilliant, thank you,' she says. 'Zachary, get me some coffee, will you? No point going back to sleep now.'

Oh, boy, do I feel awful now. It feels so icky, like we're sneaking around behind her back, like we're having an affair or something, but it truly is the opposite. Still, it never feels good lying, does it?

'Do you want a cup of tea?' Zac asks me.

'Yes, please,' I reply.

'It's cute that he remembers what you drink,' Lilac says. 'I don't even know my cousins' middle names. Listen, I'm sorry for all that unpleasant baby talk business. I guess I misunderstood what my mum had tried to tell me. What happened to you sucked.'

'Don't worry about it,' I tell her. 'It was a long time ago.'

'I can't believe you're already divorced,' she says. 'That's wild. You can't be more than thirty-five?'

Eesh.

'It is what it is,' I reply.

'Do you regret getting married so young?' she asks curiously.

Zac is safely out of earshot for the moment, so I don't mind answering.

'Absolutely not,' I tell her. 'Best thing I ever did. Happiest day of my life. We just really messed it up.'

'Do you still think about him?' she asks through a yawn.

I imagine she's just really tired and it's not that I'm boring her. Lilac doesn't ask questions if she isn't interested in the answer.

'All the time,' I admit softly.

I do think about him all the time. I really do. Even before I came here, before I found out about the divorce not being filed, I really did think about him so often. Zac was a huge part of my life; all my best memories are with him. Even when I think of my mum, and all the wonderful memories I have of her, Zac is usually present in those too. I've never been able to shake off the ghost of him.

It's not that I don't think Lilac is right for Zac – incidentally, I don't, I don't think she's a very nice person, and I definitely think Zac is far too good for her – but there's a more important reason I don't want this wedding to go ahead.

It might hurt to lie to people, but do you know what hurts more? Lying to yourself. I can't pretend this wedding isn't getting under my skin for a second longer and I definitely can't watch the love of my life marry someone else. This has to end today – and the sooner the better.

33

'Just another twenty minutes, hen,' the lady who runs the café tells me. 'I know it's all so last minute, but I really think we've pulled it out of the bag for you.'

I can tell from the flour all over her apron and the smear of what the optimist in me is going to say is chocolate frosting on her forehead, courtesy of the back of her hand.

'I can't wait to see it,' I tell her. 'Thank you. If it's half as good as this one, it will be perfect.'

'It's great,' Zac tells her. 'The coffee too.'

She hurries back into the kitchen to finish up with the cake.

Once we have it, we're headed over to the holiday cabins to send our divorce papers – our divorce papers that neither of us has actually signed yet.

It's been such a weird day so far. First of all, the motorboat wouldn't start, because apparently it doesn't do well in very cold weather, and we were told by the man who drove it that under no circumstances would it come back for us if the blizzard hit, but that's not expected until much later in the day, so we should be fine. Then, to kill a little time before heading to the café, we went for a bit of a walk, just making small talk, until it was time to head here to collect the cake, which is running slightly late, but it is a super last-minute thing, so you can't exactly expect better than the staff here doing their best.

And that's why it's weird, because this is all just so normal, just the two of us having a lovely day in a tourist town. We chatted, filling each other in on the years that have passed since we split. It sounds like Zac is doing really well at work and he couldn't have been happier for me when he heard how things were going with the business. He's never considered me boring, based on my job – then again, it was always nonstop fun when we were together (until it wasn't, obviously). You would never know this was all in aid of us divorcing.

'I tell you what, I never thought we'd do this again,' Zac says, practically reading my mind. 'Did you ever think we'd sit together in a café again, just having a drink, eating cake?'

I laugh. 'No, I didn't,' I admit. 'But if I had, I wouldn't have imagined it to be so... nice.'

'Nice,' Zac repeats back to me. 'That's one of those words that is just so... so nothing.'

'Nice is nice,' I tell him.

'Don't you remember what our GCSE English teacher used to tell us?' he starts. 'That "nice" was a word used by the unimaginative, that no one who ever said nice actually felt all that strongly about anything.'

'Mrs Horny,' I say. 'I remember using it twice in my creative writing coursework and her hitting me with a "see me" in red biro, she was that upset about it.'

'God, kids are horrible, aren't they?' he replies.

'Definitely,' I reply.

Mrs Horny's name was actually Mrs Horne. One day, one of the bad kids hilariously pronounced it that way and it stuck. Fair play to her, she had a good sense of humour, she owned it in the end. On leavers' day, she signed all our shirts 'Mrs Horny' instead of 'Mrs Horne'.

It's bizarre, when you're with someone for so many years, you have so much history together that it doesn't matter how long you go without seeing each other, when you meet up again there's no strangeness. It's like you've never been apart. I think that's one of the things that freaks me out about being single at thirty-one. It's not that I'm too old for love, or anything ridiculous like that, no one is too old, my dad is proof of that with his dating app ventures. It's the fact that the clock has been reset. Zac and I knew each other all the way through school, into adulthood; by the time we were married, we'd been in each other's lives for two decades. If I want to rack up twenty years with someone new, and I start today, I'll be in my fifties. I worry about such stupid things too, like when I hear about people celebrating their ruby wedding anniversary, I wonder, will I have enough time with someone to even do that? I mean, I could have, I suppose, if my dad hadn't found those letters from my mum, but it's not like I would have known about it, so it doesn't exactly count, does it?

'You're so sensible now,' I tell him. 'So neat and tidy and mature.'

'I'm not that bad, am I?' he replies, cringing slightly.

'It's not a bad thing,' I insist. 'It suits you.'

'You make it sound like a bad thing,' he says with a laugh. 'I feel like you're judging me.'

'No, I would never,' I reply. 'It's not a bad thing generally. I bet you'd be boring to go on a night out with, maybe, but otherwise...'

'Oh yeah? You still *living it up* then, are you?'

He says 'living it up' in such a playfully sarcastic tone.

'Try this one for size,' I start, preparing him for something spectacular. 'On New Year's Eve, I went to Rachael's wedding. I ditched it before midnight, crashed the party in the next function room instead, kissed a man I'd just met at midnight, and I woke up in bed with Kat *and* Rachael's brother – nothing happened, but still. And then the guy from midnight tracked me down just to ask me on a date.'

'Wow, okay, you are still living it up,' he says with a slight laugh. 'So, are you seeing someone, then?'

'Nah,' I say casually. 'Our date got interrupted by my dad telling me I was still married. My date said he was looking for something easy and the truth did not sound easy. I feel like I'm always going to feel like damaged goods.'

'You're not damaged goods,' Zac insists. 'If you are, then I am too. And look at me, I couldn't tell Lilac the truth either. I'm scared to talk to her about anything, she's pretty scary when she's angry, plus, have you seen her dad?'

'I've seen some of his films, he's not actually that dangerous in real life, is he? Sonny Craven,' I add, remembering his real name.

'Did you not see the one where he punched the train?' Zac replies sarcastically. '"There's only one way I know to stop a runaway train – punch the fuck out of it."'

Zac's impression of Sonny isn't too far off the mark. Somewhere between Jason Statham in *Snatch* and Danny Dyer in anything.

'That's pretty good,' I tell him.

'It's so hard not to do it around him,' he replies. 'But he'd probably punch me for taking the piss.'

'Maybe,' I reply. 'Hey, earlier, you said you had two things to talk to me about.'

'Oh, yeah.' He pauses for a second while he searches for the words. 'I saw you kiss Farrell.'

'He kissed *me*,' I quickly insist. I don't know why it's so important to me that I stress that. Well, I do, it's because I don't want him to think I'm interested in anyone else, which is completely ridiculous, so it's hardly a point worth making, is it?

'You did kiss him back,' he says. 'Do you like him?'

I scoff. 'I'm not having this conversation with you,' I tell him.

'Sorry, you don't have to,' he backtracks. 'But just know this – I know him and he's not a great guy.'

'Thanks, Dad.'

'Just looking out for you,' he says, messing with his cake fork.

'I know,' I reply. 'It's one of the things I love about you.'

Shit, why did I say that? I didn't mean it to be as heavy as it sounds.

'You love me?' he teases.

'Oh, yeah, when I think of you, David Cassidy songs play in my heart,' I joke.

'God, your mum used to rinse that CD of his in her car,' he says with a smile.

'I know! I still remember all the words too.' I really do. 'So bizarre, that "I Think I Love You" kind of wound up being our song. Man, Mum loved David Cassidy. She would have left my dad for him. She would have left me *and* my dad to run off with David.'

'No, she wouldn't,' Zac says through a chuckle, before his face falls. 'You know, I knew that I missed her, I just didn't know how permanent a feeling it would be.'

'I'm sorry,' I tell him. 'If it helps, I've had a lot longer to make peace with the news and it's never really sunk in. I still think of her all the time. She's still the first person I think of, when I have good news or a funny story. Her and...'

We fall silent for a few seconds. I sip my tea ever so slowly, busying my lips, so I don't have to think of something to say.

I do love him. So much, it hurts. So much that,

despite wondering whether I should or shouldn't tell him about Lilac's fling with Farrell, I know that I probably shouldn't. She sounded like she regretted it, like she'd made a mistake, and we've all made those in our time. I love him, and I don't want to see him get hurt, but my love for him is the same love I had when we were together. No matter how much I try to dress it up as the moral high ground, I couldn't ever rule out that I was telling him for my own personal gain, to get Zac back; I don't think I could ever quite be happy knowing that was how I'd won him back, plus there's always a chance he'll shoot the messenger.

'Are we going to talk about the elephant in the room?' Zac says, nodding towards the A4 envelope sticking out of my handbag.

'Hmm,' I reply. 'I've brought a pen with me. I guess we just need to sign them.'

I reach into my bag and remove the papers and a pen.

'You can read them if you want,' I tell him. 'But there's a sticker on the last page, showing where we need to sign.'

'Right, okay,' he says.

Zac picks the wad of papers up and then puts them down again.

'Wah!' He makes a funny face and wiggles his fingers. 'Why does this feel so… odd?'

'Probably because we've already done it once,' I tell him. 'People don't typically do this twice with the same person.'

'It's not that,' he says. 'Well, it's kind of that. It just makes you wonder, doesn't it? What if this is what your mum wanted to happen?'

'I read her letters,' I remind him. 'She knew she'd made a mistake.'

'Hmm,' he replies thoughtfully. 'We need to sign these, right?'

'You're getting married tomorrow,' I remind him, even though I wish he weren't. 'I need to send these over to my dad *today* and then Auntie Joan is going to do a rushed job for us, so that it's all done and dusted for tomorrow. She's literally working overtime to help us get this sorted. And we did have this exact same dilemma six years ago…'

'I know, I know,' he says. 'Somehow it feels even more final now.'

I grab the pen and pull the papers towards myself. Without so much as a beat, I sign my name.

'You're supposed to have witnesses watch you sign it,' he reminds me.

'Shit,' I blurt, attracting the attention of the elderly couple on the table next to us.

I was so eager to prove a stupid point. Idiot.

'So sorry,' I tell them. 'We're supposed to have two witnesses when we sign this document. I've only just lifted the pen off the paper. Would you two mind?'

They both visibly soften.

'Not at all,' the man says. He has a Welsh accent, which makes me think they must be tourists too.

'You're up next,' I tell Zac.

He takes the pen from me and sets the papers down in front of him. He doesn't look down at them, though, he holds eye contact with me.

'Sign,' I tell him.

'Are you sure?' he replies.

'What? Am I sure? What are you talking about, just sign it,' I insist.

He's prolonging the agony – and it really is agony.

Zac sighs before scribbling his signature and slapping the pen down on top of it.

'Thank you,' I say as I take the top sheet of paper and the pen and hand it to the couple.

They both dutifully sign their names. I glance quickly at them when they hand the sheet back to me.

'Thank you so much, Mr and Mrs Rees,' I say with a smile.

'You're welcome,' Mrs Rees replies. 'Perhaps you could do us a favour, too. We're here celebrating our wedding anniversary. Could you take a photo of us, please?'

'It would be my pleasure,' I reply.

Mrs Rees hands me her phone before the two of them pose together.

'I've taken a few so you can choose the best one,' I say as I hand it back, because that's just good photo-taking etiquette, isn't it? 'How long have you been married?'

'It's our emerald anniversary,' she replies proudly. 'Fifty-five years.'

'Wow, congratulations,' I tell them both with a smile.

'Are you two married?' Mr Rees asks us.

'We are,' Zac says as he smiles at me. It's one hell of a weird in-joke.

'How long?' Mrs Rees asks.

'Nearly seven years,' Zac replies.

'Well, thank you for taking our photo, we wish you many more years of happiness,' she says. 'Perhaps you'll celebrate your emerald anniversary here too.'

'I'm not sure about that one,' I reply. 'You just witnessed us signing our divorce papers.'

34

Doug, a wee Scots fella in his sixties, who works behind the desk at the holiday cabins place, has just informed us that unfortunately he isn't 'the one who knows how to use the fax machine' so we're going to have to wait until Cathy comes back to send our signed papers off. Thankfully he's let us temporarily store the wedding cake behind the counter, because I feel terrified, lugging it around. You know when you just know something bad is going to happen?

'Don't worry, we've still got plenty of time,' I tell Zac. 'I guess we just need to hang around here until she's back.'

'Typical,' Zac says. 'But we wouldn't be us if we weren't cutting it fine.'

We make our way over to a seating area and plonk ourselves down. There are a few magazines laid out, so I grab one and flick through it, but it does little to hold my attention. I feel so anxious and I'm not going to stop feeling this way until all of this is put to bed. I just want to get it over with.

'There's a solid stream of people heading into that function room,' Zac points out curiously.

I glance over at the door. As the latest cluster of people clears, they reveal a sign that reads: *Whisky tasting, all welcome*.

'Do you remember, God knows how long ago, when we went to that wine tasting?' he says with a smile.

'Ah, yes, the one Sally made us go to, because she wanted to impress that Welsh banker she was dating,' I reply. 'She said it was important we all "seemed classy even though we weren't".'

'I wanted to go bowling,' he says with a sigh.

'That was her point,' I say with a laugh. 'God, we were so wasted that day.'

'That's because you refused to spit the wine out,' Zac reminds me. 'So, I didn't either. Obviously.'

'Why would I *spit wine out*?' I say, as though it's the most ludicrous thing I've ever heard. 'I remember how mad she was at first, but how funny she found it the next day.'

'I remember how hard "Welsh banker" was to say after pushing twenty glasses of wine,' he replies with a smile. 'We had fun, didn't we?'

'We did,' I say with a sigh. 'But now you're boring.'

'Oi, I'm not boring,' he insists. 'What? I'm not.'

'Okay, if you say so,' I tease.

The look on Zac's face suggests he takes my teasing more seriously than I'm intending it. I wonder if I've struck a nerve.

'Right,' he says, jumping to his feet. He grabs me by the hand and pulls me up before dragging me in the direction of the function room. 'Come on.'

'What are you doing?' I laugh under my breath.

'We're going to this bloody whisky tasting, that's what,' he says. 'I'll show you who's boring and who isn't. It kind of sounds like you're the boring one right now.'

I laugh. It's nice to see his competitive nature is still firmly in place.

'Okay, fine,' I say. 'But I don't even like whisky, so I absolutely will be spitting it out today.'

'Chicken,' he teases.

35

Robert Vass is nothing if not a stone-cold professional.

As the whisky expert hosting the tasting today, he's having to wrangle a bunch of tourists for this entry-level Scotch tasting, and he's handling it like a boss.

While I still maintain that I don't like whisky, it turns out the more you drink of it, the less you hate the taste. I don't know if I'm a little drunk or I've removed my taste buds or it's a combination of both, but I'm rather enjoying myself. So is Zac.

'I'll race you on this next one,' he says. 'First one to neck their shot wins.'

'Wins what?' I whisper back.

'I don't know, something,' he replies. 'How about the winner can ask the loser for something? It can be anything.'

'High stakes,' I say, raising my eyebrows. 'But okay.'

'There are thousands of whiskies out there,' Robert continues. 'It would be incredibly costly to try all of them, so the most important thing to do is work out which type of whisky you like and then sample a few from that family. If you haven't yet found one that you enjoyed today, it may be that bourbon is the tipple for you.'

'How many more do you think there are?' I ask. 'I can't feel my tongue.'

'You're drunk,' Zac chuckles quietly.

'I'm not drunk-drunk,' I insist. '*You're* drunk.'

'I'm lightly buzzed,' he replies.

'What we're going to do with this next whisky is add a little water,' Robert continues. 'This doesn't water it down, it doesn't make it any less strong, it actually enhances the flavour, as drinks with very high alcohol levels can suppress flavour.'

'Jesus Christ, this is just making the drink bigger,' I whisper to Zac.

'As always, I want you to get to know this whisky,' Robert says. 'Bring the glass up to your nose, sniff it with one nostril, then the other – one will work better.'

'Can't we just knock it back?' Zac whispers.

'Okay, give it a try, and fill out your record sheet,' Robert instructs.

Zac, of course, finishes his shot (I don't think we're supposed to be doing them like shots, to be fair) much faster than I do. He smiles smugly.

I take my feedback sheet and write down: *strong*. I've basically written that for all of them. For one of the earlier ones, I simply wrote: *ouch*.

'Now, this one, under no circumstances must you drink,' Robert starts. 'I repeat, under no circumstances can you drink this one.'

Tasting the whiskies is broken up with these educational segments where Robert teaches us things about how whisky is made and fun little facts about the different ones. I never thought I'd find whisky all that interesting, but it's kind of fascinating. Plus, I really welcome the breaks from drinking it.

'You'll see this is a clear liquid, 68 per cent alcohol. All I want you to do is nose this one and write down what you can smell when you communicate with the whisky. Do not nose it too aggressively. I've lost many people in tasting groups because they nosed this whisky too aggressively. If you feel any sensations in your eyes, that's a sign you're doing it wrong. I want to know what you can smell; can you smell cereal notes? A bit of an orange tang? Perhaps you smell damp leather or sick?' Robert continues.

'Damp leather or sick?' I repeat back to Zac.

'The reason you cannot drink this whisky is because it won't be ready for at least twelve years,' Robert tells us. 'It is the whisky distilling in the wooden casks that gives it that lovely colour we're used to, wood maturing the whisky is where the colour comes from. When whisky was first produced, the people doing it didn't want to wait twelve years, so they flavoured it to try to make it drinkable immediately, and guess what? They died.'

I quickly stop sniffing the actual poison in my hand and push the glass away.

'I think I've hit my limit,' I say. I glance at my

watch and realise it's 4 p.m. 'Shit, Zac, quick. Shit, it's 4 p.m.'

'Shit,' he replies.

I grab my bag and head for the door, but I stumble over my silly drunk feet. Luckily, Zac catches me.

'Come on, let me keep you steady,' he says, linking his arm with mine.

We make our way back through to reception where thankfully a woman is behind the desk.

'Cathy?' I say, crossing everything I have.

'Yes?' she replies.

'Oh, thank God,' I reply. 'We completely lost track of time.'

'I can smell that,' she says politely.

'Doug said you could send a fax for us,' I say, ignoring her remark.

She sighs.

'Yes, okay, give it here,' she says. 'Is this your cake, then?'

'It is,' Zac replies. 'I'll take it. Thanks for looking after it.'

'Yes,' she says, as though she can't quite bring herself to say that we're welcome.

I hand her the pile of papers and the scrunched-up piece of paper I'd jammed into my purse that says where to send it.

'Back in a moment,' Cathy tells us.

I glance at Zac, who is just hovering next to me, clutching the large cake box, his knuckles turning white as he holds it so tightly.

'If it goes off okay, which I'm sure it will, you won't have anything to worry about,' I reassure him.

'I guess not,' he replies, not all that convincingly.

I reach forward and squeeze his forearm.

'There's plenty of time,' I insist. 'Everything is going to be fine now, so long as you don't drop that cake.'

'Ordinarily I'd pretend to drop it but, I don't know, I don't feel much like joking right now,' he says with small, careful shrug of his shoulders.

'Me neither,' I reply.

'Right, that's done for you,' Cathy informs me as she hands me the paperwork back.

'Thank you,' I say.

I'm grateful for the favour, but it feels like a weird thing to be thanking someone for – for ending your marriage, not that she knows that's what she's done.

'I feel like I should say a few words or something,' Zac says as we head for the door.

'There's nothing to say,' I insist, picking up the pace. 'We just need to get back over to the island so that you can get ready for tomorrow and I can get Kat and my things and leave.'

'You're not staying?' he asks.

I scoff. As I open the door for us to leave, there really is nothing to say – I'm totally speechless. It's getting dark already. I don't know why it takes me aback, it is January after all, but it's always jarring when it gets dark early, and you go in somewhere in the daylight and then leave in the dark. That's not the biggest shock though.

'So, I guess this is that blizzard they were talking about,' Zac says.

He utters these words so casually, so calmly that it only freaks me out further.

'I guess it is,' I reply.

I told you something bad was going to happen.

36

'Hi Cathy, us again,' I say brightly.

She's even less pleased to see us now than she was before.

In a series of not-all-that-unsurprising events, every bad thing that could have happened has happened. The blizzard has hit, the boats have stopped running, we're stuck on the mainland and everyone else is stuck on the island. I know, it probably sounds worse to be trapped on an island, but they're all stuck at a five-star holiday castle. We're stuck in the middle of nowhere, with nowhere to go, given that there's currently no way in or out of Tarness. Zac just called Lilac to let her know, and Sonny passed along the message that due to a severe weather warning all the roads and boat passages were closed.

Zac assured Lilac that he was going to do his best to get back tonight, with the cake, but that if for some reason he couldn't, he would absolutely be there by morning, even if he had to row himself. All things considered, optimism aside, there is absolutely no way we are getting back to the castle tonight, no chance, and while that does give us a list of problems as long as our arms, there is one really big issue that I can't seem to see past: what the hell are we going to do tonight?

'What can I do for you now?' she asks.

Charming.

'I just wondered if you had any cabins available for us,' I say sweetly.

'Didn't I just fax your divorce papers?' she replies in disbelief.

She read them?!

'Separate rooms, preferably,' I tell her. 'But there's raging a blizzard out there so at this point we can make do with anything.'

'The only availability we had left was the master

suite cabin,' she tells us. 'Which has four bedrooms in it.'

Oh, boy. That sounds expensive. I hope Zac has his card with him – he's the rich one.

'But it got snapped up today,' she says. 'You'll be hard pushed to find somewhere to stay tonight.'

My jaw drops. Why tell us, if it's taken?

'Wonderful, thank you,' I reply.

Zac readjusts his grip on the cake and we head back outside, into the cold and the dark, as it feels like night is fast approaching.

We're only standing outside the reception cabin for a few seconds before Zac just starts laughing.

'I'd love to know what's so funny,' I say, verging on the ticked off. Nothing is funny right now.

'I just find it amusing that we've been apart for years, and on the day we finally truly get divorced, it's a day that so very much feels like a day when we were together.'

'You'll have to forgive me for not appreciating the irony, it's just I'm freezing my tits off,' I point out as I hug my own body to try to keep the warmth in my coat.

'I noticed on one of the flyers in the lobby that

there's a party barn out back, they're selling tickets for tonight, some kind of club night,' he says. 'In a worst-case scenario, at least we could keep warm there for a few hours.'

'I see two problems with that,' I start. 'The first being, when the party ends, we're not only out in the cold again, but in the middle of the night this time, but also because what the fuck are you going to do with that cake, dance around it?'

Zac laughs.

'The woman who made it did say it should be refrigerated overnight,' he reminds me. 'I'll just bury it in the snow somewhere.'

'Bury your wedding cake?' I squeak.

'In the snow,' he insists. He places it down on the ground, his arms clearly tired of holding it already.

'Jesus Christ, I'm so glad you weren't so blasé about our wedding,' I say.

'Our low budget beauty was amazing, wasn't it?' he says with a smile. 'When your mum had a few too many and got on the karaoke.'

'Do you remember how upset Sally was about the karaoke, calling us uncool?' I chuckle.

'I said uncouth,' Sally points out.

I jump so far out of my skin my body temperature drops another few degrees.

'Bloody hell,' I cry out. I don't think I've ever been so freaked out in my life. Sally, Rachael and Lindsey are all standing there, right in front of us, clutching bags of what looks like food shopping.

'What on earth are you guys doing here?' I ask them.

'It's your interfriendtion,' Sally says, as though I should have been expecting it.

'Hi, girls,' Zac says with a cheeky smile.

'It's unrealistic how fit you are right now,' Sally tells him. 'But I can't get into it with you. I have to sort out this hot mess.'

'Come on, I've not seen any of you in six years, you could give me a hug?' he says.

Sally rolls her eyes but then her face softens into a smile. You can tell she's happy to see her old friend. She hugs him, then Lindsey does, then Rachael. Rachael's smile quickly drops.

'You're drunk,' she tells him. She moves closer to me and sniffs me.

'You've been drinking too,' she says. 'Okay, what the hell is going on?'

'Can we do this inside, please?' I say, my teeth chattering from the cold. 'Can we find a café or even just sit in your car?'

'We're staying here,' Sally tells me. 'I booked us the massive, fancy cabin. The plan was to call you, tell you to come here and beat some sense into you.'

'And cookies,' Lindsey adds.

'Yeah, and Lindsey brought you cookies,' Sally adds.

'Sweetening the pill,' Lindsey says with a smile.

'Okay, but can it be an inside intervention, please?' I beg.

'Fine, fine,' Sally says.

'Thank you,' I reply as we follow her. 'We're stuck here, we can't get back to the island, we've nowhere to go.'

'You'll have to stay here with us, won't you?' she says with a sigh. 'But we've only got the one spare bedroom.'

As we're walking, I feel my phone buzz. It's a message from Dad. Two words:

Papers received.

'I can just sleep on the sofa or the floor or something,' Zac suggest gratefully as Sally messes with the door key.

'Yes, you can,' she replies sternly.

'And can I put my cake in your fridge, please?'

Sally clicks her tongue and takes the cake from him.

Inside, the log cabin is simply stunning. The living space is a huge open-plan area with a kitchen section, a dining part, and a massive lounge area. The main focal point is the wood-burning stove. In front of it are two massive sofas that face each other. Behind one is a huge shelving unit overflowing (neatly, somehow) with books, board games and movies. What I'd give to spend a long weekend here, ideally alone. I can't think of anything more relaxing.

'You two, sit on that sofa,' Sally demands, and now I can't think of anything less relaxing.

'I'm sorry you felt like you had to come all this way,' I tell them, sobering up suddenly. 'But honestly, I'm handling it.'

'What is this?' she asks, nodding between us. 'He's supposed to be getting married, and you're running around town together getting drunk in the day.'

'Look, it's not what it looks like,' I insist. 'We came over here to sign and send our divorce papers and we did. It's done. My dad has the papers, they're filing them tonight, the wedding is tomorrow. The only spanner is getting stuck over here, but we'll get Zac back there in the morning, everything is going to be fine, okay?'

'Hmm,' Sally says, retreating a little. 'And that's all the loose ends?'

'Yep,' I say, sounding as confident as I can. 'Honestly, it's all under control.'

'It does sound like it's all in order,' Rachael chips in. 'Where's Kat? At the bottom of the loch?'

'No,' I say with a laugh. 'She's fine, she's been great. She's really helped me.'

'We're supposed to be your best friends,' Lindsey pipes up, like a kid who just caught her dad putting her Christmas presents under the tree while he's munching the mince pie she'd left out.

I purse my lips. Is now really the time?

'Are you?' I ask, so I guess now is the time. 'We never have fun nights out, not like we used to, and you never invite me to hang out with you any more.'

'Only when it's couples stuff,' Rachael insists.

'But it's always couples stuff,' I remind her. 'You leave me out all the time.'

'You know what it's like when you're mar...' Sally's voice tapers off.

She was going to say married, wasn't she?

'I don't think that's fair,' Zac replies. 'I know what you're thinking: what do I know? We hardly know each other any more, but when Pops and I were married, it was still the five of us, all the time. *We* were best friends.'

'We've grown up,' Rachael tells him.

'Why?' he replies. 'Surely you still have time for your friends? Surely you can still hang out and have fun without it being a his 'n' hers event?'

'Well, we've got some wine,' Rachael says. 'Now we know you've got everything under control, we could have a few glasses together? If we're all stuck in here anyway.'

'I've got a better idea,' Zac says as he scootches to the edge of his seat. 'There's a club night in the party barn. Let's go.'

'A club night?' Sally says in disbelief. 'We're married ladies. We're too old for a club.'

'You're just proving Poppy's point,' he says

smugly. 'Plus, I didn't get a stag do, so we'll say this is it. You guys are my oldest friends, after all.'

'It might be fun to let our hair down?' Lindsey says hopefully. She was always the first to crack. 'When was the last time we had a night out, without the boys?'

'I suppose this might be our last chance,' Rachael chimes in.

Usually, if you can get two of them on board, you can get all three.

'Okay, fine, fine,' Sally concedes. 'It's a good job I brought some nice clothes.'

She sounds like she's giving in, but I can see that little glimmer of excitement in her eyes.

'I might have something you can borrow,' she tells me. 'You can't go out like that.'

Sally giveth and Sally taketh away. I don't even care because, for one night only, and the last time ever, the old gang is back together. Let's have some fun!

37

'I'm going to say something, something that I don't usually say, and then I'm never going to say it again, okay?'

Sally slurs her words, confirming just how drunk she is, and it's a level of drunk I haven't seen her since... probably before I got married.

'Okay,' I say. 'What?'

We're in the party barn which, honestly, is actually a lot of fun. I was a bit nervous when we got here and they said it was an eighties-themed party but the music is great, the atmosphere is spot-on and the cocktails are *amazing*. We've all certainly had a fair few.

'This night out was a really, reeeeally good idea,' she says. 'You were right, about us not having as much fun as we used to. That's the bit I won't say again. You. Were. Right.'

'I appreciate you saying that,' I tell her.

'I appreciate that Zac is queuing at the bar for my drink because I can't stand,' she cackles.

She can stand. Kind of. Just not very still for very long.

'I appreciate you as well,' she tells me. 'I'm starting to think you might be right.'

'You just said that,' I tell her.

I notice, over her shoulder, that Rachael and Lindsey are low-key dirty dancing, in the centre of the dancefloor, to Survivor's 'Eye of the Tiger', which is a bizarre sight, but it wouldn't have been ten years ago.

Sally slaps me hard on the arm. Ow! She never did know her own strength when she's had a few.

'Not that,' she insists angrily. 'Something else. You're right about us being boring now, and leaving you out, but you had it right, you're the one who knows things and stuff.'

I'm not quite following everything she's saying but I get what she means.

'I didn't say you were boring,' I tell her. I thought it, but I never said it.

'Are we boring, though?' she asks.

'Kind of,' I admit.

She slaps me again.

'See, you're right. We left you out and that's on us, but we're going to do better, we just talked about it in the loo, okay?'

'Okay,' I say with a laugh.

We'll see if sober Sally agrees. We are having a pretty amazing time, though. Honestly, it doesn't feel like a day has passed since the four of us were doing this every week. And, best of all, not one of them has mentioned any of their husbands once.

'While we're being honest,' she says, leaning in. Oof, I can smell the Cosmopolitans on her from here. 'Zac still loves you.'

I'm taken aback. I wasn't expecting her to say that.

'What?' I reply.

She snorts.

'Don't give me that fake coy rubbish. We're too

drunk for that. He still loves you. And, mots wore…' I think she means what's more, '…you still love him too. You love each other. I catch him staring at you and when I don't catch him staring at you, guess what? You're staring at him. And you're still so clearly perfect for each other. If we're being honest, you should never have broken up.'

'You know why we broke up,' I remind her.

'I do,' she says. 'But you shouldn't have.'

'You didn't tell me that at the time.'

'No one was telling you anything at the time, were they?' she says, implying I wasn't interested in listening to what anyone else thought. 'But you should have stuck together, got through it together.'

'Thank you, Jerry Springer,' I reply with a roll of my eyes.

'Ah don't give me that,' she slurs. 'You know it's true. Zac is… perfect, hello, thank you.'

I realise he's standing next to us, holding our drinks, but I don't think he heard much else.

'Here you go,' he says.

He carefully hands Sally her drink but, as she takes it, she spills a third of it.

'This is a bit stingy, isn't it?' she says, noticing how not full it is. 'I'm taking this back. Excuse me.'

I don't know if she's doing this to leave the two of us alone together or if she genuinely didn't realise it was her who spilled her drink.

'I thought you said that these three weren't any fun any more?' Zac says, sitting down next to me.

'They're not,' I reply. 'At least, they weren't. We seem to be a lethal combination; we bring out the worst in them.'

'Or the best,' he says with a smile. 'It's nice to feel like old times, isn't it?'

'It is,' I admit.

'We were great, weren't we?' he says with a smile. 'I can never quite believe just how many amazing memories I have with you, this lot, your mum and dad. In fact, all of my good memories seem to have you in them somewhere.'

'Well, I'm here at your wedding, aren't I?' I point out. 'So why change the habit of a lifetime?'

He laughs for a second but then his face falls.

'I think about our wedding all the time,' he admits. 'All the time. I can't ever forget it – even when

I'm not thinking about it, something reminds me of it.'

'It was an amazing day,' I say with a smile. 'Mum used to say it was the happiest day of her life, more so than her own wedding day.'

'God, I miss your mum,' he says. 'And your dad. Does he still live in the same place?'

I nod.

'I feel like I should call in and see him sometimes,' Zac says.

I'm sure my dad would love to see Zac but that would be weird, right?

'Oh my God,' Zac blurts.

'What?' I reply.

'Listen,' he insists. 'It's "True Colours" by Cyndi Lauper. It's the song you sang at our wedding. See? I'll never be able to forget it.'

'It's a weird coincidence, I'll give you that,' I tell him.

'Will you dance with me?' he asks.

'What?'

'Dance with me,' he says. 'Come on, everyone else is dancing, look, even your friends.'

I glance over at the dance floor. Rachael and

Lindsey are dancing with each other. Sally is dancing with a man who must be in his seventies, who looks as drunk as she does.

'Come on,' Zac prompts.

'Okay, go on then,' I say, like I'm giving in, but it's not like that at all.

I would love nothing more than to just enjoy a nice, nostalgic dance with Zac, on a lovely night out, and that be that, but it's more than that for me. I miss him. I want to touch him. I want to feel his arms around me.

I follow him to the dance floor, where he wraps his arms around me. At first, I try to keep a bit of distance between us but, practically against my will, our bodies get closer together while we dance.

Zac raises his hand to move a piece of hair from my face and gives me a giant static shock. He laughs awkwardly. I do too. I know, it's just one of those things but, come on, there are literally sparks flying between us right now.

Like Sally, I hate to say it too, but she was right. Zac and I never should have separated. But there's not much I can do about it now, is there?

38

13 JUNE 2016

I am absolutely positively shattered.

I'm not complaining, the fact that I'm so tired is a sign that I'm working loads, and I'm working so much because things are really starting to pay off with Dad's company. We're no longer just a local shop selling locally made frames to local people, oh no. We're shipping frames all over the world, and sourcing new and cool materials from all over too. But as tired as I am, I am even prouder. Dad and I are absolutely crushing it.

I do look forward to getting home at the end of the day, usually craving a nice bath and a bit of Netflix on the sofa before an early night. It's nice, having a bigger house, a bigger sofa, a bigger bath, a bigger bed. It just feels so empty without Zac here.

My taxi drops me off and drives away. It's late, like 10 p.m., but I'm used to getting home late, and heading into an empty house.

Except, is it an empty house? I can see through the front door that there's a light on at the top of the stairs.

Shit, am I being burgled? Because I am way too tired to be dealing with burglars tonight. I'd probably just walk past them, get into bed and ask them to shut the door on their way out.

I go to unlock the door but it's already unlocked, so I open it quietly and peer inside. In the middle of the hallway, I spy two shoes, as though they've been kicked off and left.

Is that...

I drop my bag and close the door behind me before running upstairs.

'Hello?' I call out.

By the time I reach the landing, I see who it is. It's Zac, standing in the bedroom doorway, holding a bunch of roses.

'Hello,' he says with a smile.

'Oh my God, what are you doing here?' I ask him as I run over to him, throwing myself into his arms. 'You're supposed to be in London, working.'

'Dylan gave us all the evening off,' he says. 'I think my trial run is going really well. I told him I wanted to surprise you; he's a great guy.'

'I'm certainly surprised,' I tell him.

I genuinely am so pleased to see him, more than I have been in a long time. Things have been so difficult between us since we lost the baby.

I know some people think I'm pathetic, I can tell. They're always so heartbroken for you when they find out but then, when they hear it happened so early, their tone changes, they think you should be over it by now, that it was never really a thing to begin with.

It doesn't make any difference to me that it was early, that I didn't know if it was a boy or a girl. When you find out you're pregnant, the first thing you do is start planning for the future. Being pregnant isn't the thing, it's the baby that comes after, and that's all you think about. Sure, I'm not mourning someone I got to know or had even met, but that's not the point. It's the potential I feel robbed of. Our baby could have been anyone or anything. Sometimes, when I'm just going about my day, and I remember that it happened, I start to wonder what could have been and it makes me so sad.

Zac feels sad about it too, I know he does, but it's different for him. He doesn't seem to dwell on it like I do. He's trying to be proactive, to look to the future, but I can't help but look backwards. We argue all the time these days.

I feel so guilty. Zac wants to try again but I've had to make him promise to stop mentioning it because it just gets me so upset every time. Other people suggest trying again too, as if it's the cure, to just try again. But I'm so scared of it happening again. And I feel even more guilty when I think I can just have another, as though it cancels out the one I lost.

I'm just not over it yet. I'm trying, I really am, but I'm still finding it hard. Why did it happen to me? There are pregnant people everywhere. I see people I went to school with constantly posting baby pictures on Facebook. What is it about me? What did I do wrong?

'Obviously these are for you,' he says, handing me the flowers. 'And, if you'll just come this way...'

I follow Zac into the bedroom.

'Here's a bunch I killed earlier,' he says.

There are rose petals all over the floor, and all over the bed.

'And if you'll follow me this way...'

I'm right behind him, into the bathroom, where a strip of rose petals lead up to an amazing-looking bath that he's run for me. There are rose petals in the water, candles everywhere, it's an absolutely romantic dream. I've never seen anything like it in real life.

'Here's what's going to happen, you're going to get in this bath,' Zac starts, removing my coat before unbuttoning my blouse. 'And you're going to have a nice long soak while I make dinner.'

He unhooks my bra and lets it fall to the floor.

'Your favourite sweet and sour chicken will be ready when you are; there's a bottle of champagne chilling and then there's a stack of profiteroles that even you'll have trouble taking down.'

'What have I done to deserve this?' I ask him through a grin.

Zac drops to his knees and pulls my skirt down. Then my knickers. Then he places one long, lingering kiss on my hip.

Zac and I never used to be able to keep our hands off one another until you know what, and then sex became this strange, awkward thing; something that I feared. I can't blame Zac, because he would try, but I would feel so uncomfortable and then so guilty, and then I would start crying and no one wants to shag a crying girl, do they?

Tonight, though, tonight feels different. It's unexpected, purposeful but not forced. For the first time in a long time, I feel excited.

Zac takes me by the hand and helps me into the bath. As the warm silky water covers my body, I can't help but moan. I feel like I'm being transported back to before – God, for once, I don't even want to think about it. Zac places a hand under the water and strokes my tummy and it feels like all the tension between us is just washing away.

'Aren't you going to get in with me?' I ask him, biting my lip, just to make sure I'm being crystal clear about what I want.

'Nope,' he tells me with a cheeky smile. 'You're

going to relax. Totally relax. Then we're going to eat dinner – even if it's only because I made it from scratch, so someone is eating it – and then, and only then, am I going to throw you over my shoulder, carry you back up these stairs, throw you down on the bed...'

'Ugh, dinner is going to be torture,' I tell him. 'But it all sounds gorgeous, so I guess we'll find it under expert level foreplay.'

'Sounds good to me,' he says, his hand moving down my body a little, teasing me. 'And, who knows, maybe if the night is going well, and you fancy it, perhaps we could finally think about trying again?'

I smile and wiggle under his hand until... wait...

'Try again?' I say, curiously.

'Yeah, try again, for a baby,' he clarifies. 'I was wondering if it maybe might be—'

I quickly sit up.

'Get off me,' I tell him.

'Pops, come on, it was just a suggestion,' he says quickly, trying to calm me with his hands.

'That's what all this is?' I say. 'Some kind of weird mating ritual?'

'Look, forget I said anything,' he says. 'Don't let it ruin a good night.'

'Except it already has,' I tell him. 'I'm sick of telling you, I can't do it again, I don't know if I will be able to do it again and the one thing, *the one thing*, I keep saying is to please stop asking. You can't even do that.'

'It was misjudged,' he says. 'I'm sorry. I won't ask again, okay?'

'Can you pass me a towel, please?' I say softly.

Zac does as he's asked.

'I'm sorry, Pops,' he says again. 'I really won't mention it again.'

'Except you said that last time,' I remind him.

'What do you want me to say?' he asks, his tone shifting into something harsher. I can see that he's frustrated. I get it, it makes sense, all he wants is to give it another go and all I want to do is go back in time, to before the first time...

'I think we need to take a break,' I say.

'Well, obviously I'm not going to say that,' he replies, thinking I'm answering his question.

I don't want to be away from Zac, of course I

don't, but right now all he wants is a baby and I can't give that to him. Perhaps, if we spend a little time apart, we'll realise what's important.

'No, I'm saying it,' I tell him. 'I think we need to separate.'

39

First it was Lindsey because her feet were aching. Rachael was the next one to drop out because she was knackered from the long drive here. Finally, Sally called it a night and then it was just me and Zac. It's funny, whenever we used to go on nights out, this is the exact order we used to grow tired of partying in. Zac and I have always been quite well matched.

It turns out that, as pre-drinks go, smashing shots of aged malt whisky isn't the one, because I feel really drunk. Zac is the same, though – see, perfectly matched. At this stage, staggering back to the cabin, I'm not sure which one of us is holding the other up.

I think we're leaning into one another, creating perfect balance between us. Thankfully, the snow has stopped falling and the path has been cleared so we don't have that to contend with.

It takes me a few seconds of messing with the keys to get the door open. When I finally manage it, I stumble through the doorway. Zac somehow has his wits about him just enough to reach out and grab me by the belt of my coat, stopping me from face-planting the floor. He starts laughing. Then I start. Then I remember that the girls are probably asleep, so I place one hand over his mouth while I bring my other hand's index finger to my lips to shush him. I look into his eyes until the sparkle dies down a little, showing me that he's calm and that he's going to be quiet.

'Get to bed,' I whisper. 'You're getting married tomorrow.'

'Can I talk to you?' he whispers back.

'What?' I reply.

'I need to talk to you,' he says.

'Let's go to my room,' I reply. 'The girls will be mad if we wake them.'

I take Zac by the hand and lead him to my bedroom – something I've done a thousand times after a night out, but never just to talk.

I open the door quietly and close it behind us carefully. The last thing I need is another inter-friendtion.

I plonk myself down at the top of the bed, resting my back on the wooden headboard.

'What's wrong?' I ask him.

Zac sits down next to me.

'I think I'm making a big mistake marrying Lilac,' he says.

The second the words have left his lips, he puffs air from his cheeks, so much air it must make him instantly lighter.

'What?' I reply. 'Don't be daft. You're marrying her in like twelve hours.'

'I'm serious,' he replies.

'Look, this is partially on me, I've turned up here out of the blue, dumped a ton of crap on you, I've distracted you, and now I've given you a taste of your old life – when we were all young and fun – but it's not like that any more. We've all grown up.'

I don't know what else to say.

'It's not you,' he insists. 'I've been worrying about

it for a while, not knowing what to do. It's just... it's not right. It's not easy, not like we were.'

'We weren't easy,' I remind him.

'We were until we weren't,' he says. I know what he means. 'We were perfect. Remember when you told me you were pregnant, and you freaked out, because you were scared, and you were worried we wouldn't be good parents?'

I nod.

'I remember telling you we'd be just fine, because you were just like your own amazing mum, and that any kid would be so lucky to have you because you were the kindest, sweetest, most amazing person I'd ever met,' he continues. 'And that night, when we had that long talk, I saw something change in you. Your eyes looked different, your smile changed – you even sounded different. All of a sudden, you wanted to be a mum and I couldn't wait to have a family with you. Then, when your miscarriage happened, I saw those lights go off again, and it switched a few others off at the same time. I just wanted to give you that feeling back and I'm sorry. I didn't do the right things at the right time. Of course, you needed all the time you needed, and I see that now.'

I feel my eyes welling up. I wasn't expecting this tonight.

'I felt like we'd planned our future, in those weeks, because all we would talk about was life when the baby arrived and then, when it didn't, it felt like we lost that life we'd planned too. I appreciate you saying all this now, I really do, but it doesn't change what you have with Lilac,' I remind him.

'What I have with Lilac,' he says to himself. 'Things between me and Lilac are not good. Six months ago, I found out she cheated on me, just after we moved in together.'

Oh my God, he knows! He knows and he's still marrying her.

'When I found out, she said it meant nothing, that he'd confessed his love for her because she'd got serious with someone else – with me. I didn't want to bail just because things were difficult, so I stayed and we chatted and eventually she proposed. She said she wanted to show me how serious she was about us and it felt like a good idea at the time, but things aren't great. Every day I see sides of her that I don't like. She seems meaner or more selfish than she used to, and I wonder if I turned a blind eye to it before, but now, now that we're talking about spending the rest of our lives together, these things matter. I don't want to get this wrong again. And she takes it all out on me. She's terrified I'm going to cheat on her to even the score. She keeps tabs on me, checks my phone – she's the reason I didn't get to have a stag do, I wasn't allowed.'

Zac leans forward and places his head in his hands.

'And I'm not right for her either, I know I'm not; she's always trying to change me, telling me how to dress, how I should look – insisting on calling me bloody Zachary, which I hate, because it's not my name.'

God, I just want to hug him. He doesn't sound happy at all.

'I'm sorry things aren't great,' I tell him. 'And I'm sorry if me turning up has rattled you and dragged up old anxieties.'

'I was going to tell you not to worry, that none of this is your fault, but I'd be lying if I said you being here hadn't at least reminded me that once upon a time I had real love. Is it really worth getting married for less?'

Seeing Zac this upset reminds me of, well, the first time we got divorced. I know how he feels. It's that inner turmoil. Am I making the right decision? Am I bailing because things are difficult or because it's what I want?

'I've missed you,' he tells me. 'All these years, I've never stopped thinking about you. That's not right, is it? To never get over someone?'

I sigh. I know exactly what he means because I feel it too.

'I'm the same,' I confess. 'The problem is that we didn't break up because we stopped loving each other. Usually, at least one person wants the relationship to end. We were just too sad. Too messed up. Both so wrapped up in grief with no idea what to do for the best. We didn't break up, we just broke away.'

'No one has ever come close compared to you, or the feelings I had for you – the feelings I still have for you, Pops. I've been kidding myself, thinking I could find that with someone else.'

I turn to Zac, hoping the right words will find my lips, but instead it seems like Zac is going to find them first. Our faces hover no more than thirty centimetres apart. As much as I want him to kiss me, I know that we can't.

'Do you want to watch TV?' I ask him. 'We shouldn't be having this conversation when we're drunk.'

'Okay, sure,' he says. 'But my mind is made up. Lilac and I aren't right for each other. I'm going to have to tell her tomorrow it's over.'

40

Remembering whisky expert Robert Vass telling us not to drink the 68 per cent alcohol whisky, I'm starting to wonder if I might have ignored him and drank it anyway. Either because this is one of the worst hangovers I've ever had in my life, or because I died and now, I'm trapped in my own personal hell.

I've just woken up, lying on my bed with Zac, where we must have fallen asleep watching TV, except at some point I've rolled over and rested my head on his shoulder. I've only been awake a matter of seconds, but I feel frozen in time. I know that I need to move but I don't want to wake him up. I don't want him to know that I've snuggled up to him in my sleep – or he might even think I've done so consciously, which looks even worse.

What I need to do is slowly lift my head and pull away from him but, just like old times, it feels like he draws me in, like I feed off something – whatever it is about him that has always made me feel so comforted. I don't want to move, but I know that I have to.

I slowly lift my head a centimetre or two, just enough to break contact, and I'm about to pull away when Sally hurries in through the bedroom door. When she clocks us on the bed together, she frowns.

'Nothing happened,' I insist quickly as I sit up.

Zac wakes up. He looks disorientated for a few seconds before all the pieces of the puzzle slowly start falling into place for him.

'Shit, did we fall asleep?' Zac says. 'Shit! What time is it?'

'You've got bigger problems than that,' Sally tells us. 'There's an American man called Farrell here. He says he's come to, quote, "save the day".'

'Oh, God,' I blurt. 'Honestly, this looks worse than it is, I'll explain later, but everything is fine. Just distract him.'

'I already told him Zac is in the bathroom,' she says. 'So, hurry up.'

Sally closes the door behind her.

'Right, we need to get you to your wedding,' I tell him.

'Pops, I meant what I said last night, this marriage is a mistake,' he says firmly. 'She cheated on me, she's possessive, she isn't nice to you or Nanny May even though, as far as she's concerned, you're my only family. Everything has just come to a head this week. And since you've turned up, knowing that I've never stopped loving you, if there's a chance for us…'

'Let me stop you there,' I say. 'There's no way I'm letting you do this for me. Not a chance. If you're not happy, then do something about it, but not for me.'

I love him. Always have, always will. But me turning up here was not about stopping his wedding and ruining his relationship so I could have him back. If he wants to walk away from this, he has to do it himself, for his own reasons.

'Believe me, Pops, this isn't just for you, okay? I've had cold feet for a while,' he insists. 'Things have kind of gotten out of hand, I've been too scared to say or do anything – Sonny will literally punch me like I'm a train or a Kraken or whatever ridiculous thing he always seems to defeat with one big punch in his movies. I've been trying to get out of this for a while.'

'Oh, really?' I say in disbelief as I hurry what few things I have in this room together.

'Yes,' he insists. 'Really.'

I head into the bathroom to use the loo and wash my face quickly, although I get the feeling that whatever is plastered all over my face this morning isn't going to shift with a bit of tap water.

'I've been sabotaging the wedding, Pops,' he says through the door.

I flush the loo, wash my hands and open the door.

'What?'

'I've been doing little things to throw the wedding off slightly, to buy myself some time, to work out how to get myself out of this – I started doing it before you arrived, it's nothing to do with you. I've been trying to stop things for months but bloody Sonny and his bloody movie... He's been rushing everything, making all the plans – doing things for the wedding but only because they'll be good for his film. I haven't known how to stop it.'

I think Zac is telling me this to show me that it isn't in fact because of me that he wants to call off his wedding, that he was building up the courage to do it anyway, but that's not what I take from it.

'You've been messing with the wedding stuff?' I say, because I can't believe my ears.

'Yes,' he says. 'So, believe me, this isn't because of you.'

My heart drops. Zac has been doing all these things. Cancelling the cake, hiding the rings, destroying Lilac's dress. I think it's the last one that upsets me the most. I don't like the girl and she definitely doesn't deserve him, but to soak her wedding dress in a red liquid is just cruel and unnecessary.

'I thought you'd grown up,' I tell him. 'You're still that immature twenty-four-year-old I married – and divorced – who couldn't cope with things so he sabotaged them.'

I grab my things and head for the door.

'Pops, wait,' he says.

'No,' I reply. 'Let me make this clear: I want

nothing to do with you. So why don't you just marry Lilac today? If you ask me, you two deserve each other. You're just having cold feet, Zac. Just grow up and get on with it.'

I walk through the door, closing it behind me.

'Well, good morning, gorgeous,' Farrell says.

'Good morning to you too,' I reply with a smile. 'How did you get here?'

'Zac told Lilac you were here,' he says. 'All the roads are still closed and the motorboats are out of action. I rowed here and I'm going to row you back.'

If all the roads are still closed, and my things (including Kat) are back at the castle, then I have no choice but to go back there.

'You rowed here?' Lindsey blurts.

The girls are all sitting on the sofas.

'Yeah,' he replies. 'It's no biggie. Plenty of room, if you guys are coming too?'

'You should all come,' I tell them. I turn back to Farrell. 'They're old friends of the family. I think it will do us all good, to see Zac tie the knot.'

'We did only book here for the one night,' Sally says. 'The wedding is as good a place as any to wait for the roads to open.'

'Awesome,' Farrell says. 'The more the merrier.'

'Farrell, can you help me get the cake out of the fridge, please? While we wait for Zac to finish up in the bathroom. Must be pre-wedding nerves.'

I say all this loudly, so Zac knows it's his chance to sneak out.

'Okay, sure,' he says as he follows me to the fridge. 'You know, we haven't talked about the kiss we shared the other night. I've never kissed a secret agent before.'

'Let me stop you there,' I say. 'Before you say another word, I need to be honest with you. Kat made that up, about me working for MI6. I actually run the family framing company. She lied because most people think it's boring, but it's a really successful company, and I'm really proud of it.'

I smile. For the first time that felt really good to say.

'Wait, you're not a secret agent?' he says.

Wow, he clearly isn't either, if he didn't get that.

'Nope,' I say. 'And I'm sorry for going along with it but, like you said before you kissed me, I shouldn't let my baggage define me. Anyway, I just wanted to be honest with you.'

'I feel so violated right now,' he says. 'I thought you were cool and interesting, that you might be a worthy match for me, but you're telling me you make boxes?'

'Frames,' I correct him. 'Fucking sick frames.'

'I'm going to be honest with you, because you seem nice enough,' he starts. 'I only really kissed you to make someone jealous and now it seems like maybe they're not interested in me any more, so… yeah. We should stay friends, though, yeah?'

Why do I feel like I've just been dumped by the man who shagged my ex-husband's fiancée?

41

After one hell of an awkward boat trip back over to the island I, unfortunately, have no choice but to attend the wedding of my ex-husband. With no way out of Tarness until the snow is cleared later, and checkout from the cabin being at eleven, there's nowhere else for me or my friends to go, so here we are, at the wedding, with only minutes to spare.

Sonny grabbed Zac the second he walked through the door, to get him suited and booted, while the rest of us, in the smartest clothes we could get together between us, were ushered into the ceremony room.

Kat is sitting at the front, on the groom's side,

with Nanny May on her right and a space for me on her left. When she spots Sally, Rachael and Lindsey in tow, her face falls. The girls sit at the back while I head for my seat at the front.

I take in the ceremony room as I make my way down the aisle. It's a cold, dark room, just like the rest of the castle, with red and black flowers everywhere. It's so dreary and depressing, not like a wedding at all. It's the sort of non-traditional thing you see on Instagram, which makes sense, given that it's Lilac's job, but it doesn't exactly fill you with romance. Then again, maybe I'm immune today.

'What are that lot doing here?' Kat asks me as I take my seat.

'Oh, they came up to throw me an interfriendtion,' I say, like it's the most normal thing in the world. 'But we ended up going on a night out, just like old times, and it was actually a lot of fun. They've said they're going to do more to include me again and I made sure that Rachael knows how wonderful you are. She's going to make more of an effort with you – she'll have to, if she wants to be my friend too.'

'Whatever,' Kat says with a shrug, but I notice the

corners of her mouth turn up slightly. I think she's enjoying having a friend just as much as I am. 'So, did you sort everything out?'

I notice Sonny and Farrell escorting Zac to the altar, one either side of him, and I know they're not forcing him but I can almost appreciate what he said about feeling like he's being ushered through the motions. He looks terrified. He's fidgeting on the spot. I stare at him, hoping to catch his attention, because suddenly low-key yelling at him and telling him to just do it makes me feel like part of the problem. What Zac needs is a friend, someone to talk to, but I was so caught up in not wanting to be the person who ruined a marriage that I left him to it.

'Here Comes the Bride' starts playing and the muscles in Zac's face tighten so much he doesn't look like himself any more.

'We sent the papers,' I tell her. 'But, as far as sorting everything out goes, I feel like I've maybe made things worse.'

Zac looks so good in his suit. It fits him perfectly – I'll bet it was expensive. When he married me, he wore trainers and he ditched his tie the second the ceremony finished, but neither of us cared. And

Lilac, wow, she looks stunning. Even soaked in blood, that dress would still look incredible, never mind the fact she always looks like there's a filter on her flawless skin. They make one hell of an attractive couple, it's almost a shame they're a total mess.

Lilac walks down the aisle with Sonny and takes her place next to Zac. Zac looks at her, unable to hide the terror in his eyes. I can just about make out her narrowing her eyes at him before taking his hand.

'Please be seated,' the wedding official says.

Wow, I hadn't even realised I'd stood up with everyone else, to be honest, it's one of those things you just do on autopilot. In my defence, I'm pretty distracted.

The wedding official cracks straight on.

'Good afternoon, ladies and gentlemen. Let me begin by welcoming you all here today to the snowy but stunning Castle Tarness for the marriage of Zac and Lilac. Today marks a new beginning in their lives together and it means a lot to both of them that you, their family and friends, are here to witness their wedding vows and celebrate their marriage with them.'

The room is silent, of course it is, but the tension in the air is so thick I can't breathe. I can see how uncomfortable Zac is, like he's just picking his moment, waiting until he can find the words he needs to say.

'Now, for the Ts and Cs,' the official continues. 'One of my duties is to inform you all that this room in which we are all gathered today has been duly sanctioned according to law for the celebration of marriages. You are here to witness the joining in marriage of Zac Hunt and Lilac Strong. Finally, you all know how this bit goes, if any person present—'

'Yeah, no, okay, I do,' Zac blurts.

Oh, bloody hell. He didn't even let the guy get to the 'speak now' bit, which is where you usually expect an interruption, well, that's what movies have taught me, at least.

'Erm, what?' Sonny says.

God, you can see the anger building up inside him. Not even a beat for a little bit of context – Sonny Strong is about to go full Jack McVey.

'I'm really sorry, Lilac, I can't marry you,' Zac tells her. 'I've been trying to get to you, to talk to you, since I got back this morning, but Sonny and Farrell just rushed me into my suit and up to this altar. I'm so sorry, I just can't do this.'

'Of course you can,' Sonny insists firmly. 'Crack on.'

Zac holds Lilac's hands and looks into her eyes as he speaks. I can tell he feels awful that it's taken him so long to pluck up the courage to say the words, but he's got to say this.

'I can't marry you because I'm already married to someone else,' he says.

Well, he didn't have to say that!

Lilac drops his hands.

'To who?' she asks.

'To her,' Zac says, pointing me out. 'And I'm still in love with her.'

Okay, he definitely didn't have to say that bit! All eyes are briefly on me before they're back to Zac.

'What the fuck?' Sonny shouts. 'Your cousin? You're married to your cousin? You're in love *with your cousin*? I should punch a hole through you!'

Wow, that really is his thing.

'Everyone out of the room,' Sonny demands. He turns to me and points. 'Not you, though. You stay.'

Sonny Strong is genuinely terrifying. I'm not surprised Zac was too scared to back out of the wedding. He's not going to punch a hole through me, is he? *Is he*?

Zac exhales deeply and runs a hand through his hair. Everyone has vacated the room apart from me (I wouldn't dare!), Zac, Lilac, Sonny, Cherry and even Farrell has hung back.

'Okay, confession time, obviously she's not my cousin,' Zac says. 'We got married when we were twenty-four.'

'What? So, why pretend she's your cousin?' Lilac asks. 'And why invite your wife to our wedding? Why would you even agree to marry me if you were already married?'

'He didn't invite me,' I say, starting up sort of quietly, finding my voice as I go along. 'And he didn't even know that we were still married – we did get divorced, six years ago, but due to a, erm, clerical error, it was never finalised. I only found this out days before I turned up. It was never my intention for any of this to happen. The idea was I would get him to sign the papers and be on my way, leaving you two free to get married. Zac only lied because he didn't want to upset you.'

Lilac doesn't look impressed with this explanation. In fact, she looks even more confused.

'But he said he was still married to you – so why didn't you sign them?' she asks.

'No, no, we did,' I insist. 'We signed them and sent them.'

'Actually, that's not strictly true,' Zac says. 'I couldn't do it, Pops.'

'I saw you sign them,' I tell him. 'And I saw them being sent – Dad said he received them.'

'I signed a fake name,' he confessed.

Oh, boy.

'You come to my daughter's wedding,' Sonny starts as he approaches me, with a *Godfather* meets *Snatch* vibe. 'And you convince her fiancé not to marry her?'

'It wasn't like that at all.' I turn to Zac. 'Tell them. Tell them how I insisted you weren't to call your wedding off for me. You said it was the whole Farrell thing that was the real reason, nothing to do with me, didn't you?'

Farrell's ears prick up at the mention of his name.

'What?' Lilac chimes, her voice wobbling.

'He told me that, even though he forgave you for

the whole Farrell thing, that it was the main reason he didn't think he could marry you,' I say.

I know this is none of my business, but I need to save my own skin here. I'm not going to be the person taking the fall for this mess. This lot were screwed up long before I got here.

'The Farrell thing?' Zac repeats back to me.

'The affair or the one-night stand or whatever you want to call it,' I say quietly. Suddenly I feel bad having this conversation in front of Lilac's parents, but this is the final showdown of this 'movie', clearly.

Zac turns to Lilac and his expression morphs into something much angrier.

'You told me it was someone you worked with,' he says to her. 'It was him that you slept with?'

As Zac points angrily at Farrell, it's Sonny who sees red.

'That's it, I'm punching someone,' he says.

'Sonny, no,' Cherry says, like she's talking to a disobedient dog. 'Sonny, stop.'

'You slept with my daughter?' Sonny says as he approaches Farrell. 'We treat you like you're a part of this family – you're like the son I never had.'

'I'm out of here,' Zac says, heading for the door.

'Sonny, no,' Cherry tries again but it's too late.

Sonny lunges at Farrell who obviously, being a stunt man, is more than used to combat like this. Farrell ducks out of the way, causing Sonny to plough his clenched fist into a stone pillar. His punch sends the pillar flying across the room, which makes me flinch, because I'm expecting the castle ceiling to come down on us – maybe he does have super human strength and it wasn't so weird, when he punched that train! Except it becomes immediately evident that the pillar is a movie prop, but the solid wooden bench that Sonny winds up hitting his fist on, on his way to the floor, is not.

'Fucking movie props,' Sonny rants. 'It's costing me a fortune, things getting destroyed, the bloody dress going missing.'

Cherry runs over to comfort him.

'The bloody dress?' Lilac says.

'The dress for the movie,' he says. 'We needed a blood-soaked one for the bride, so I just ordered two of yours... had someone soak one in blood.'

'Ohhh,' she says. 'I thought someone had ruined my dress – I bought another one.'

'Another dress?' he says angrily. 'A third dress?'

'Hardly the issue, Dad,' she replies.

'You're never seeing that boy again,' Sonny blurts.

'Which one?' Lilac asks.

'Both of them,' Sonny replies as he cradles his hand to his chest.

'But… I love him,' Lilac says.

'Which one?' Sonny asks.

Jesus Christ, it's like a bad episode of *Jerry Springer*.

Lilac looks at Farrell, then back at her dad, then she turns around and runs.

'What a fucking mess,' Sonny rants to himself. 'What an absolute shit show.'

Farrell skulks off in the other direction, lest he actually gets smacked – I'd kind of like to smack him myself, to be honest, but I'd only hurt my hand.

I make my way to the back of the room and through the doors. Kat, Sally, Rachael and Lindsey are waiting there.

'Is everything okay?' Sally is the first to ask.

'Yes, I just need to talk to someone,' I tell them. 'I'll be back.'

'Zac?' Kat calls after me.

'No, Lilac,' I call back.

42

It doesn't take me long to find Lilac in her room, sitting on her bed, sobbing, clutching a pink and orange glass vase.

'Can we talk?' I ask softly.

She just nods.

I sit down on the sofa opposite the bed, rather than sitting down next to her, just because I've seen what her family do with their fists.

'Lilac, I promise you, I only came here with the best intentions,' I tell her. 'I found out we were still married, learned that Zac was marrying you soon, and rushed here to get him to sign the papers – and did. Well, I thought we both had, until just now.'

'It's not your fault,' she tells me. 'Or Zachary's. It's all my fault.'

Lilac pours the contents of the glass vase on the bed next to her: two rings.

'Are those the rings that went missing?' I ask.

She nods, pursing her lips to hold back the tears.

'I didn't want to go through with it either,' she says. 'I love Farrell. I have since the day I met him but... well, he's like a brother to me. I knew Dad would flip. After Farrell and I slept together, I panicked, and I proposed to Zachary to try and fix things between us, but I think they've been over for a long time. I just got so swept up in the wedding, and doing the right thing, and... I don't know.'

'Listen, if you love Farrell, and he loves you too, and you're good for each other, then it doesn't matter what your dad thinks,' I tell her. 'He says Farrell is like family, like a son to him. Well, if the two of you ever got married, then Farrell would be Sonny's son, of sorts, so maybe remind him of that fact.'

Lilac sniffs.

'That's a good idea,' she says. 'You're actually much smarter than you seem but I guess that will be your job, right?'

'I'm not a secret agent,' I tell her. 'I sell picture frames.'

'That's really boring,' she laughs through her tears.

'It's been said before,' I say with a smile.

'I should go find Farrell, shouldn't I?' she says. 'Tell him how I feel?'

'Absolutely,' I say.

'And, I guess, better to love someone who is like a brother to you than marry your cousin, right?'

'That's too many jokes,' I tell her with a laugh. 'Come here.'

I give Lilac a big hug.

'It's been lovely to meet you,' I tell her. 'I'm sorry for causing trouble.'

'I think it may all have been for the best,' she replies. 'You should tell Zac how you feel, you know. If you still feel something.'

I just smile at her before I leave.

Out in the hallway, in the family wing, I bump into Zac.

'Well, that went well,' I say sarcastically.

'Yeah, it's not my favourite wedding,' he replies.

'Want to come up to my turret for a chat, before Sonny punches me off the island?' I ask.

He laughs.

'Sounds good.'

As we approach the spiral staircase, we catch Kat coming down it.

'There you are,' she says. 'They've got one of the boats started. We should get out of here while we can.'

'Absolutely,' I say. 'Reckon you can hold them off for ten minutes?'

'Oh, yeah, of course,' she says with a jokey sarcasm as she walks off. 'I'll show them a boob or something.'

'She might be my favourite cousin,' he says as he follows me up the stairs.

'Mine too,' I reply.

Zac and I sit down, me on the bed, Zac on the desk chair.

'Lilac and Farrell,' he says. 'I never saw that one coming.'

'Are you upset?' I ask.

'I feel stupid, more than anything,' he says. 'I can't believe he acted like he was my friend – I let

Sonny talk me into having him as my best man. You're looking at me like you want to say "I told you so".'

'I did tell you to sort things out before the wedding,' I say, not quite saying I told you so, but heavily implying it.

'Yeah, well, I didn't get chance,' he replies. 'But it sounds like we were both thinking the same thing – me and Lilac, that is. I don't know if you're thinking the same thing as I am.'

'I'm wondering why you didn't sign the papers,' I say.

'Because I love you,' he replies. 'Because I didn't want to break up the first time, because I've never been happy since, and because you turning up here felt like someone was giving me a second chance.'

'I love you too,' I tell him. 'But – and I can't believe I'm saying this – I do want that divorce.'

Zac looks deflated.

'First of all, I owe you an apology, because when you said you were trying to stall the wedding – which is turns out Lilac was doing too – I wrongly assumed you'd done things that were way worse than you had, like ruining Lilac's dress.'

'I would never do that,' he insists. 'She loves that dress. I'm certain she'll keep wearing it.'

'It turns out she thought the movie prop dress was hers,' I tell him. 'But, even though you didn't, I don't want to get you back by ruining your wedding and stealing you – even if you two were headed for a break-up anyway, you know?'

'I get what you're saying,' he replies. 'But doesn't everything happen for a reason?'

'Maybe,' I say. 'But if I'm going to get a happy ever after with you, it isn't going to start like this.'

'So, what happens now?' he says.

'I'm going to go find my friends, I'm going to get on that boat, and I'm going to go home,' I tell him. 'You're going to write your phone number and email address on that notepaper behind you, and I am going to send you divorce papers, which you're going to sign properly, okay?'

Zac just nods before turning around on his chair and doing exactly as he's told. He folds the piece of paper in half and hands it to me. As I take it from him, he grabs my hand, pulls me close and kisses me.

Of all the kisses I've had since Zac and I split – which, admittedly, has not been many – the second his lips touch mine, as corny as it sounds, it feels like my heart starts beating again. Like mouth-to-mouth resuscitation. He's the cure for every horrible feeling I've been left with since we lost our chance to become parents, since we broke up. His lips on mine and his hands on my body make me feel like I'm home again, or at least shows me how to get there. When he finally lets me go, it's like removing part of a circuit. The light goes out again.

'Are you sure?' he asks me.

'I am,' I tell him. 'Not now, not like this.'

'Well, I guess I'll see you around then, Pops.'

'See you around, Zachary,' I say, lightening the mood a little with his fancy fake name.

I tuck the piece of paper in my purse, grab my bag and leave. I get halfway down the spiral staircase and stop in my tracks. Am I really doing the right thing here? The man of my dreams is a matter of feet away from me, he wants me back, and I'm leaving?

I carry on down the stairs, deciding to go with my instincts, heading for the boat and not looking back.

43

'It's fucking freezing,' Kat blurts.

'Well, we are in Scotland, and it is January, and there was a blizzard yesterday,' Rachael tells her politely. I can tell she's doing her best to put up with her, even though she doesn't like her, but that's just because she doesn't know her. The two of them are family, they should be friends.

We're currently standing in the car park, as in, the only car park in Tarness, saying goodbye for now.

'Anyone can tell he's still madly in love with you,' Sally tells me.

I filled her in on pretty much everything on the boat ride back to the mainland.

'I love him too,' I tell her. 'But no one wants to start – or, I guess, restart – a marriage like this. To be honest, it would be crazy to just get back together after all this time. I feel like we need to get to know each other again, start from scratch, if we stand a chance.'

'Wow, maybe you have grown up,' Sally says. 'Just keep that super fun, immature side of you, please? Because, honestly, last night was the most fun I've had for years.'

'Your wedding wasn't that long ago,' I remind her with a smile.

'Don't tell my husband,' she says, kissing my cheek. 'See you back home.'

'Yeah, see you there,' I say. 'We'd better get going, while the roads are open.'

I turn to Lindsey and Rachael and hug them too.

'Last night was a top night,' Lindsey says. 'Just like the good old days.'

'I'm starting to feel like I missed out on something,' Kat says, pulling a face.

'Well, you can come on the next one,' Rachael tells her. 'Because girls' night is going to be a regular thing.'

We all hug and say our goodbyes; Sally, Rachael and Lindsey getting in Sally's car, and I'm travelling back with Kat.

As I load my bags into her boot, I spy the envelope with the divorce papers poking out. I take them out, curious to see what he wrote.

I flick to the signature and the name to see that's he's written the date as our wedding anniversary, and the name he's signed? David Cassidy.

Mum would have loved this.

* * *

The first thing I notice, when Kat drops me outside my dad's house, is the baby blue Ford KA parked on the driveway. That is not my dad's car.

I walk up to the door when it hits me. Shit. It must be his new lady's car.

I begin to turn around when I hear my dad's voice.

'Come in, the door is over. Open.'

'Erm,' I say, mostly to myself.

'Sorry, I mean, come in, the door is open. Over.'

The blue ring of a smart doorbell, which wasn't there before, catches my eye.

'Wow, you're in the twenty-first century now, Dad,' I say. 'You'll have a robot vac next.'

'You can get robot vacs?' I hear him say to the person next to him.

I feel so awkward, knowing they can both see me, but I can't see them.

'Poppy, come in,' Dad tells me. 'I'll put the kettle on.'

I take a deep breath and open the door. I suppose this had to happen sooner or later; I just wish it wasn't today.

Sitting at the kitchen table, next to my dad, is a woman in her sixties. She's small – tiny, in fact – with a smart up-do and an impressive face of make-up. I wish I could blend my contour like that, I usually just look like I've got bruises.

'Darling, this is Dora,' my dad says. 'Dora, this is Poppy.'

'Hello, my love,' she says warmly.

'Hi,' I say, suddenly feeling like a kid.

'Your dad has told me so much about you,' she

says. 'And, wow, what a fantastic job you're doing with the business. He's so proud of you.'

I almost recoil. Someone who knows about my job and doesn't think it's pathetic, or at least isn't saying so if they do.

'Your dad said you've been away,' she says. 'I'm sure you've got lots to catch up on. I brought a cake, you're both welcome to eat it. I'll go, leave you to catch up, but it would be nice to get to know each other sometime soon.'

'Yeah, that would be nice,' I say. 'Please don't feel like you need to go just because I'm here, though.'

'Oh, not at all,' she insists. 'I was just saying to your dad, I think it might be my tea time.'

'Why don't we all have dinner together?' I say. 'Then we'll see about that cake.'

I smile. If Dora can make an effort, then so can I.

'I could nip to the chippy down the road?' she suggests. 'I'll go pick them up while you catch up with your dad.'

'Sounds like a plan,' Dad says. 'Marvellous. Let me get you some money.'

'Don't be daft,' she says. 'It's just a few chips.'

Dora flashes us a big beaming smile before she leaves.

'Okay, she's lovely,' I tell my dad.

She is. I know I felt a bit weird about it all, but I can see how happy he is, and she seems great, and good for him, and it's about time he was happy.

'I have good judgement,' he replies. 'Most of the time.'

'Did you hear back from Auntie Joan about the divorce papers?' I ask him.

'I never sent them to her,' he replies. 'David Cassidy?' He smiles. 'Your mum would have loved that.'

'That's what I thought,' I say with a smile. 'So, once again, I thought I was divorced and, once again, I am not. One divorce is enough for anyone, I can't go through a third.'

'You don't have to,' my dad says.

'Oh, believe me, I do,' I reply. 'I did this whole speech about starting from fresh which, I don't know, it sounded like a good idea at the time, but I do love him, and I do want to be with him, and being around him only confirmed that. Bloody Mum and her bloody meddling.'

'I can't let you talk about your mum that way,' he says seriously.

'Sorry Dad, you know I love her, and I know she's not around to defend herself, but this is such a mess.'

'This is my fault,' he says.

'How is it your fault?' I ask.

'I'm afraid, in your mother's absence, I may have taken matters into my own hands, and taken a leaf out of her book, as well as taking a few sheets out of her old printer,' he says.

I pull a face.

'Dad, what are you talking about?'

'I wrote the letters,' he says. 'I wrote them after you came here, after Rachael's wedding, when you were talking about how much you missed Zac. I went on the internet, like I said, to try and find him, that's when I saw he was getting married again, and that's when I knew I needed to get you in a room with him, because if you didn't face him now, you would never get the chance, and if you didn't then you always would have wondered, always missed him at parties, always struggled to find "the one".'

'What?' I shriek.

'I thought I was doing what was best, and then I

thought, well, what would Mum do? What would she want me to do? And this is what I came up with. You are divorced, darling. This was all just a daft old romantic trying to make his daughter happy again.'

'Dad... I'm so... so... bloody hell, I think I'm impressed,' I blurt.

'You're not angry with me?'

'I... probably should be? I don't agree with your methods – and they are absolutely Mum's methods, so well done there – but I think you were right. I did need to face him. I think it's done me a lot of good.'

'So, I take it he didn't get married?' Dad says.

'Nope,' I reply. 'To be honest, that whole thing was a mess, I didn't need to turn up to ruin things, it sort of imploded without me.'

'Any spoilers on the set of the new Sonny Strong movie?' he asks curiously.

'You don't watch those?' I reply in disbelief. 'He's fighting the Loch Ness Monster in this one.'

'And I thought his literally jumping over a shark, before punching it, was jumping the shark,' Dad muses.

I smile before my face falls again.

'Zac said he loves me,' I tell him. 'And that he wants us to try again.'

'And what do you think?' he asks, taking my hand in his. 'What do you want?'

'You remember Mum said that Zac and I had wandered down different paths, and if we were really meant to be, our paths would cross again?' I say.

Dad nods.

'Well, I think I'm going to give that one another try,' I tell him. 'This time, without any of *your* meddling.'

'I'll keep my nose out this time,' he says. 'Scout's honour.'

'You were never a Scout,' I say. 'But I'll take it.'

An unfamiliar chime rings.

'Oh, that'll be Dora with our tea,' Dad says excitedly. 'Here, look.'

He holds up his phone to show me a live feed of the front door. There's Dora, smiling for the camera, enthusiastically brandishing a white plastic bag.

'Thanks for giving her a chance,' Dad says. 'I always knew you would but still, it must be hard for you, so I appreciate it.'

'I might tell her you're married, just to stress test your relationship,' I tease.

'I'm never going to live this one down, am I?' he replies.

'Not this year,' I reply with a smile.

God, I can't believe it's still only January. This has been the longest year of my life. Rachael's wedding, New Year's Eve, feels like forever ago.

That's when I remember, while I was in Scotland, I got that message from Fred, asking about another date. I open it up and punch a reply.

Hey, sorry about that, I'm back home now. Still fancy that date? Just so you know, I wasn't actually away with work, I had to go see my ex-husband, to make sure we were definitely divorced – we are. Speak soon x

See, what you do is, you don't give away anything in the message preview, by always typing a bunch of stuff first. That way, if they see something they don't like, and don't read it, you'll never know for sure that they definitely saw it. I watch as Fred's status changes to online and then my message shows as 'read'. A few seconds later, he's back to offline. Well, that settles that one then, a little bit of baggage, a dose of honesty, and he's not interested.

As opportunities arise for life to keep on that same path, the one that leads me away from Zac, things just keep popping up in the road, making me want to retreat back to him. I'm going to keep going, though. I'll give Zac a chance to heal from what happened with Lilac, and I'll wait to see if we find our way back together. We'll see what happens when he finds out we are actually divorced, and have been all along, won't we? Half the battle, since our split, was wondering what if? What might have been? What could I have done differently? Was Zac happier with someone else? Now that I can see more clearly, I'm going to take some time, I'm going to focus on myself for a bit, and see what happens.

For once, though, I'm genuinely excited about the future again.

44

SIX YEARS LATER

I walk down the staircase and turn the corner to find a pile of shoes spilling out of the cupboard under the stairs.

'Shoes everywhere,' I call out. 'I guess I'll put them away, shall I?'

I don't know who I'm talking to. I find myself doing that a lot these days. So, this is wedded bliss, huh? Picking up crap, talking to myself.

But, if I'm being honest, I love it. I love my husband, I love my messy house – I love my life.

I head into the living room. Jack is sitting on the sofa with his feet up.

'Did you leave shoes all over the floor *again*?' I ask him.

'I was looking for something,' he replies, his eyes fixed firmly on the TV.

'We talked about this,' I say softly, not wanting to sound like a nag, but kind of sounding like one anyway.

He pulls himself to his feet, heads into the hall and starts frantically throwing shoes into the cupboard. It's not a great system but, I suppose I didn't say I wanted them put away tidily, did I?

'Love you, Jack,' I tell him.

'Love you,' he replies.

Shoes finally all out of sight, he resumes watching TV.

I walk through the open-plan room to the kitchen area and sit down at the island.

'He's just like you, you know,' I say.

'Is he?' Zac replies. 'I was a horrible four-year-old, by all accounts. Jack's an angel.'

'Well, he's like you now,' I say with a laugh. 'He leaves mess everywhere and hides it instead of tidying it. And all he wants to do is watch TV... you're right, he is cute though.'

Jack is his dad's double. They've got the same eyes, the same hair, the same cheeky little smile. And, my God, they're so cute together. When they sit on the sofa together, watching *Spider-Man*, the same expression on their faces, both drinking little cartons of orange juice through tiny straws, wow, it just makes everything feel worthwhile.

'Are you looking forward to Grandad and Dora babysitting you tonight?' Zac calls out to Jack.

'Yeah,' he replies. 'They give me sweets and let me stay up past my bedtime.'

'Oh, Grandparents of the Year,' I say sarcastically to Zac. 'To be honest, he could have said they give him beer, I don't care, I'm so excited for our anniversary night out.'

I'm kidding, obviously. About the beer part, at least. I am so excited for our anniversary though.

'Are you sure you don't mind that we're not going to be alone?' he asks. 'Are you sure you don't want to do something romantic?'

'Hey, we promised we'd all have a crazy night out every month with the girls and their husbands, and we've stuck to it, and we're all a lot happier for it,' I say. 'Plus, Kat is supposed to be bringing her new boyfriend.'

'And how do you think he's going to react to a bunch of thirty-somethings who get pissed on cocktails and sing karaoke terribly in a desperate attempt to hang on to their youth?' he asks.

'Erm, he's *Kat's* boyfriend,' I remind him. 'He's going to be on board.'

'Fair enough,' he says with a laugh. 'Well, I'm going to get ready.'

I watch as my gorgeous husband walks across the room.

'Are my black shoes in here?' he asks, opening the cupboard under the stairs. Shoes spill out all over the floor. 'Shit.'

He swears under his breath, but Jack hears and cackles with laughter.

'Oi, come here, you,' Zac says. 'Help me put these shoes away properly.'

Jack rolls his eyes before forcing himself to his feet again. He definitely gets his attitude from me.

It may have taken me a little longer than expected, with a few bumps along the way, but everything finally feels as it should be. Zac and I are stronger than ever and Jack is the best thing to ever happen to us. I'm sad that my mum never got to meet him, or see me and Zac back together, but I know she would be so happy for us, and that she would've been the best grandma in the world. Dad and Dora aren't doing a terrible job though, and we're going to see Nanny May next week, who Jack loves – he also loves that she has a pool he's allowed to play in.

'Hey, you don't fancy leaving a bit earlier and going to the cinema first, do you?' Zac asks, joining me again. 'Romantic movie for two.'

'What's on?' I ask him.

'*Not Dead Yet II*,' he replies.

I throw a tea towel at him

'Oh, come on, in this one Jack McVey fights a haunted house,' he teases.

It's funny, but it's probably true.

'Maybe some other time,' I say, wrapping my arms around him, kissing him on the lips.

'Okay, I really am going to get ready this time,' he says. 'And my black shoes weren't in there. Could you find them for me, please?'

'Do I have to do everything in this house?' I joke. 'Of course I will.'

I kiss him again.

Honestly, domestic life is the life for me. I love running around after the boys, cooking, cleaning, being stuck in a never-ending cycle of DIY. And, of course, I'm still running the business, but from my office at home. Dad and Dora are always going off on trips and things. It's so nice to see him so happy. I think Mum would have been happy for him too – well, I know she would, despite always joking that if she died first, Dad had to become a monk.

When I think about Mum, how she was here one minute and gone the next, sometimes it freaks me out, it makes me panic that life is short and that one day it could be me who disappears, leaving Zac and Jack in a house full of mess and a floor constantly covered in shoes, but I don't dwell on it for long. I'm so happy with everything I have now, I'm going to live in the present and try to make wonderful memories for Jack so that he'll always have those, even when I'm gone. At least that way I'll live with no regrets, just like my mum did.

ACKNOWLEDGMENTS

A super huge thank you to the absolutely brilliant Boldwood Books. Thank you to Nia, the best editor on the planet, to the wonderful Amanda, and to everyone else on the team who work so hard on my books.

Thank you so much to my readers, and to all the reviewers on my blog tours, for all your support and lovely reviews. Your kind words mean so much to me.

A massive thank you to my family and friends for their love and support. Thanks to Kim, for always being incredible, to the wonderful Aud for all her love, and to Pino for his support. Thank you so much to James for always being on hand with the tech/emotional support – whichever I needed (usually both). A very big thank you to Joey for helping me out and saving the day (you're my hero). Thanks to Rachel for taking a mental trip to 2006 with me. Shout-out to Darcy, my furry assistant, for always being right next to me when I'm working.

Finally, the biggest thank you of all goes to my husband, Joe, for always being so wonderful. From helping me sort out my office to just generally keeping me sane, I couldn't do this without him. Love you, fella.

MORE FROM PORTIA MACINTOSH

We hope you enjoyed reading *No Ex Before Marriage*. If you did, please leave a review.

If you'd like to gift a copy, this book is also available as an ebook, digital audio download and audiobook CD.

Sign up to Portia MacIntosh's mailing list for news, competitions and updates on future books.

http://bit.ly/PortiaMacIntoshNewsletter

Discover more laugh-out-loud romantic comedies from Portia Macintosh:

ALSO BY PORTIA MACINTOSH

One Way or Another

If We Ever Meet Again

Bad Bridesmaid

Drive Me Crazy

Truth or Date

It's Not You, It's Them

The Accidental Honeymoon

You Can't Hurry Love

Summer Secrets at the Apple Blossom Deli

Love & Lies at the Village Christmas Shop

The Time of Our Lives

Honeymoon For One

My Great Ex-Scape

Make or Break at the Lighthouse B&B

The Plus One Pact

Stuck On You

Faking It

Life's a Beach

Will They, Won't They?

No Ex Before Marriage

ABOUT THE AUTHOR

Portia MacIntosh is a bestselling romantic comedy author of 15 novels, including *My Great Ex-Scape* and *Honeymoon For One*. Previously a music journalist, Portia writes hilarious stories, drawing on her real life experiences.

Visit Portia's website: https://portiamacintosh.com/

Follow Portia MacIntosh on social media here:

facebook.com/portia.macintosh.3

twitter.com/PortiaMacIntosh

instagram.com/portiamacintoshauthor

bookbub.com/authors/portia-macintosh

ABOUT BOLDWOOD BOOKS

Boldwood Books is a fiction publishing company seeking out the best stories from around the world.

Find out more at www.boldwoodbooks.com

Sign up to the Book and Tonic newsletter for news, offers and competitions from Boldwood Books!

http://www.bit.ly/bookandtonic

We'd love to hear from you, follow us on social media:

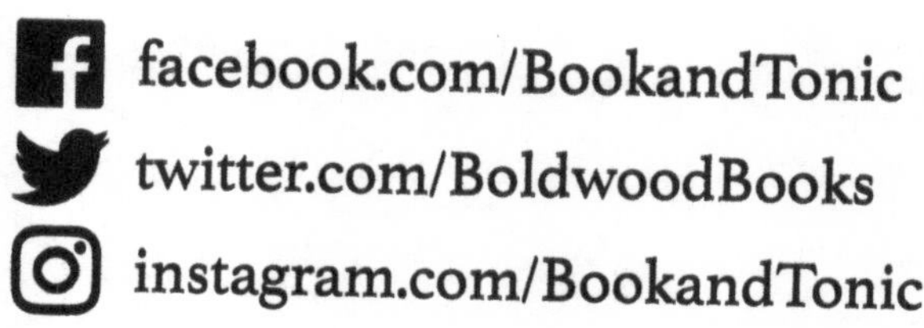

Lightning Source UK Ltd.
Milton Keynes UK
UKHW022228300122
397898UK00003B/280